HAGAR OLSSON (1893–1978), a member of Finland's Swedish-speaking minority, was for over half a century a forthright and influential presence in Finnish cultural life. Her friendship with the poet Edith Södergran, cut short by the latter's early death, was crucial to Olsson's development as an author and reviewer. Highly conscious of international literary trends, she introduced many new writers to a Nordic readership, and was in the vanguard of Finland-Swedish modernism alongside such names as Elmer Diktonius and Henry Parland.

Olsson made her fiction debut in 1916 with the expressionist novella *Lars Thorman och döden* (Lars Thorman and Death), and went on to publish a further twenty-one prose works in a variety of genres, among them the futurism-inspired photo-novel *På Kanaanexpressen* (On the Canaan Express, 1929). She also wrote plays, including *S.O.S.* (1928), a defence of pacifism and disarmament. She is probably most remembered for her novels *Chitambo* (1933) and *Träsnidaren och döden* (1940; *The Woodcarver and Death*, 1965) and the memoir *Kinesisk utflykt* (Chinese Excursion, 1949).

SARAH DEATH has translated Swedish literature of many periods and genres, including works by Lena Andersson, Kerstin Ekman, Selma Lagerlöf, Astrid Lindgren, Sven Lindqvist and crime-fiction writer Håkan Nesser. Her most recent translation was *Letters from Tove*, the correspondence of Finland-Swedish author and artist Tove Jansson.
She has twice won the George Bernard Shaw Prize for translation from Swedish, and in 2014 received the Royal Order of the Polar Star for services to Swedish literature.

Some other books from Norvik Press

Johan Borgen: *Little Lord* (translated by Janet Garton)

Karin Boye: *Crisis* (translated by Amanda Doxtater)

Kerstin Ekman: *Witches' Rings* (translated by Linda Schenck)

Kerstin Ekman: *The Spring* (translated by Linda Schenck)

Kerstin Ekman: *The Angel House* (translated by Sarah Death)

Kerstin Ekman: *City of Light* (translated by Linda Schenck)

Vigdis Hjorth: *A House in Norway* (translated by Charlotte Barslund)

Sigurd Hoel: *A Fortnight Before the Frost* (translated by Sverre Lyngstad)

Svava Jakobsdóttir: *Gunnlöth's Tale* (translated by Oliver Watts)

Henry Parland: *To Pieces* (translated by Dinah Cannell)

Ellen Rees: *On the Margins: Nordic Women Modernists of the 1930s*

Klaus Rifbjerg: *Terminal Innocence* (translated by Paul Larkin)

Edith Södergran: *The Poet Who Created Herself: Selected Letters of Edith Södergran* (translated by Silvester Mazzarella)

Kirsten Thorup: *The God of Chance* (translated by Janet Garton)

Dorrit Willumsen: *Bang: A Novel about the Danish Writer* (translated by Marina Allemano)

Chitambo
The Story of Vega Maria

by

Hagar Olsson

First published by Holger Schildts förlag, Helsingfors, 1933 as
Chitambo: romanen om Vega Maria

Translated from the Swedish
by Sarah Death

Norvik Press
2020

Originally published as *Chitambo* in 1933.

This translation and afterword © Sarah Death 2020.
The translator's moral right to be identified as the translator of the
work has been asserted.

Norvik Press Series B: English Translations of Scandinavian
Literature, no. 81

A catalogue record for this book is available from the British Library.

ISBN: 978-1-909408-55-5

Norvik Press
Department of Scandinavian Studies
UCL
Gower Street
London WC1E 6BT
United Kingdom
Website: www.norvikpress.com
E-mail address: norvik.press@ucl.ac.uk

Managing editors: Elettra Carbone, Sarah Death, Janet Garton,
C. Claire Thomson, Essi Viitanen.

Layout: Essi Viitanen
Cover image: *Eydtkuhnenin tyttö II (Girl from Eydtkuhnen II)*, 1927,
Helene Schjerfbeck.
Finnish National Gallery.

Norvik Press gratefully acknowledges a grant from the Finnish
Literature Exchange, which has made this translation possible.

We would also like to thank Åbo Akademi for granting permission
for translation and publication of this work and the Finnish National
Gallery for allowing use of the Helene Schjerfbeck painting on the
cover.

Contents

* in the text indicates endnotes on pages 179–186.

A torn-out page

I have never understood the concept of spring cleaning. Good God, how pointless to imagine you can clean away all trace of life's cruel ravages! You only find you have ripped open everything that ought to have been left there in merciful oblivion and turned the entire contents of your desk drawers and hiding places upside down, coming across letters, objects and memories that sear you and that you would much rather never have set eyes on again. Profoundly agitated, disturbed by the shadows of the past and the peculiar forms and figures that supposedly represent your previous self, you wander around rooms, between tables and chairs that are not in their usual places, noting for the umpteenth time that your life has been wasted and that nothing on earth will help you to get it in order.

And why did I start rummaging among those old papers? I hardly know what I am doing now. A loose page, torn from a book, fell into my hands, and it was enough to disconcert me utterly. A picture, an illustration from an old book about the heroic feats of explorers. I have propped up the picture on the desk in front of me and cannot tear my eyes away from it. How farcical! Sometimes I laugh, sometimes I cry, beside myself with anxiety and bewilderment. If I close my eyes, I see a blue horizon and dazzling white sails, always the same vision, and I do not know where it comes from. If I open my eyes, I find hopeless chaos on my desk, papers from today and from heaven knows when, from the dawn of time. And reigning supreme in the midst of it all is the picture of David Livingstone, working on his diary somewhere in the jungles of Africa.

9

It feels so strange to sit here and look at that picture. As a child with wide and shining eyes I was transfixed by it as if it were a miracle of secret grandeur, impenetrable and mysterious. But oh, I know so much about David Livingstone now, know the details of all his journeys. He opened up the path to the interior of Africa, and did so at the cost of his own life. I don't know why that picture so entrances me. I sense the same mood descending on me as when I stared at it with the eyes of a child. Perhaps they are still hidden somewhere inside me, those eyes filled with wonder?

A state of disorder beyond words! And just when I needed to muster all my strength for the reorganisation at work. My room is in as much disarray as if I were about to set off on a long journey. It will not do. I've got to concentrate. Resolutely chase all my memories out of the door, lock away the papers. Livingstone, Mr Dreary... Just lock them away, and let that be an end to it. They are welcome to stay untidy as far as I am concerned! I have no business with them. I have my job, and an important job at that. I must be in a fit state for work tomorrow.

See, see, the white sails!

Mr Dreary is not happy
in his home

Mr Johan Dreary, my father, was quite an unusual man. It is hard to say what made him unusual – he was not consummately evil, still less high-minded and noble enough to stand out from the crowd. Nor was he possessed of a brilliant mind, though he had talent and a quick wit. He did not distinguish himself from the rest by any particular quality. No, what made Mr Dreary so surprising was rather his blend of mutually incompatible qualities.

To take one example, he was incredibly miserly, so miserly that it was a great torment to him to spend even the smallest sum, whether on the housekeeping, on clothes for his wife and child, or on his own expenses. I felt genuinely sorry for him every time I saw him having to part with money. He complained loudly and his expression grew as wretched and confused as if you really had relieved him of all he possessed. If any of his friends or business associates found themselves in temporary difficulties and foolishly asked to borrow money from him, he would break out in a string of terrible curses and swear on the salvation of his eternal soul that he could scarcely afford his daily bread. He would wave his arms about, his eyes fixed in wild anguish on his petrified visitor, and eventually work himself up into a furious rage. Having put the supplicant to flight, he would be in excellent spirits when he came in to see my mother and me. He was never more pleased with himself than at such moments! He positively sparkled with good humour and the usual outcome was that he took me somewhere especially exciting that evening.

On the other hand, he ruined himself by standing surety for all manner of dubious characters who consciously cultivated a certain mystique and made their activities appear in a fabulous light – individuals brooding on strange inventions or dreaming up crazy plans for the redemption of mankind in some respect or other. He was ready to assist anybody at all who could present him with a sufficiently fantastical story. Prophetic lunatics and miracle-workers, down-at-heel students with *idées fixes*, fools and social outcasts with delusions of grandeur, who imagined themselves party to secrets which made the rulers of the world fear and persecute them – this was his clientele. And above all, inventors! There was nothing that charmed Mr Dreary more than the notion of someone 'inventing' something. These gentlemen unrolled their designs with an air of mystery, making Mr Dreary swear a solemn oath not to reveal their secrets, and then began to expound in fanciful terms on the wondrous properties of their inventions. Mr Dreary listened, eyes shining, all the more charmed because he did not understand a word of the technical details. He delighted in financing such schemes.

It is a mystery to me where he found these characters. He had his own eccentric ways, Mr Dreary, and it wasn't easy to check up on him. It was by being inquisitive, listening from behind the door and peering through the keyhole that I discovered what little I do know. If he happened to be in really high spirits, he would occasionally drop me a hint of what he was up to, on condition that I solemnly promised to say nothing to my mother. But most of it I picked up for myself, through vigilance and keen powers of observation. I was terribly interested in my father's activities. To me he seemed so enigmatic and majestic. I was convinced that his undertakings were preparations for splendid exploits and that the world would one day see him for who he really was.

It was a time when our country found itself richly endowed with individuals full of ideas, as the many new tiers of its population were propelled into the work of culture by the first light rays of popular education which, strangely refracted, reached even into the deepest levels and darkest corners. There were plenty of inventors to throw themselves with playful ease into the most difficult technical problems, not least the challenges of *perpetuum mobile*, and plenty of prophets to foretell the imminent advent of God's kingdom. Sooner or later, by some obscure means, most of these found their way to Mr Dreary's room. He received them with open arms – and an open wallet. No matter how many times he had been disappointed, he was instantly prepared to be enthused once more. He loved these people, they appealed to his imagination and added a delightful dash of irrationality to his petit-bourgeois existence. I witnessed in astonishment the way Mr Dreary handled his money in their company, as if it held no value for him. A hundred marks, a thousand marks – it was as if he suddenly had no appreciation of monetary value, and had never felt it in his soul. He played with money as if he were a child, extravagantly and carelessly. Yet his soul had recently been martyred by a five-mark note my mother had only been able to prise from his hand by the shedding of tears!

This made an indelible impression on me. Young as I was, I somehow grasped that the entertainment value of these people's projects and passing enthusiasms lay in their futility, just as the tedium of necessary expenses lay in – their necessity. Mr Dreary's secret patronage became as precious to me as it could ever be to him. I felt as though it made our house distinct from every other house in the world. In my imagination I saw it standing at the centre of some vast and mysterious enterprise which one of these days was going to change the whole world and elevate my father to power and glory. Whenever anything disagreeable happened to me outside home, like being told off at school or quarrelling with my playmates, I would think to myself: nobody knows our secret.

My mother saw the whole thing in a very different light. Mr Dreary's capacity for squandering money on risky ventures while he and his family were obliged to live in the most straitened of circumstances was a source of perpetual discord between him and my mother. The age-old universal conflict between woman's instinct for safety and man's appetite for adventure was played out in its sharpest focus within the modest walls of our home. He, of course, carefully concealed

13

his every step from her, partly because he knew she would object and make a fuss, partly because he loved mystification for its own sake. But through her own private intelligence channels she would nonetheless glean something of what was going on. She would go around as usual for quite a time, white and stony-faced as she mentally geared herself up, which cowed Mr Dreary. If she had had the sense to keep it up she would have retained her advantage over Mr Dreary. But at the first hint of an argument between them, things would come to a head. She would pour out all she knew, whatever she had been told or had fathomed, alternating all the while between tears and dark threats, sometimes begging him to desist, sometimes painting him as an inhuman monster driving his wife and child onto the street.

This gave Mr Dreary a welcome opportunity to play his trump card. With a series of fiendish facial expressions that a first-class actor might have envied him, he instructed her to pack his most essential possessions. He would leave right away; he asked nothing better! As he was such a useless breadwinner for the family, the best thing would be for her to find another husband. He would not stand in her way. She had never understood him, nor appreciated him. There were people who understood him better. And with that, he would make a grand exit – without any baggage, naturally. The following morning he would be back for coffee, delighted at having played her such a trick.

Those lonely nights weighed heavily on my mother. Her misfortune was that she could never get used to these episodes. She lacked imagination, and believed Mr Dreary was in deadly earnest. I could never contain my surprise at her despair whenever he left us like that. She would drift from room to room, weeping and reproaching herself. She always took it equally hard, no matter how many times the tactic was repeated. Her endearments when he returned were touching, and all the more so because she was not in the habit of expressing such emotions. Her behaviour turned Mr Dreary's perpetual threats to leave us into a genuine vice. It was a threat permanently hanging over her, a cruel reminder of the insecurity and transience of human existence.

Mr Dreary was very popular among his circle of friends, despite his tight-fisted reputation. He rarely invited anyone round, but was always receiving invitations. A celebratory gathering without Mr Dreary was unthinkable. There was no one in and around town as smart as he was! Who else could tell preposterous stories, make such biting and witty comments, or mimic other people the way he could? Mr Dreary had real talent – as an actor, a clown, a joker. I have to some extent inherited his skill in dissimulation, but my mimicry is merely a pale imitation of his. The versatility of his elastic facial contortions, the diabolical gleam in his eye and the crushing expressiveness with which he gave one of his customary caricatured renditions of a situation or mimicked an individual – all these were exceptional, and impossible to reproduce. With his sparkling energy, his agile wit, the pyrotechnics of his whole personality, he was able to enliven the spirits of even the most sluggish and ruminant band of tipplers. His name, Dreary, was generally considered a fine joke. Were it not for the fact that he had expounded to one and all on the subject of his family line, people would probably have thought it was a name he had assumed – just to make them laugh. And no one ever referred to him by any name other than Dreary. I do not think I ever heard anyone call him Johan. I have often reflected that this, like so much else, showed how solitary he was at heart – this merry carouser. We are solitary types, we Drearys.

My mother never addressed him by his first name, either. Dreary, was all she called him. And she had better reason to do so than his cronies. At home, he truly was dreary. A dyed-in-the-wool misanthrope who viewed life without a single glint in his eyes. The land in which he lived was the most wretched of lands, the age in which he lived the basest and most evil of ages, his friends the most untrustworthy to tread this earth, his family the most ill-starred of all families. He could come home in excellent spirits, but would never fail to find cause for dissatisfaction with the government or the socialists or European politics as a whole, within ten minutes of his arrival. Once he had begun painting everything in the worst possible light, he would rapidly warm to his own words and find himself inspired. Before long he would see no limit to how terrible things were, how badly they were being handled and what consummate rogues people were. If he found no other outlet for his irascibility, he would discover a curtain hanging crooked, a hair that had accidentally strayed into his food, or some oversight in paying him due attention – and with that, his evening's entertainment would be assured: no one had such an impossible wife as his, nor such hopeless children! It was one of Mr Dreary's idiosyncrasies, whenever he was angry and really wanted to humiliate his family, to refer to 'his children' in the plural – he, the father of a single child, and a girl at that. There was implied scorn in this that we both felt intensely, my mother and I.

I have often wondered what it was that caused this total transformation in Mr Dreary's character as soon as he was within his home. And I have speculated that an individual with such a soaring imagination will inevitably find his shabby and constricted domestic circumstances distasteful. On coming home he must have been acutely aware of his incarceration, condemned to this dining table, this plush sofa and this ageing, unimaginative woman who simultaneously vexed him to the point of spiteful retort and bound him with ties of secret affection.

Admittedly with someone like Mr Dreary there is no justification for drawing logical conclusions; inconsistency was his only truly reliable character trait. But I, as his daughter, had been in a position to study him in detail and at length, and think I can venture to assume that his home and family were to him a visible and permanently painful testimony to his wasted life. A person with a vivid imagination is generally inclined to consider his life a failure, because life, the longer one lives it, inevitably tends towards mechanical repetition and stagnation, while the imagination craves perpetual new nourishment for its creative urges, perpetual new leaps into uncertainty. The tedium of the form of living accorded to him must have caused my father a great deal of suffering – the only inheritance he had from his own parents was a spirit of adventure and the restlessness in his blood.

The irascibility and tendency to abrupt changes of mind said to be a hallmark of the northern races is particularly characteristic of that crossbreed of obscure origin which inhabits Finland. A breath of wind from the Asian steppes blows in across our country from the east and sings its broody, passionate songs in our wild, remote forests; in the west, the sea surges over us, its sparkle opening our coasts to the appetite for daring feats and the urge for adventure. This country is well suited to the rearing of adventurers and dreamers – individuals with no sense of proportion and balance, who stake their lives on a whim and would sooner sacrifice their well-being than suppress their craving for the impossible. This was my father's heritage. His forefathers were adventurers, as far back as one could trace them – and Mr Dreary had devoted tireless interest to researching his own family tree. Swedish seafaring blood and Karelian horse-dealer blood combined uneasily in his veins, firing up his imagination but making him personally incapable of bold action and risky gambits. His breast was a battlefield for wild and untamed temperaments, vainly attempting to find an outlet for their excess of vitality in his weakened blood. The depths of his being were home to flinty-eyed Vikings staring towards foreign coasts, greedy for danger, loot and pillage. They echoed to the loud-mouthed rowdiness of Karelian marketplace heroes who had gone to trade with Russia, returning in the spring with gaudy cloth and an air of sinful lust to women who quietly hummed ancient folk songs as they moved between cottage and cowshed.

Mr Dreary was very proud of his heritage and never entirely gave up hope of one day coming into his own and changing his life utterly. He was a weak character who could only endure the monotony of his days and the shackles of his most immediate duties by dreaming of the big day when everything would change and his life would suddenly take a different course – not by his own efforts, but through the intervention of unforeseen events. Only once, as a fourteen-year old, had he seized the rudder of his own fate and run away to sea. His father had at that time, after a stormy youth, settled down on a farm some way inland, and forced his son to work the soil. At this, Johan Dreary left home, never to see his father again. But his seafaring career, like so much else in his life, ended ignominiously. Clumsy and clueless, with a weak and nervous constitution, he was not remotely suited to the profession, and moreover had to suffer the shame and torment of seasickness.

After that sharp lesson, he never repeated his attempt to be master of his destiny. His occupations were many and varied, for he seized any opportunity that arose, but never with any thought of drawing up a conscious plan for his life, still less carrying it through. He did not acknowledge his setbacks, always blaming everything on 'circumstances'. By way of compensation, he naively overrated himself. He would imagine, the way children often do, that a brilliant future awaited him. The fact of his own insignificance did not worry him in the slightest, for he was unshakeably convinced that he was a man singled out by destiny. He had merely to bide his time. One day, by means of some apparently chance occurrence – a fortunate constellation of those mystical 'circumstances' – his great qualities would spring to light and his journey to the stars would begin. No reverses or humiliations could break him and, in any case, he took nothing in earnest but his own fantasies. This lent his nature its irresistible light-heartedness, its supreme independence. As he stood in his empty home after one of his many bankruptcies, looking out of the window with a smile on his face while his wife wrung her hands in despair and his child wept tears of diffuse anxiety, perhaps there was a look in his eye that had a touch of the little Corsican* about it, after all.

Unfortunately, dismal reality offered no hint of where the great opportunities might be lying in wait for him. Mr Dreary was one of those somewhat shady businessmen of whom the world is full, a small cog of dubious value in the capitalist distribution machine. He never attempted anything major.

For him, the important thing was to get by on a succession of temporary jobs – while waiting for something that never happened. He ran one or two small companies in various locations and lines of business, whatever came to hand. He easily tired of a job and would then be beguiled by the certain prospect of quick, easy profits on offer in some other trade. Earning money was for him, as for people in general, the sole aim of any enterprise he set up. His redeeming feature was that he never invested his soul in any of this. Everything he did was intended to achieve something else. The money he earned by so-called honest means and greedily saved – it had another purpose. When the time came, it would show its true worth; destiny would provide a pointer to what it should be used for.

At the time of my birth, Mr Dreary had started to take an interest in antiques. This was a job that gave him greater gratification than anything else he had ever tried. It appealed to his artistic sense to handle such beautiful objects and it satisfied his ambition to be viewed as a connoisseur. He settled in our capital city and there, in two dark rooms in an old building, he opened the business that became known to all Helsinki residents as 'Dreary's Antique Shop', and which for me, also a Helsinki resident, became the centre of the universe. This was Mr Dreary's golden age. By the time I took possession of the shop as a living world of the imagination, sordid reality had already done all it could to destroy its lustre and charm. As the years passed, the shop took on an ever more motley and battered air. Behind its pompous sign, a less imaginative observer than Mr Dreary or his daughter might even have seen in their mind's eye the familiar, depressing title of 'General Store'.

With his shop, Mr Dreary struggled with an existence from which every trace of gloss had vanished, one that could only be endured as an interregnum – a waiting period of the kind that fate imposes on all those whom it has singled out to accomplish some amazing feat. In terms of its sign, at least, Dreary's Antique Shop defied the ups and downs of perfidious

chance, and through the years Mr Dreary's private nameplate
continued to read:

C.J. DREARY
Antique Dealer

Mr Dreary would not have relinquished this title for the
world. Had he done so, it would also have meant relinquishing
his rightful claim to a more brilliant existence than the one
which hateful circumstance had temporarily allotted him.

My soul is troubled by contradictory names

Naturally I was born in 1893. Everyone knows this as the proudest year in the Nordic nations' history of polar exploration. It was when Fridtjof Nansen set out on his world-famous voyage to the North Pole aboard the *Fram*. Mr Dreary viewed this as a personal honour and a sign that destiny had its eye on him. He immediately assumed I was born for great things and shrewdly realised that he ought to foster the same absurd fancies in my mind, too.

His marriage had threatened to take as ignominious a turn as his other enterprises: it had remained childless for a number of years. Not that Mr Dreary particularly craved offspring, but he realised that having once ventured into marriage, one should have some results to show for it, and anything else would be a fiasco. Admittedly he had no cause to reproach himself in this case, having personally not lifted a finger to bring about the marriage. He had merely become aware of the dreamy girl at carpenter Hearty's in Nystad. She was so dainty and pretty, so coy, and those big, sad eyes melted Mr Dreary's heart. He scarcely knew how it happened, but one day he brought the girl some flowers. And heaven knows, that was all it took. There sat her father, there sat her mother, and in agonies of embarrassment, Mr Dreary handed over his flowers to the girl. By the time he left, he was betrothed. He was rather surprised, yet at the same time relieved: the whole question of marriage had always hung over him as something one had to prepare for, weigh up, and make a serious commitment to. The fact that this, like everything else, appeared to take care of itself, was a good sign. Which made it all the more tiresome to encounter the subsequent hitch over children who were, after all, part and parcel of it all.

But late in the autumn of 1893, when I let out my first cry, he instantly understood, of course, why it had taken so long. It would not do for the firstborn child of a man like him to arrive in just any year, the way other people produce their offspring. He was utterly engrossed in Nansen's expedition that year. He had minutely followed the preparations, rejoicing in King Oscar's generosity – 'there's a king who takes his duties seriously!' – and, around midsummer, when *Fram* had weighed anchor, he went about bragging as though he were the one actually setting sail for the far north and destinations unknown, into seas through which no vessel had ever ventured*. There was a perceptible change in him; he grew bold and manly, and assumed a stern tone of command, such as would be suitable on deck in rough weather.

But Nansen was away for a long time, nothing was heard of him, and fate offered Mr Dreary no clue as to the feats for which he himself had been chosen. He had an uncomfortable feeling that everything threatened once again to remain in its old rut, the shop to remain the shop, a little better one day, a little worse the next, and Mr Dreary to remain Mr Dreary, a little more cocksure one day, a little more subdued the next. Just as his sense of elation began to go decidedly flat, along came the baby girl in October! It did not take long for Mr Dreary to observe that something extraordinary was going on. Not only was the child born in that notable year, but it also first saw the light of day on the thirteenth. Now everyone knows that the number thirteen is linked to remarkable things, and in 1893 the number was even more remarkable than usual, because the members of Nansen's expedition also numbered exactly thirteen. In some unfathomable way, Mr Dreary connected my arrival with his own dreams of greatness, and he wasted little time in implanting them in my soul. Even as I lay in my cradle in my earliest days, the mysterious aura of destiny hovered about my head. A delightedly grinning face, mobile and surprising, was permanently bent over me; gestures, facial contortions and astonishing expressions found their way into my dreams and drew my waking soul into the magic spell of singular expectations before it even had time to detach itself fully from the darkness from which it had emerged.

Mr Dreary threw himself body and soul into my upbringing. In actual fact, I gave him a very welcome opportunity to make some changes. The room in which I began my existence was altered beyond all recognition. No item of furniture was permitted to stay where it had been before; the rugs were rearranged on the floor; a special corner with a little desk, a little chair, a little bookcase and a little globe was set up for me long before I – a wriggling bundle – had the remotest need of these objects. In Mr Dreary's hands, a destiny began to take shape long before its bearer had any part in it. He had imagination, Mr Dreary, but of a rather singular kind. To my mother's horror and to ridicule from their entire circle of acquaintances, he decorated the wall above my white cot with pictures so far from appropriate for a child's mind that they could only be considered offensive. They were wild, thrilling pictures, which etched themselves into my mind forever. I have certainly developed a sense of personal ownership of them, and been influenced by them in a way quite different from the obligatory guardian angels and fairytale princesses deployed to keep other infants happy.

The most glorious of them all were the ships. They inhabited my imagination from my youngest years and I know they are slumbering for all time in the depths of my being, those beautiful, restless birds, the spirits of adventure, waiting for the wind to fill their sails. They were not just any ships, the ones with which Mr Dreary adorned my walls. They were ships of destiny, ships of heroism and conquest. Seeing them, one instantly knew that they were en route to something great and mighty and terrifying. I particularly remember a three-master with magnificently billowing sails, making landfall on a desolate Antarctic coast. Chill, glittering water around its keel, encircled by vast expanses of ice and snow, and the slender rigging against an endless grey sky. The uncannily suggestive aspect of that picture was the sinister and mysterious way in which the ship was pitching and tossing. Amidst such petrified, impenetrable wastes this impassioned tossing, an expression of its will to press forward despite the opposition of the elements and gods! In my mind I always linked this image with the most gruesome picture I had on my wall. Its backdrop was a towering, night-black wall of rock, a fantastical outline besieged by birds, an agitated mass of flapping wings, and on the ground beneath there were three small mounds of earth, rather comical in shape. Despite their amusing shape – they looked rather like three nesting ducks – these filled me with inexpressible dread. 'The Three Graves on Beechey Island'* read the caption under the picture. I did not know what graves were, but I could still tell from the picture what was going on, and I had no need to ask anyone what the scene showed. It is truly terrible to think how much a small child knows.

By contrast it was a real joy to absorb myself in the engraving depicting 'The Death of Cook on 14 February 1779'*. It was full of life, movement and wild rhythm. A waving palm tree, a stormy sky, and on the ground a band of wily, hot-headed savages charging forward to surround the lone white man in soldier's uniform. I loved such pictures with a passion. Even before I had any conscious understanding of what they portrayed, I was carried away by the passionate rhythm of their gestures, the wild and horrible expressions, the tense, highly-charged atmosphere of the situation. Mr Dreary would sometimes take down a picture of that kind and show it to me at close quarters. It made me shriek with delight.

But there was one image of a completely different kind, a very tranquil picture, which was closer to my heart than all the rest and which meant that my earliest years on this earth were spent in the shadow of a sense of great and majestic mystery. The picture was pinned at the head of my bed, just where a guardian angel should rightfully have had its place. On the floor of a curious hut with partially built walls sat a man, legs crossed and stretched out in front of him. He had a large book open on his lap. In his right hand, resting on the open book, he held a pen. He was sitting rigidly upright and staring straight ahead. Outside, two bearded and turbaned characters in long garments could be seen putting their heads secretively together and looking at the solitary man inside the hut. 'Livingstone Works on his Diary', the picture was called. The man's oddly stiff position, the mysterious strangers' knowing gazes and above all the eyes staring into space and the distant, ecstatic look on his white face made an irresistibly eloquent impression. The poor, solitary figure radiated a loftiness of purpose that no shimmering angel wings or fairytale princes' crowns could have instilled. Long before I knew anything of David Livingstone's exploits or could even piece together the difficult words in my ABC book, knowledge of the supreme power of the human spirit streamed in some unfathomable way from this picture into my soul, exerting a compelling power and expectation over the life of my imagination. Even today I still keep that modestly and clumsily executed picture as a precious memento of the time when Mr Dreary, so blithe and foolish, introduced me into the society of lofty minds after his own fashion. The picture's uneven edge points to it having been torn out of a book - who knows, perhaps some lavish, costly volume – and this touches me more than anything else, telling me as it does that Mr Dreary shunned no sacrifice when it came to surrounding the new arrival with symbols to arouse the soul's desire for all that is great and majestic in existence.

I am inclined to believe that this picture has been one of the most significant symbols in my life. Later, after I had experienced the errors and disappointments of youth, the indelible impression it made on me in my earliest childhood drew me to find out what this David Livingstone had said in his diary. I discovered a spirit that had testified to itself: 'In the glow of love that Christianity inspired, I resolved to devote my life to the alleviation of human misery' – and I cannot deny that such words lent fuel to a fire that was already burning in my soul. A fire that had never been fed enough and could never be satisfied! At times of deep depression and despair I tell myself the flaw in my life is that my desire was directed from the outset towards goals too lofty for a spirit of modest proportions and worthless character. But there are moments when all this is forgiven me – my weakness, my incapacity and my conceit – and, like an echo from deep, mysterious forests, my childhood answers me:

'Mankind must want the great and the good! Everything else is a matter of chance.'

This aphorism from no less a man than Alexander von Humboldt*, printed in large and magnificent letters, was pinned up over my little desk, where I was absorbed in the mysteries of my ABC book and other learned texts. And I must say that it appealed to me far more than the gloomy biblical quotations and religious homilies (such as the – to me – insufferable 'Thank you God for everything') that I saw in the homes of my playfellows. The interplay between cause and effect is here, as ever I suppose, impossible to tease out, but one thing is certain: whenever I feel most at ease in life and filled with the rhythm of my own destiny, I return in my mind to the room that Mr Dreary so thoroughly refurbished in my honour. I linger there, refreshed, as if in the rightful home of my spirit. If I look around me at the walls, I find the same symbolic script as the one carved into my own heart. I see the exhilarating pictures, imagination's passionate promises, I see the strange jagged outlines of unknown coasts, and as if to accompany all this I hear my father's tales of men who defied death in the virgin forests and on the world's oceans in order to chart and name a single little spot on the surface of our earth, men who had penetrated the Arctic regions where the cold snuffs out all life but the most fiery of all: human thought.

The guidance Mr Dreary offered me on this great voyage of discovery could not but arouse my mother's deepest disgust, especially as I was a girl, which only made it worse. Implanting such thoughts and fancies in a girl could lead to nothing but misfortune and ruin. That much she knew. But Mr Dreary paid no heed to such trifles. Boy or girl signified nothing to him, it was enough that I was born under an adventurous star. I was at any rate a living being who brought change, plans and hopes, a new character on the stage, around whom he could gather his dreams and high-voltage expectations.

With the holy act of baptism itself began the succession of conflicts between my father and my mother that was to make my growing-up years so strained and divide the world of my childhood into two hostile camps. My father had decided that, in commemoration of the remarkable year of my birth and to set a seal on my unique position in life, I was to be christened with the admittedly odd-sounding yet no less solemn name of Fram. Naturally, my mother was in despair. She initially said nothing, concentrating instead on recruiting allies in preparation for the expected clash. In women's usual foolish way she took her laments to the neighbours. They listened, mildly amused and mildly scandalised. The most well-disposed tried to persuade her it was just a joke on Mr Dreary's part, while the malicious did all they could to egg her on. Mr Dreary gave a surreptitious sneer of satisfaction and thought: let the old women prattle, but the girl shall be called Fram! He derived indescribable pleasure from being able to cause my mother and her godly friends this vexation. The more scandalised they were, the more clearly he sensed his superiority to his surroundings.

It was not until the very day the holy rite was to be performed that the storm broke. My mother cried and pleaded and wrung her hands, but nothing helped. Mr Dreary remained unmoved.

In tears my mother carried me to my christening. She quietly informed the godparents that in the name of God the child was to be called Maria Eleonora, which was a Christian name, fitting in all respects. Everyone breathed more easily, thinking that Mr Dreary had relented. He went round with a genial smile, greeting everyone cordially. But when the vicar arrived, Mr Dreary raised his voice and announced that the girl was to be called Fram, pure and simple. His expression and bearing were dignified as he made a statement of some length, setting out the views that had led him, the girl's temporal guardian, to this choice. The speech left an atmosphere of general despondency. The vicar and the godfathers were cowards, of course, merely exchanging furtive glances. But one of the godmothers, our immediate neighbour Miss

Jonsson, normally a great favourite of Mr Dreary, stepped resolutely forward and declared that she thought it a heathen name and wanted no part in such an affront to the female sex. Mr Dreary danced with rage and asked if the girl was his or Miss Jonsson's. An out-and-out scandal loomed. Thinking of my later life, I find it absolutely typical that I managed to cause a scandal at my first ceremonial entrance into the Christian cultural community.

The vicar finally felt obliged to step in and mediate. He cast about desperately for a name that would be more fitting for a baby girl while still fulfilling Mr Dreary's principled wishes. In awkward situations, people often get brilliant ideas, and this certainly applied to the vicar. In a flash of inspiration, the name Vega suddenly came into his mind. Wasn't *Vega* just as illustrious a polar expedition ship as *Fram*, in fact more so! And after all, it was too early to tell how things would go for *Fram*. News could come in any day that the ship had gone down with the loss of all on board. Mr Dreary had not thought of that. He grew pensive and looked crestfallen. No, *Fram* was nothing to cheer for yet, said the vicar, warming to his theme, but Nordenskiöld's *Vega*, well, that really was a name to reckon with. A name with which to sail into the storms of life. What was more, Nordenskiöld was a fellow countryman, an illustrious son of Finland.

The vicar had no need to say more. His words had plucked at the most sensitive string in Mr Dreary's heart. Moved, the latter thanked the eloquent clergyman for drawing his attention to these symbolic particulars. And then he uttered the words:

'Let the girl be called Vega.'

For a moment, a breathless hush fell over the place. But Mr Dreary was all too taken with this new idea to let it slip by in silence. On the spot he improvised a rapturous speech to the glory of *Vega*. He described her voyage around Asia and Europe, initiated his listeners into the problem of the Northeast Passage, afforded them glimpses of Spitsbergen, Novaya Zemlya, the Kara Sea and Cape Chelyuskin somewhere above my downy head, briefly sketched out the lives of the Chukchi, with intimate moments around the whale-oil lamp, lovingly lingered over a Samoyedic knife with an exquisitely worked haft made of a walrus tusk, and ended with a description of the dazzling festival of light with which Stockholm had celebrated *Vega*'s return. As he paused for breath, the vicar seized his chance and baptised the baby. Mr Dreary was seeing such splendid visions and taking such intense pleasure in his own flights of fancy that he did not even notice as, without further ado, the vicar additionally took the name suggested by my mother and baptised the girl Vega Maria Eleonora.

On discovering this betrayal afterwards, Mr Dreary immediately took steps to annul the additional names. With great gravity he staged a ceremony in which he, in his capacity as godfather and guardian, solemnly revoked the names Maria Eleonora, with the natural consequence that it became my mother's ambition to mount guard over them. She never called me anything but Maria. My father called me Vega. The cat, which incidentally was the only witness to the solemn annulment ceremony, said only miaow, and he was the only individual on whose neutrality I could fully depend. This naturally put our friends and acquaintances in a very awkward position. At first they tried to laugh it off, but they soon found that the conflict over names in the Dreary household was not to be taken lightly. To show their respect for Mr Dreary, his cronies used the name Vega, while my mother's friends kept strictly to Maria. Some people avoided calling me by name at all.

For me, it was a tragic situation. I was dimly aware that a battle for my soul was underway and that the two names symbolised unknown forces that seemed set on ripping apart my embryonic and anxiety-ridden self, which knew neither its own foundation nor the name of its own being. I became aware at an unnaturally early age of the strained internal conflict which presumably prevails within every human being and is perhaps the innermost incentive in each individual's struggle for form and learning, but which is seldom made so brutally manifest at such a defenceless age. My subsequent life has also proved to be unusually disharmonious. I have never been able to settle into calm co-existence with other people. I have lived my days in precarious balance, prey to sudden shifts of emotion, like a sailor in squally weather. A stab of rebelliousness goads me whenever reconciliation with the world and other people comes within reach, and I scarcely have time to harvest the fruits of my work or my intimate liaisons before their taste turns sour. That spirit of discord hovering above my innocent head at my christening has followed me in matters great and small, forcing me to destroy anything I have built up and to disavow things I have myself declared sacred. It seems to me that Vega, my father's irreverent child, has claimed the prize from Maria, my mother's gentle, considerate daughter.

I do not know which of the two names I should curse. My yearning for Maria's safe, sheltered and self-enclosed world – a world located so close to the ground that all its entrenchments hold fast and no cosmic shaking can be detected there – is something I have never been able to overcome. When I see the lucky individuals who have 'their own little corner on earth', where invisible walls of love and understanding protect them from the fiercest winds, I say to myself: you too could have had all this, if only you had known how to make the most of happiness when it was on offer. Instead you now have the self-reproaches and stifling sadness of your lonely evenings. But when I then look more deeply into their happiness and see the price they have paid for it, see the harsh indifference to all the distress and loneliness that cannot penetrate the protecting walls, then I think: oh, the human heart does not exist for this. In my mind's eye I see a broader, deeper, more all-encompassing spirit of community, one that is not built on shutting out, and – like a chill breeze running through my soul – the awareness dawns that this spirit of community is only to be won by hazardous ventures and great losses. From this I deduce that I am at the core of my being a Vega and that my father had hit the spot when he named me for the unknown and dangerous reaches beyond the boundaries of what lies closest to hand.

Long before this had come home to me, and before I had any opportunity to grasp the import of the fateful words 'the die is cast', I made my instinctive choice. By the time I went to secondary school – the first milestone on my conscious route to education – and after a feverish, agonising and emotional examination of the matter, I opted definitively for the name Vega.

Macedonia proves too small for me*

Mr Dreary could, incidentally, have hit upon many other names to put in place of the unfortunate Fram, if only he had been given a little time and not been caught off guard by the vicar in the middle of the ceremony. The ships that had set sail for uncharted oceans offered various splendid names to choose from. Just think of the proud squadrons with which Ferdinand Magellan embarked on his perilous passage. *Trinidad! Concepcion! Victoria!* What glory surrounded those names! I would willingly have borne every one of them. How readily the names which school tried to imprint on my mind have evaporated, while those that Mr Dreary taught me in those joyful, school-shirking lessons of the imagination will never be erased. The passing years have only enhanced the beauty of their symbolic sheen, which now has the lustre of old gold.

I can still keenly feel the shiver of sensual pleasure that would run up my spine as I sat on my stool at Mr Dreary's feet, listening with bated breath to his tales from the history of intrepid seafarers' feats. Only the highest heroism had the power to satisfy me, and tales that had no death-defying element left me completely unmoved. Mr Dreary himself derived indescribable enjoyment from these moments. As the situation came to a head and the starving and desperate crew threatened mutiny, he would suddenly go quiet and give me a meaningful look. I would quiver with excitement and my little heart would pound, yet I remained rooted to the spot and did not say a word, but kept my eyes fixed on his lips. Then he would stand up and strike a bold pose, as one would on deck in a challenging situation, staring death in the face, and declaim some incredibly heroic phrase uttered by the leader of the expedition:

'Even if I have to eat the leather wrappings of the ship's spars, I shall not give in but will complete my task.'

We both loved such lines with a passion. They constituted the eagerly awaited climax of our story, and once it was finally reached we would fall into one another's arms, overcome by an inexplicable emotion neither of us could control. We could hear the wind's song in the ropes and rigging of the ships, and it was always the same wind, singing the same intoxicating song: intrepid feats are calling us, calling us... This was the wind that filled your sails, you *Trinidad*, *Concepcion* and *Victoria* of my childhood!

It was certainly not at home, in the blandness of Gräsviksgatan, that these dramas were played out. Oh no, nothing ever happened there, except the usual routines. It was in Mr Dreary's shop, or to be more precise, in the dark little inner room that was supposed to be his office.

If you only saw me at home or at school, you would probably think me the decorous daughter my mother had wished for, a true Maria. I slept my way through life in that world. A burden weighed on my body and my soul, I felt tormented by my clothes, my plaits, my duties. This deep discomfort made me apathetic, which I assume to be the precondition for decorous conduct in childhood. My mother did everything to train me into domestic virtues, the only virtues a girl in our circles was felt to need. She placed particular emphasis on dusting. This loathsome ritual was performed each morning with meticulous thoroughness under the stern eye of my mother, with the consequence that I came to hate every piece of furniture and every ornament in our home. I detested all these things so profoundly that I would gladly have administered a kick or dashed them to the ground, had not fear held me back and forced me to do my rounds with a subservient expression, dusting and polishing in an idiotic and senseless fashion. If only the operation could have been left for a few days, at least for God's sake a slight layer of dust would have settled and one would have felt there was some purpose in what one was doing. But no, the whole point of so-called women's work is that it is supposed to be so delicate as to be invisible! Total meaninglessness is the defining characteristic of all tasks considered constitutionally suitable for women.

It was just the same with what they insisted on calling handicraft – as if women had ever been entrusted with any craft of the brain! Patching and darning were just about all right, I suppose. Not that those were much fun either; it was slow, fiddly, finicky work like everything else in the home, but at least it was a form of needlework worthy of human beings, compared to all the ridiculous cloths and monograms and embroideries one was expected to toil over. Cross stitch and stem stitch, running stitch and backstitch and crows' feet of every imaginable kind, all of them fiendishly devised to lend meaninglessness some pretence of meaning. Once the hole had been darned or the worn area patched, at least one had the satisfaction of having done something rational. But all those cloths that not a single person needed, which were stored away in piles in drawers and taken out once a year for airing – they were the real handicraft. It was in their intricate patterns that Mrs Dreary and her friends invested all their feminine ambition. They made a great show of them whenever they gathered together, and woe betide anyone who had 'forgotten their sewing' and simply took a seat at the table without that pretext, to listen to the gossip and drink coffee. There would be a pursing of lips and a concession that it could happen to anybody and one didn't always have a suitable piece of work to hand, but the tone and the looks said all too clearly that this was the hallmark of a slut. They knew what sort of person she was. Handicraft was in actual fact much more than it claimed to be; it was one of the great symbols of propriety, an indication of the owner's position in society, a guarantor of respectability, conscientiousness and virtue.

In this company I had to sit, demurely bent to my needlework in an unbearably strained position and, moreover, under close scrutiny. My hair was so tightly scraped back that my scalp ached, my nose shone from incessant washing with soap and water, my underclothes were so thick that I could barely move, my dress was so tight and my neckline so high that a straitjacket would truly have come as a relief. The ladies smiled with satisfaction and said: 'What a credit your daughter is to you, dear Agda'. In this company I learnt to detest my sex. From the dull indifference inside me, the first combative stirrings rose slowly but surely to the surface of my consciousness.

I fervently envied all boys. Couldn't I constantly hear their wild howls out in the yard, while I was trapped with the old maids? Didn't I see them freely prowling the streets in their robber gangs? Weren't they always up to strange and wonderful antics, producing from their pockets the most tempting objects: knives, magnifying glasses, ends of rope, pipes and God knows what else, all of them things that only free individuals have at their command, to use as they make their assault on life. Who would think of seating them with a piece of needlework in a circle of chattering womenfolk? Who would force them each morning to dust where there was no speck of dust! The bitterness slowly advanced into my heart, while they bound my soul more tightly with every passing day, the way people bound the feet of little Chinese girls. Like me, they initially found this very painful, while their feet adjusted.

A time was to come when I would feel the same pain over again, for the opposite reason. That was when I myself, in desperation and with clenched teeth, began to undo the binding – determined at any price to make myself capable of standing on my own feet. All at once I realised what upbringing means, for a boy as well as for a girl. I realised it is a long procedure involving much pain when a free creature, a child, is to be fitted into a prison system, and yet more pain when this creature starts to free itself from its prison with its own bloodied fingers, so it can finally stand there as a mature human being. Parents and teachers only have a share in the former hurt, the latter part we must inflict on ourselves. That is probably why it so often fails to happen.

At school, too, sluggish indolence was my only means of defence! I went through my primary years as if in a dream.

I was shunted from class to class in my sleep, automatically, as if I were some component in a machine on the production line of an efficiency-driven factory. I was considered very backward, developmentally impaired, and that really does not surprise me. Decades later I can still feel the drowsy apathy that sat there on my brain, purring its way through lessons. I was present, yet profoundly absent. I obediently submitted to the rules, laboriously learning the bare essentials of what was prescribed, but nothing got through to me, nothing took on life and shape in my imagination. The first little breath of wind from the regions of my soul dispelled that existence like mere shadow play. Nothing stayed in my memory – everything there just fused together, without colour, without contour, into an empty grey, a shrouding, characterless fog. That was how utterly I was able to distance myself from a world that did not belong to me.

In the street or on a train or bus, I occasionally happen across people who tell me with a beam of delight that they were classmates of mine at primary school. I look at them quizzically, like beings who have suddenly fallen from the moon, and with the best will in the world I am unable to locate a single recognisable feature. The only one of my classmates I can remember from that time is a pale boy in a black velvet jacket with a turned-down white collar and a big, black silk bow under his chin. He was top of the class, a conscientious, well-brought-up boy, much troubled by nerves. I can picture him vividly, but only in a single situation: he is standing at his desk, giving his astonishingly correct and concise answers in a strained and nervous voice. His pale face is so white against the black jacket, his voice trembles, the fingers with which he is supporting himself on the desk tremble. I do not know why he, of all people, made such a deep impression on me, for I am sure we had nothing to do with one another outside school. I have not seen him since, but many a time I have caught myself wondering what became of him, the star pupil. Things have doubtless gone badly for him, I think at times like those. Perhaps he died long since.

This melancholy little link, the shadow of a shadow, is all I have left of my early days at school. It was only much later, when I had turned sixteen, that I awoke from my dream and school became a reality for me. By then I had entered a new phase and the dream world of my childhood had vanished like a mirage.

What surging anticipation filled my world of dreams! Its master was Mr Dreary – the very same Mr Dreary who at home did nothing but carp and express his dissatisfaction with everything and everyone, except when he gave way to one of his completely gratuitous fits of rage. They recurred with periodic regularity but were nonetheless impossible to predict. At moments like that I feared him as one fears thunder, storm and conflagration. His hair was all over the place, his face contorted and his eyes glazed with a fierce, wild look. I hid in the wardrobe, shaking, and burrowed my head in among the clothes to avoid hearing those terrible words. But the curious thing was that none of this fear persisted or attached itself to his person. With the safe psychological assurance of a child I was able to differentiate between his normal self and the demonic spirit that took hold of him at times like that, putting him 'beside himself'. He was never as happy and dewy fresh as when he had just recovered from one of those outbursts! It happened in the blink of an eye; he simply shut himself in his room for a little while – ten or fifteen minutes at most – and when he came out again, his face would beam with childish satisfaction, his hair would be neatly combed flat and the gold chain would glint mysteriously across his stomach. He wandered cheerfully about the apartment, patted me on the head and told funny stories, especially from his younger days. He was so braced by his encounter with elemental rage that he could not understand anyone having cause for a surly countenance. If he detected any, he would look utterly offended and make a speedy exit in the role of family martyr.

These sudden switches were among the most surprising things about Mr Dreary; I never got used to them, and they would break over me each time with the fascination of something beyond belief. When he emerged from his room like that, as gleaming and freshly scrubbed as a child, I felt great tenderness for him. I sat completely still, not moving a muscle, but my eyes filled with tears and my little heart trembled with happiness. My papa, I thought. It is impossible for me, with the words of a fully-grown adult, to express all I felt at that moment in terms of affection, pride and unfathomable security: my papa.

When the two of us crept out to his shop in the evenings, I awoke to my real life. My numbness melted away and with it all the troublesome and inhibiting elements of my mind. I capered along the street, weaving to and fro, free and relaxed, babbling on about everything I saw on the way and shrieking with delight every time I encountered some handsome animal – a horse or a nosing dog. Their shining eyes were the loveliest things I knew. All the dog owners in that part of town knew me, and they knew my habit of taking every opportunity to capture their pets and lovingly press their damp muzzles to my own overheated face. But my true bosom friends were the cab drivers. Mr Dreary was a talkative man and liked to stop for a while on our walks to exchange a few words with them. They were such a droll lot, the old cabbies, real characters who had grown used to taking a philosophical and phlegmatic view of the world from their high driving seats. Many a time they would laboriously dismount from their majestic perches and hoist the little girl aloft so she could stroke the horse's nose. Their splendidly ruddy faces and rusty bass voices were quite frightening at close quarters, but their screwed-up eyes peered so kindly and their great paws held me as gently as if I were at my own nurse's breast. Sometimes they would put me in the cab, and that was really something! After a triumphant look at any passers-by I would swiftly close my eyes and imagine myself being driven round town.

A great deal could happen on the way to the shop, but underlying every event along the road lay the excitement of being en route to the biggest adventure of the day. Everyone knows how unassuming Mr Dreary's shop was, but for me it was the world. Just that: 'the world', in the sense one might use the word to speak of discovering a world. The place has been pulled down now, like so many other old buildings in our go-ahead city, and replaced by a newer, more practical one, but I cannot pass its former site without feeling a thrill of expectation. As my eyes scan the smart façade of the new building, which tells me nothing more than that this is where people with aspirations to modern comfort live, I see in my mind's eye the two little rooms where it was so quiet and dusky that all the spirits populating my imagination were clearly to be seen. The strange, hazy time of my childhood is resuscitated; even as I hurry about my business it comes to meet me with a feeling that is both carefree and full of anxiety:

'In the beginning, the world was an adventure for humankind, everything that lay beyond the perimeter of what was immediately known was a billowing home of the imagination, a playground for the fabulous creatures of myth – but the furthest reaches were the realm of darkness and mists...'*

For some inexplicable reason, on these occasions my father would always cross the outer room on tiptoe, as if he had entered someone else's shop without leave, and this drove my excitement to almost unbearable heights. In the end I couldn't control myself, but dashed headlong into the dark office and hid in a corner, trembling. There I would stand wide-eyed, staring out into the darkness until my father came and put on the light. He would close the door to the outer room carefully and quietly, so quietly, and then, slowly and with real reverence, make himself at home in our little nook. In our language, it was never referred to as anything but the cabin. Mr Dreary kept all his curiosities there – miniature ships made by some seafarer for his bride in his spare time, mysteriously encased in glass, like the longing that had given them their form, souvenirs from foreign lands, shells that surged like a whole ocean when you put them to your ear, and curious old books, among them some extremely rare editions in Spanish and Portuguese, accounts of the incomparable feats of the Conquistadores.

Muttering to himself and mumbling inaudible words, Mr Dreary would go round the room, myopically fingering the spines of his books. Anyone listening as keenly as I did could hear in his grunts the wild singing from South America's virgin forests and the Cordilleras' fearsome gorges, the Aztecs' battle cry at the bloodbath of Tenochtitlan, or the roar of the Spaniards' cruel and rapacious hordes in the fortune-starred valley of Cajamarca. After long and careful deliberation, Mr Dreary would draw out a volume, weigh it portentously in his hand and say: 'Pip!'* At that I would creep out of my hiding place and sit down on my stool at Mr Dreary's feet. The moment had come when Mr Dreary and I could find compensation for everything that was denied us in everyday life. Our ignominy and humiliation, our insignificance and obscurity were known to all – our pride and secret exaltation could be read only in one another's eyes as they met in the cabin on the exploit-filled voyage.

For the most part, neither of us could read the words in the foreign books, but it was of no consequence. Mr Dreary knew the main elements of all the stories – I have no idea where he learnt them – and anyway, why do we have imaginations if not to not to supply from our own minds what we lack in knowledge? And it made the old-fashioned trappings, strange names and, above all, the illustrations even more appealing to us. They were the only tangible props Mr Dreary and I required for staging our dramas. However much the world later devoted itself to feeding people's imagination with pictures, executed with all the technical refinements of photographic art, presented in ultra-modern montages, I have never seen any images to compare with those I saw in the cabin as I crouched over those heavy, yellowing volumes that I could only safely balance on my little lap with the greatest effort.

Who, now, can show me the picture of a ruler like Montezuma, the proud king of Mexico? There he stood, in full-length portrait, with one hand extended invitingly, as if just giving the order for the fabulous gifts that were to be handed over to the white stranger. No one can imitate that gesture.

No other picture can, as this one does, evoke the notion of godlike power and immeasurable riches, of nobility which even in the picture conveys the feeling that no mortal would dare look up at this face. Alas, such potentates no longer exist! And where can I now find pictures that infuse my breast with such a powerful fighting spirit, such a passionate desire to wreak vengeance on evil, as the depiction of noble Inca chief Atahualpa's execution? At later points in my life I have seen appalling pictures from the never-ending chronicle of mankind's cruelty and destructive urge, but these have only darkened my mind with deep pessimism and robbed me of my faith in what is good. Yet when my child's eye was fixed in fascination on the picture of the tortured Atahualpa, his terrible fate did not remotely depress me. In overwrought exaltation I clenched my fists and gritted my teeth, absolutely determined to become his mighty avenger. I dreamt feverish dreams about the vengeance-bound expeditions I would one day lead, when I grew up. I would liberate the unfortunate Inca people, defying a thousand deaths and superhuman dangers, and woe betide those who had committed any misdeed. Woe betide all those who had plundered and tortured and slain the innocent of this world! My weapons would strike terror into them all, wherever they were found. It goes without saying that Mr Dreary keenly supported the grandiose plans I was turning over in my mind. When he saw my blue eyes sparkling with righteous anger and my little hands clenching convulsively, he would give a leap of delight and shout in a high, shrill voice to an invisible audience: 'That girl has guts. She takes after her father!'

For some reason I can't recall, Fernando Cortez was my father's particular favourite. He never tired of describing how brave and bold he was and the way he could fire up his troops to achieve the impossible. He put everything into his role as Fernando Cortez. His face, otherwise as mobile and changeable as his whole nature and almost clownish in its exaggerated grimacing, suddenly seemed recast in a completely new form: stern, purposeful, unflinching. A new light illuminated his brow – the starry halo of the chosen one. I gazed up in dread at the hero as he gave his orders; a gesture of his hand was all it took for me to hear the steely clink of weapons from his camp in Veracruz.

'If I have worked hard,' he thundered, 'and staked everything on this enterprise, it is out of thirst for glory, which is a man's noblest reward.'

The voice was not Mr Dreary's. Fernando Cortez himself was addressing me. I stood ready to follow him into pale death. My whole body would tremble and I would feel my lips whiten and my mouth go dry, though I was stricken not with fear but with the flames of ambition.

Whatever else can be said about the education imparted to me in this peculiar way by Mr Dreary, it was not designed to mould a harmonious character. I still cannot fathom how I endured the physical tension with which my little body was charged on those heroic evenings in the cabin. My imagination was entirely focused on what was dazzling and unusual; for me, nothing else even remotely existed. It seemed natural to me that I had been singled out for greatness, and there was no limit to the wonders that fate held in readiness on my account. I felt my great calling burning in me, literally trying to burst out of my breast! How could I, an avenger of Atahualpa, a ruthless dispenser of justice, be expected to apply myself to dusting or hunch over pulled-thread embroidery or plug away at Bible history? In my imagination I always saw myself as the central figure in amazing and incredible events, which opened the eyes of those around me at a stroke and made my family realise who I really was. Bowing, they offered me their homage, and I took inexpressible pleasure in reading the immense surprise on their faces. The sweetness of these fancies can only be imagined by those who have tasted them in person; the danger in such poison is only perceived by those who have fallen prey to it themselves. This is the source from which they sprang, the disquiet and restlessness that have dogged me throughout life. I have never managed to keep what I possessed – it always seemed so small and insignificant in comparison to all I did not possess! I never felt satisfied with who I was, for I could perpetually see the dim mirage of who I really should have been – of my unutterably beloved and ardently craved but always elusive other self!

Once I grew up, so I believed as a child, I would automatically become one with that mysterious other being, suffused with all the power and glory that attended it. Hosts would join me, friends would spill their lifeblood for me and the sign of victory would shine on my brow. It is probably the dream of 'when I grow up' which constitutes the charm of childhood and which makes all those who have long since abandoned hope of ever growing up so eager to return to their early years. And it was probably this dream that helped me endure the tension of an existence in which I was daily flung in exaltation to dizzying heights, only to plummet brutally to earth the next moment at the sound of an angrily ringing alarm clock in Gräsviksgatan.

In the late evening, the walk home was certainly easy and enjoyable! I was in such a state of elation that I did not even feel the ground beneath my feet, still less spare a thought for the sordid morrow. Mr Dreary was on sparkling form, his ideas rocketing skywards as we walked hand in hand. Back home I immediately slipped into bed and pulled the quilt over my ears so I could truly feel that I was alone with myself, in my own lair. I lay there in the soft warmth and continued mulling over my dreams of greatness. Now, strangely enough, in the soft dark embrace of night, their character was completely different from what it had been in the storm-tossed world of the cabin. That convulsive fighting spirit dissolved in the warm bed and female nature asserted itself in secret and seductive ways. Fernando Cortez was pushed aside, edged out by the image of the crowned donna Marina, the loveliest of the slave women the defeated chieftains presented to their conqueror.

'She became the Spanish commander's mistress,' Mr Dreary once happened to say.

He had no idea what a deep impression this casual remark made on me. The mysterious word 'mistress' sank into a still lake in the depths of my being, generating much disturbance and dreams full of foreboding. It hinted at something of which

I was mysteriously aware, yet had no knowledge of. Lying there in my bed, a little bundle, I extended fine, quivering feelers into the surrounding darkness and a vague feeling of sensual pleasure filled my internal organs. I instinctively understood that this was something I would have to find out about entirely on my own. It was something I had to conceal even from Mr Dreary, my only confidant. A shiver ran through me as I curled up and pressed my knees against my chest; then I fell asleep, smiling at the approaching conqueror.

I had a cruel awakening. When one falls from the outermost edge of a cloud, floating free in cosmic air, to an oppressive existence in a petty-bourgeois setting, it is a hard and heavy fall. With bitterness and amazement I observed my mother's behaviour: she forced me roughly out of bed and hectored me about my laddered stockings, about the washing up I was to help with and the homework she had to test me on in a tearing hurry before I went to school. Outwardly demure and obedient, but with a hard heart and tight lips, I performed my duties. Sorrowful and embittered, I resheathed my sword. In this world, no one had any idea who I was.

Sullen and low-spirited, a little girl with tightly plaited hair and a shiny nose made her lethargic way into the classroom.

Intermezzo in the street

Today something dreadful happened to me. I could barely drag myself home, so shattered did I feel, and all my hard-won composure has been blown away. My heart feels like an inflamed boil in my breast, the heart I had believed dead, and with a heart like that I cannot shut myself inside the room of my memories.

It is the twenty-ninth of April today – the day he left me, many, many years ago. How the waters of Strömmen glittered, that day in Stockholm! People were leaning casually over the parapet of the bridge, staring down into the water, at the gleaming catches in the fishermen's lift nets, at the playful beauty of the birds, at the circles of their own trivial and meaningful thoughts. A many-coloured shoal of happy young people in new spring outfits promenaded along Strandvägen, giving the impression from a distance that showy flowers had suddenly blossomed from the tarmac, and along the quaysides the boats out to the islands, freshly spruced-up and keen to be underway, displayed their white spring finery. It was a wonderfully mild spring day, like today, with a sunlit golden haze in the air and a dash of chilly freshness in its bright blue shades. I stood on Norrbro bridge for a long time, looking down into the water like all the others, at the gleaming catches in the fishermen's lift nets, at the playful beauty of the birds. The people around me came and went, but I stayed on, alone in an unfamiliarly lovely city.

I was waiting for Tancred. But he never came. He had left me.

When I went out today, my mind was empty and quiet, as the mind of a resigned individual will be. I was not thinking about that, had not remembered what day it was. It all lay so infinitely far back in time. My childhood and my adventures with Mr Dreary felt much closer to me. I sat down for a while on a bench on Esplanaden, watching the children, the plump, cooing pigeons and the workmen digging the border round old Runeberg* to smarten him up for May Day. Then I thought: I shall take a stroll down to the harbour to see the terns flying.

I passed Kapellet restaurant and saw that the place had opened its doors for the spring season. I was thinking about this just as I stepped out onto the pavement by the market square – and almost collided with a man, who seemed confused and raised his hat in an absent-minded way, not looking at me, before he went on his way into town. Before I consciously had time to register anything, I suddenly felt intensely weak and lightheaded and had to lean against the doorpost to stop myself falling. My eyes followed the hunched and shabby figure and in terrible pain my heart screamed: It's him! This pain did not think, did not reflect, it simply screamed. I had nothing in my head but the thought that once he reached the next street corner he would disappear from view and the great emptiness would engulf me forever. I wanted to shout, cry out, call his name, but no sound could force its way through my burning lips. At the corner of Alexandersgatan he took a left turn and I saw him no more.

I came round to find myself lying on the ground, surrounded by a crowd of curious people, and the kind woman at the lemonade stall offered me a glass of cold water. It was a delicious and refreshing drink. I got to my feet and walked without too much difficulty to a nearby bench from which, in the middle of sunny Esplanaden, among playing children, smart young people and quietly dozing old ladies, I could resume battle with my crazy heart.

'What do you want of him?' I said. 'You know all that is over, dead and buried.'

'Can't you see he's free again,' yelled my heart. 'He's out of his prison! He's mine. I love him.'

'Didn't you see the way he looked? Preoccupied, down at heel, a shadow of his former self. If you went up to him he would turn his eyes away, like a stranger.'

'What do you mean,' shouted my heart. 'It was Ta!'

'Don't you remember how he left you that time, without a word?'

'It was my own fault,' cried my heart. 'I shouldn't have tormented him the way I did, I should have loved him, understood him, helped him!'

And I couldn't prevent the tears starting to run down my cheeks. It felt good to cry properly after so many years of desperately restrained yearning. The tears fell so quietly and imperceptibly, without any anguish, without any sobbing.

There stood the beautiful old building on Västra Trädgårdsgatan, thinking genially of its former friends. When spring came, lending the windowpanes that strange glint, it would often stand there deep in thought. It withdrew into itself and listened to its inner music. People passing would say to one another: 'Look, what a beautiful building. Just imagine living in a house like that!' They were not sure what they meant by it. They were by no means unhappy with where they lived, and if offered the chance to move they would undoubtedly have had to think very hard about it. But that wasn't really what they meant. There was something special about that house. Here in Västra Trädgårdsgatan there were so many other lovely old houses of equally exclusive pedigree, but no one ever nurtured dreams of living in them one day. This house was so gaily coloured that it made you think of the south, of palm trees and gondolas and that sort of thing. And it was in such an attractive position, no other houses opposite, only an opening to Kungsträdgården park and the springtime. The old lime trees around the fountain must already be coming into bud. So why not go that way home, pause for a while under the limes, feel the spirit of spring.

I could see that the old house paid no heed to those passing by. It did not spare them a glance. It was thinking of its own children, how they had fared in life. Its big, benevolent eye, which had watched over them all, started to fill with tears as it remembered all those who had vanished and been seen no more. The little blond-haired boy who sat so still at his window on the first floor, why did he never come back? Where had they taken him? He was so beautiful, and his smile so captivating that it lit up the whole house. He never ran on the stairs and was never to be heard shouting, or making too much noise when he spoke. He was a real dream child for a lovely old house with a distinguished façade. In those days the man with the beautiful hands lived up on the top floor; he and the child would make secret signs to each other that no one else properly understood. He had gone now, too, and his music had fallen silent. It was only at moments like these that the memory of his music would run like a shiver through the old house and bring an instant change to its physiognomy. It was illuminated by the light of devotion and one could see that the whole house was tuned to the key of C minor. I could hear him playing myself, mysteriously and as clear as day, and for the first time in all these years I summoned the courage to let my thoughts take me into our little attic room, mine and Tancred's, which was above his apartment. Nobody was as good to Ta as he was, least of all I. It is strange to think of how many good people there are here in the world and yet how little they can achieve, how little they can 'help' anyone heading to their doom.

'None of you understood him,' said my heart in a sudden cry of despair. 'He lived alone among you, hiding what was deep inside him. Now I would understand him!'

'We tried to help him as much as we could,' I said. 'His talent ...'

'You loved his career, but not the man himself, his life, his fate!'

'I wanted what was best for him, I swear.'

'You wanted your own vanity, nothing more,' my heart cried, so loudly that anyone could hear it. 'I want to go back to him, make it all up to him, share his misery and destitution. I love him!'

'Too late,' I said bitterly. And emptiness gaped like a chasm before me. I dragged myself home with heavy steps.

All night I have been brooding on why my life has turned out such a failure, why I have managed to do so many bad things when I wanted to do good, why my love, to which I devoted myself so ardently, has grown toxic to me and to the one I loved. It is already getting light outside, day is dawning on the street. On the pavement opposite I can see three adolescent girls walking past in caps, one red, one green and one blue. It looks comical, and I fleetingly wonder where they have come from and where they are going at this early hour. But the magical light of the sky does not reach my heart and I feel alone, excluded from the secrets of the cosmos.

I can find no answer to my questions.

Days of convalescence

Naturally I should have been prepared for this!

When I thought about it, I realised of course how different Mr Dreary had been of late. It was clear that his mind was filled with thoughts and plans in which I had no part. He seldom had time for me any more, a succession of odd visitors came and went, there were long deliberations behind closed doors and it all seemed very hush-hush. He said not a word to me about all these activities! This hurt me deeply. I had been blithely assuming I would be his fellow conspirator. I had turned fifteen, hadn't I, and would be leaving school? Was I not now mature enough to test my arms' strength, my stamina and my bravery in some risky and glamorous venture!

One evening, when Mr Dreary seemed particularly exhilarated after one of those sessions, I summoned up my courage and asked him:

'What are you planning, Papa?'

To my utter astonishment, he replied:

'Womenfolk don't understand that kind of thing.'

I was so disconcerted that it was only once I was alone in my bed, my shame hidden from the world, that I felt able to think over his answer properly. My thoughts circled in agitation around that word 'womenfolk', which had somehow smuggled its way between my father and me. I didn't want to be classed as 'womenfolk'! I hated the very word. I felt instinctively that it would separate me from all that I most fervently desired, the great exploits, the glorious honours and distinctions, the wild and perilous life out in the wide world. My free highwayman's heart felt insulted to its core. I clenched my fists and gritted my teeth in impotent defiance and took a holy oath never to join the ranks of womenfolk. But I ended by bursting into tears, the apprehensive and bitter tears of a child at the first creeping sense of disappointment.

Even so, I rushed with glittering eyes and a trusting heart straight from the ceremonies of my last day of school – human beings never cease to amaze – up the steps to Mr Dreary's shop, waving my grade certificate like a victory banner! He wasn't there, which was aggravating, but did not rouse my suspicions. Nor was he at home, though that was nothing to wonder at, when he had so many irons in the fire. I had to resign myself to taking coffee and buns with the female company my mother had invited in honour of the day. But Mr Dreary's absence certainly took the shine off proceedings. 'My, how time flies,' said Aunt Emma. 'Little Maria's a grown-up lady now.' 'Ye-ees,' said insufferable Aunt Mili in her slow and sanctimonious way, 'God's will be done.'

Well that's that then, it's started, I thought. But then, fortunately, worldly Miss Jonsson interjected a sensible verdict on my dress.

'The girl doesn't look bad, but the dress is frightful,' she said bluntly.

Embarrassed silence, general scrutiny of my person. I was suffering indescribable agonies, but determined to endure anything now I had so unexpectedly found an ally in the bitter battle with my mother over what I wore.

'Presumably you're not intending to put her in a nunnery, my dear Agda,' said Miss Jonsson, and gave a resounding laugh at her own wit.

'I'm bringing my daughter up to be decent,' my mother said haughtily.

'Thank God someone is taking a stand against vanity in these times of ours,' lisped Aunt Mili with a venomous look at Miss Jonsson's showy outfit.

Why was my papa taking so long? It felt so awful being consigned to the old biddies on such a day. Their chatter ran past my ears, until I suddenly jumped at the sound of a question:

'Well, little Maria, what are you intending to do now school is over?'

As soon as I heard the question I truly understood that school was over, that the excruciating torpor, the endless lesson times were over, and life could begin at any moment. A fiery blush stained my cheeks and my heart thumped so violently I simply could not stay in my seat. I jumped up and leapt foolishly into the air. Unaware of my own actions, I clapped my hands and gave a shout of joy. Before I could feel the floor beneath my feet again, I heard my mother's sharp exclamation:

'Maria, really!'

Then I saw that everyone was staring at my skirt as if witnessing something totally beyond belief. And it was beyond belief, of course, for a young girl to behave like that before the very eyes of her mother and all the other ladies, ripping her pleated skirt on a treacherous chair leg, which for some unfathomable reason was sticking up into the air instead of being planted on the ground.

My outbursts of joy often have disastrous consequences of that kind. Some evil omen always likes to slip in whenever I let myself go and shout hurrah! But I was heedless both of bad omens and of my mother's ominous expression. I was expecting Mr Dreary at any moment. I was expecting him in greater suspense than ever before, like a gambler who has staked everything he owns on a single card.

The longer he tarried, the more eager my absurd anticipation grew. The fantasies of my childhood years rose up inside me, more indistinct yet more insistent than ever, manifesting themselves physically as a glowing internal heat that almost took my breath away, a craving that could no longer withstand its own excitement. Nothing definite had ever been said about my future, but the entirety of my peculiar double life was built on the implied presumption that one day I would make a total break with the trivial life of school and home, jettisoning it like some ridiculous disguise and donning instead the suit of gleaming metal that Mr Dreary had selected for me in the armoury of the imagination.

I considered it self-evident that my schooling would end at the intermediate level. Though I did not really dwell on it or nurture any specific plans, the conviction grew within me that now was the time for my life to begin in all its glory, now the hour had arrived for the sweeping change that my whole disposition, the action of my thoughts and the direction of my fancies desired. Centre stage in this dazzling shift of scene stood Mr Dreary. This was why I was waiting – with my far from brilliant school-leaving grades and my shredded dress – in quivering anticipation of his arrival. Arrogantly I delighted in the fact that the hated dress had been ruined – it was rags and nothing more! Arrogantly the laughter bubbled inside me as the old ladies enquired what I was going to do now – what I was going to do *now*! Pitiful old ladies! Mr Dreary could be there at any moment. 'Well then, my girl,' he would say with a wink of secret complicity, 'this is it.'

But Mr Dreary did not come that evening, nor the next day, nor the next evening. He stayed away for a whole week, which had never happened before. This was the time when my mother finally fell into the hands of the Pentecostalists, so worn down and defenceless had she become. She went eagerly to the Tabor church meetings* every evening God gave, staying out until late at night. She came home with her eyes red from weeping and a strange, absent brightness in her look. She scared me. It chilled me to the heart to regard the stony immobility of her thin, white face, with that gaze which was turned on me yet seemed not to see me.

For my part, I was living in a wonderful state of liberation and divine lightness. I revelled in having the evenings to myself. My spirit expanded, at rest and yet mighty, filling the small rooms, filling the world and the universe. I breathed deeply and felt blessed, and for once entirely in harmony with the rhythm of the days and nights, with the cosmic melodies of light and dark. I did not confide my sensual pleasure to anyone. Whenever the doorbell rang I did not answer; I sat so still that only those who can hear a human breath or see the pathetic death struggle of a mosquito on a blade of grass could have perceived my presence. I often guessed it was Fridolf trying to pay me a visit, but I did not want to see him at all. In my heart there was no one but Mr Dreary. I was waiting for him. The longer he delayed his arrival, the more significant this waiting time became. It was plain, of course, that his peculiar disappearance on my red-letter day could only mean one thing: sensational preparations were in progress. I fully and firmly believed, even at my age, that my papa was not at all who he seemed to be, but was in league with great and secret things which he would reveal to me in the fullness of time.

When Mr Dreary finally appeared, as nonchalant as ever, as if he had merely missed dinner, I could see at once that he was much changed. He regarded me with a peculiar look of unfamiliarity, as if he were seeing me for the first time. I momentarily felt a self-consciousness verging on alarm, but then the laughter bubbled up inside me and I thought to myself: You don't fool me so easily, you old ruffian! Accustomed as I was to all the rules of the game, I gave nothing away, but adopted a solemn expression. He asked for my report and pretended to be absorbed in examining the inadequate grades. He adjusted his face into troubled furrows, gave a sniff or two and nervously fingered his gold watch chain. I waited impatiently for the moment when I was to run into his arms and hear him depict the wild and beautiful future awaiting the two of us.

Then Mr Dreary looked up:

'Well Vega, you haven't inherited your father's gift for scholarship.'

A little gurgle in my throat indicated that I appreciated the joke and knew what was going on.

'There's no point your taking the higher school certificate.' This he fired off with a grimace, looking at me over his spectacles.

'No,' I answered with an energetic shake of my head, still thinking he was putting on a grand show.

Then Mr Dreary tossed my report onto the table and stood up:

'You can help out here at home for now. Then I suppose I shall have to try to find you some kind of job in an office.'

With these astonishing words, he left me. He disappeared out into the hall. Paralysed by the most intense anticipation, I waited for the funny little sign that would transform this ghastly drama into a game played by two young rascals enjoying a kick-about with their own fates. But Mr Dreary was so strangely silent out there in the hall. Was he really putting his coat on?

'Make me some sandwiches please, Agda,' he called to my mother in the kitchen, and was out of the door in an instant.

That was the last line delivered on the stage of my childhood's great drama of adventure. And with that line, the brilliance that had surrounded Montezuma, Atahualpa and Fernando Cortez vanished. With that line Mr Dreary vanished from the world where he had been the absolute monarch with all the resources and opportunities in his hand, vanished from the lonely and misled heart of a little girl. I never stopped loving him – jealously and unjustifiably, as one loves the people whose weaknesses one has exposed – but my heart suffered so much in the process that it would have been better for it never to have possessed such an idol.

I was still lying there staring wide-eyed into the darkness when I heard my father put his key into the lock. Once again a tremor ran through me; I held my breath and waited. But he went straight to his bed. I curled up in mine as if it were a protective nest and gentle sleep came to blow away my suffering, the way a mother blows away the pain in a child's pinched finger.

The next morning I was the last person to imagine anything nice would happen to me that day! Or that anything nice would happen to me ever again, after that. I was reluctant to wake to the new day at all, there was no point getting up and dressing and – well, how was I supposed to occupy myself? It was not as though I had anything to live for. I heard my mother bustling around the kitchen. I heard my father cough and clear his throat in the next room. All at once he started whistling and began to wash with a great deal of splashing and snorting. I heard all of this, but every familiar sound was like a stab to my heart. It was if I stood outside it all and everything had lost its purpose.

I closed my eyes and thought about the way it used to be on Sunday mornings and school holidays, when I would lie there lazily as I was doing now, listening with a blissful sense of anticipation to every sound indicating that Mr Dreary was in vigorous morning action. At any moment a bristly head would thrust itself round the door and pull a horrible face to announce that it was time to weigh anchor and cast off! However changeable the weather over the course of the day, at least one knew that as long as Mr Dreary had his health and strength, the ship would be commanded with dash and vim. Now it was so strangely empty around me, I had nothing whatsoever to wait for and the snorting and splashing in the next room did not have the same friendly ring to them as before. It was a torment to me to lie there and hear these people going about their usual activities as if nothing had happened, while I plummeted down into a bottomless chasm! There was such a dull, unnatural throbbing inside my head, office and housekeeping, housekeeping and office, and when an incautious movement made me conscious of a splitting headache I could feel it drilling away at a single point. It drilled insistently and meanly at just one word: womenfolk, womenfolk, womenfolk...

I must have been dozing for a while when I came to with a start and saw my mother standing by my bed, solicitous and good-humoured the way she could sometimes be when her heart had been calmed and softened by Mr Dreary's return from some menacing escapade. She was bringing me coffee in bed, the nicest thing I know! I sat up at once and said something I was not in the habit of saying: Mama! She made a clumsy and touching attempt to enact a little fantasy, keeping one hand stiffly extended behind her back and proffering the coffee cup with the other as she fluttered her eyelashes and bowed deeply with her whole body. I almost knocked over the cup in my eagerness to reach for what she was hiding behind her back. Luckily I was saved such a mishap at this solemn moment and was able to retain my dignity and unclouded sense of happiness as I received into my hand the first letter ever brought to me by an unknown messenger from the big wide world.

I could hardly believe my eyes when I saw the large envelope and read the address written on the front in delicate, elegant lettering: *Miss Vega Maria Eleonora Dreary*. Ideally I would have liked to hide the letter under my pillow to open later in private, when I could devote myself fully to its unimaginable mystery, as the rituals of such an occasion demanded. But my mother could not contain her curiosity and that was therefore out of the question! So I opened it solemnly in her presence and laid it on the bed in all its splendour.

Kangais, 31st May 1909.

My dear child!

Here is your paternal grandfather writing to you to extend an invitation to visit fair Kangais in the heart of beautiful summertime Tavastia before I close my old eyes and take my rest from this earthly journey. Many a time I have thought I would like to see my grandchild for God has, I believe, allowed you to thrive and grow up a good girl, and the others have no girls but only boys. You need bring nothing with you and with your mama's permission I would like you to come whenever you will to visit your old grandparents.

Yours,
C. A. E. Dreary

Speechless with astonishment, I stared at my mother. Kangais, Tavastia, grandfather ...

These were all new and amazing concepts to me, unknown worlds popping up out of nowhere, appearing magically at the very moment everything around me had turned so oddly grey and small. Never in my life had I heard anything of a grandfather, of Kangais or Tavastia! How funny that Mr Dreary had a papa, it had never occurred to me. My head was pounding and throbbing more insistently than ever and suddenly the thought ran through me: Papa! This is his doing!

He kept all this secret just to make it a nicer surprise. That's so like my papa!

With a bound I was out of bed and on my way to his room brandishing the letter so I could finally, finally give him that hug from the bottom of my heart. So, none of it had been meant seriously! He had led me up the garden path, deceived me with office and housekeeping and other nonsense! A little cry of delight forced its way out of my brimming heart and I had to stop for a moment in the middle of my room to truly savour how much I loved my papa. My head was spinning from sheer joy.

Then my mother rushed after me, grabbed me by the nightgown and whispered, her eyes wide with horror:

'Hush Maria! Not a word to your father, remember that!'

Something in her expression made me realise something was not right here and the terrible suspicion crept over me again. Somewhere inside me it hurt so much and I would have fallen to the floor if my mother had not taken me in her arms. She swiftly pressed me to her breast, stroking my head with a tender, nervous hand. I could feel how timorously she did it, as if not convinced she had the right. It was the first instance of any gesture of affection between my mother and me, if I exclude the time before I had any awareness of such things. The tears ran silently down her cheeks. She always cried when she was happy, my mother.

'You feel so hot, Maria. You aren't ill, are you?' she said in sudden anxiety.

You aren't ill, are you?

It sounded so flat to my ears, so utterly forlorn. I was conscious of feeling very tired and everything seemed so empty and strange around me. I was dreadfully cold. After being tossed for days and weeks between endless expectation and darkest despondency, my little heart was now shivering in fits of cruel disappointment. As if through a fog I saw my mother seated on the edge of the bed, surreptitiously dabbing her nose now and then with the corner of her apron. She explained everything to me: how Mr Dreary had once run away from home, and since then had refused to see either his father or his mother, or his younger siblings, and could not even bear to hear them mentioned; how this behaviour – offensive, unnatural and unchristian as it seemed to her – had made her suffer too, and furthermore, grandfather's property was very grand, he had sold off some forest land, and a visit to him there would certainly be no bad thing, if the occasion arose. But Dreary of course could not abide a word being spoken of all this, he was so unreasonable in many respects, simply impossible to comprehend. But behind Mr Dreary's back she had written to the old couple in complete secrecy to tell them of my arrival in the world, and had continued to keep them informed of all major events thereafter. And now look how kindly my grandfather had extended his invitation!

'But what shall I tell Dreary?' she kept asking herself in alarm.

I listened, but it was plain that these were matters that did not concern me. Now and then I looked at her in astonishment. This Dreary, this man she feared so much – could she mean my papa? Was he hostile? To me?

I closed my eyes and abandoned the effort of finding any kind of clarity in this inexplicable tangle. The conflicting emotions in my breast settled into a sweet, restful state of numbness. The days and nights merged into a melodious lullaby, a gentle purring in my brain, where my fever lay like a soft and silky cat, its eyes glinting through narrow slits.

'My girl,' 'My darling little girl,' and similar endearments reached my ear through the loud roar of hot, feverish blood. Whenever I opened my eyes I saw my mother's face bending over me, the light of her gentle devotion directed towards me. I smiled at her and sank back into my torpor, secure in my sense that a patient, steadfast spirit was watching over me. Sometimes a snatch or two of her hymns and prayers would reach me and I softly repeated the words to myself. They had such a beautiful, solemn ring.

It was by no means with mild phrases about God suffering the little children to come unto Him that my mother sought to fortify me in my arduous time of sickness. On the contrary, she fed me the most full-bodied religious sustenance, sometimes in such potent doses that they should have been enough to waken the dead. Despite her sectarian sentimentality she had in her character a good helping of the genuine Protestant austerity that does not shrink from calling the Evil One by his proper name or – if necessary – throwing some hard object after him. As she sat there by my sickbed, blissful at having her daughter entirely to herself but beset by the horror of losing her to implacable death, she instinctively turned to the most robust incantations her battered old hymn book had to offer, words saturated over centuries with the profound quaking of the human heart when confronted with the transience of life and the abrupt ending of its joys:

> Oh sinner, safe and so secure while resting,
> In sin's sleep and death's torpor long since nesting,
> Awake, arise, mark well: your time is nigh,
> See, God still views you kindly from on high.
>
> What is your life? A stream time soon will banish.
> What's your desire? A dream that soon will vanish.
> Your strength? A prop collapsing in a day.
> What's gold, possessions? Just three trowels of clay.*

'Three trowels of clay.' I repeated to myself with solemn dignity. It gave me unutterable satisfaction to say such words – the more cheerless, ominous and terrible they sounded, the more impressed I felt by their truthfulness.

My mother would lower her otherwise reedy voice to the deepest pitch as she sang this hymn of eternal damnation:

> Consider too the torment grim and horrid
> One godless suffers; flaming depths so torrid
> Where no redemption waits since he is doomed,
> Where he will burn, yet never be consumed.
>
> Body and limbs – shake, shudder, quake and quiver,
> Hair – stand on end; my thoughts – plunge like some river

Into the abyss, and see the torment glower
That all erodes, yet nothing will devour!

I shook, shuddered and quaked as I lay there in my bed,
burning up with fever, listening to Lasse Lucidor's words as to
the clamour of impassioned humanity: 'Where he will burn,
yet never be consumed' – 'that all erodes, yet nothing will
devour!' As the words fell from my mother's lips she, too, grew
in my eyes in stature and power, her face sometimes looming
over me like a cloud, sometimes enigmatically disappearing so
all I saw were two glowing eyes in the darkness, darting from
side to side. She sang the hymn over and over again and each
time my lips would repeat the words. Thus we, a lonely woman
and a girl child locked in her battle with death, in terrible and
solemn words shaped by an unhappy poet and sung through
the centuries for comfort and edification by congregations
with death in their hearts, deposited all our fear and frailty
and our deep sense of abandonment, as if in bowls of black
granite.

I shall never forget this hymn.

While my illness lasted, it was as if Mr Dreary vanished
from my consciousness. Once or twice I deliberately fixed my
awareness on his presence, but I sensed he was only briefly
in the room and did not belong there. Mr Dreary did not like
sick people; he was, quite simply, afraid of them. Every time
anyone fell ill, even if it was only with the slightest of colds,
he made a terrible fuss, deploring what he saw as the extreme
indifference shown to the poor invalid by everyone else. He
fetched all the medical books in the house, made a keen, close
study of the symptoms and determined which were the most
interesting theories about what it could be. Clearly there
was something serious concealed behind those apparently
innocuous symptoms. In nervous agitation he would issue his
prescriptions, bring out bottles of dried-up medicine he had
secreted away, come rushing in with the thermometer to take
the patient's temperature, make a great business of ordering
compresses and hot-water bottles. And throughout all this,
his pitiful and accusing voice would exhort the patient not

to lose heart. Once he had thoroughly worn you out with his admonitions and long-winded tales of other cases he had seen or heard of, he would suddenly vanish from the scene and take great care to have no further dealings with your person, if you were exhibiting any signs of being seriously ill.

My mother was completely different. She seemed initially quite indifferent, talking about anything but the illness. How you appreciated Mr Dreary's sympathetic words then! But if it proved more protracted and painful, you could feel assured that she would not stir from your side, whatever happened. And you would forget Mr Dreary – until you got better and began longing for him to poke his head round the door and pull a funny face.

This time, overcoming my serious bout of illness with the help of potent spiritual sustenance and the adventurous resilience of my own soul, and slowly emerging from my torpor, I did not long for Mr Dreary. Oh, my longing was for something completely different! Clouds came blowing over me – of agony and delight such as I had never tasted. Mr Dreary's betrayal drilled so excruciatingly into my heart, but from the pain itself, life's red sap spurted in all its turbulence and longing – onward, onward. Beneath my pillow lay the letter as the pledge of a thousand new possibilities, a message imbued with a host of meanings, from regions unknown. Mr Dreary entered and left my orbit with no capacity to touch my soul or fire my imagination. Sometimes he would sit down by my bed for a little chat, but I did not particularly enjoy this, and listened to his jokes with only half an ear. I had the letter under my pillow and he knew nothing of the wonderful thing that had happened to me. Quite simply, he stood outside it. It was so extraordinary and unfamiliar for Mr Dreary suddenly to be left on the outside of great events – what pain, what bliss!

Whenever both my parents happened to be together in my sickroom during my days of convalescence I would often look surreptitiously from one to the other, as one steals looks at strangers whose secrets one is keen to decipher without them noticing. I wondered how it had actually come about that

I was their child. The whole thing was highly amusing and absurd! I would have vastly preferred to be alone, and found it disturbing to have them near me. When I was on my own I could lie as still as I wanted, completely quiet and unmoving, not even pretending to do anything. Lying like that, eyes closed, I felt so indescribably light and free, like a bird in an expanse of sky. It was sheer heaven to lie there in that way!

One day, when my mother felt I was strong enough to bear a hard blow, she told me I would have to put the trip to Kangais out of my mind. Mr Dreary did not want it, she said; it was impossible. She had not dared to tell him about Grandfather's letter, but she had cautiously touched on the idea of letting Maria go to Kangais to regain her strength after her severe fever. Mr Dreary had been wild with rage, saying that if the girl went to Kangais she would have to stay there too, and it would be best for her mother to go with her. He would not stand in the ladies' way – please go ahead! Have a good time and tell my father that Carl Johan Dreary isn't man enough to feed his own wife and child! But don't come back afterwards! Stay there and live on the old fellow's charity! My mother had naturally beaten a swift retreat, declaring it was only a passing fancy and on reflection she could see very well it was a stupid idea and not at all appropriate. This had happened several days earlier, but my mother was still in a state of alarm as she told me about it and made me swear never to say a word about the letter to Mr Dreary.

'Dreary would be so angry I don't know what he might do,' she said in deep distress.

I listened to her with a superior smile. So Mr Dreary would be angry, would he, I thought to myself. And the little steel spring inside me quivered and felt its power. Before I knew it, the decision to defy Mr Dreary grew to maturity at lightning speed within me. My helplessness was overwhelming and my dependence manifest, so lacking was I in physical strength, but inside me a mysterious process of liberation was underway. A new little personality was faintly stirring in the unconscious depths of my being, like a foetus in the womb of the mother-to-be, and its vibrations filled me with deep and happy anticipation. When my mother anxiously demanded the letter – she wanted to destroy it so it could not fall into Mr Dreary's hands – I laughed in her face, something I have never had the courage to do before or since! Of course this incensed her and she approached the bed with cold determination to seize it from me. Then I reared up like a tigress and threw myself desperately on top of the pillow beneath which the letter lay hidden. I pressed myself to it with a passion and uttered a reckless cry of: 'I won't give it up, I won't give it up!' – and I am sure that as I did so I felt the same frantic ecstasy as if I had said: 'You shall have it over my dead body!' In that letter lay my new life, beckoning me with a 'Come, Vega, come!' Taking it from me would have been like tearing the heart from my breast.

Furious, my mother left me – as my partner in crime she dared not bring matters to a head. I was left alone with my booty. It was like receiving the letter all over again. It filled me with secret joy that no one realised how much it meant to me. I held it tenderly to my breast and fell into a happy slumber in the knowledge of having fought a great battle.

My Tavastian odyssey

I spent the whole train journey to Tavastehus feeling like a princess in disguise. I was so wrapped up in my new role as an autonomous personality that I neither saw nor heard what was happening around me, still less did I spare a thought for the misfortunes I was leaving behind me at home. With a look of superiority and self-importance on my face I sat in my corner, as straight-backed and stiff as a newly discharged grenadier, surveying the assembled company, none of whom had any idea what I had done, or what unyielding forces moved within me. A pride beyond words possessed my mind. Had I not by my actions proved that I was far from being just any girl, to be placed sometimes here, sometimes there, in the home or in an office but otherwise ignored. One of the tribe of womenfolk! I did not belong with the womenfolk, no I did not! I was Vega Maria Eleonora Dreary herself.

The scenery slipping by and the chatter in the railway carriage could not reach me. Although it was my first long journey – what did I care? I was wrapped up in a drama far exceeding this in excitement and significance. Over and over its scenes passed before my eyes, over and over I became engrossed in its thrilling details, savouring every little fluctuation with godlike gratification. How prettily and sanctimoniously I had written to Grandfather to tell him how difficult it would be to make the journey because my papa thought it too expensive! What dazzling good luck I'd had in being the only one at home when the postman brought the registered letter! That had not occurred to me, and things could easily have gone instantly awry. But fortune favours the bold. Fortune had been on my side all the way through, ever since I took the decision, cost what it might, to get myself to Kangais. How felicitous and elegant my departure from home that morning had been! Not even the cat suspected anything. I truly had to laugh at the thought of it.

But my laughter faded when I found myself on the station platform at Tavastehus. I just stood there, looking at all the people walking past me. Everything was so awfully unfamiliar and not a single person took any notice of me. They rushed off as if they all knew where they were going and nobody came up to me and asked if I was Vega Maria Eleonora Dreary, not a one.

I suddenly realised it was terribly empty all around me. It was as deserted as only a station platform can be after all the trains have left and all the people have gone home. I felt the tears burning my eyes as a lump formed in my throat. I made a most pitiful princess, standing there mournfully with my suitcase on the station platform at Tavastehus, crying. Grandfather was meant to be meeting me here with his carriage and pair. I had pictured that carriage so vividly in my mind's eye: the snorting horses, the gaily-coloured reins, the bright metal fittings. As I stepped from the train it would be there waiting, everybody would see it and cast envious glances at me as I climbed in with a smile, while the coachman saluted and Grandfather flung his arms wide. But everything was so different now, with no sign of any carriage, any coachman or any grandfather. I was left standing alone in a horribly strange place, with indecision, anxiety and alarm constricting my heart. What had I done? I had left home without leave and what would Papa say and how would Mama explain the matter? By now, everything would long since have come to light, and here I stood. What should I do? Going back home was unthinkable! Papa would slam the door in my face. And anyway, I could not bear such humiliation. No, there was no way back now! All I could do was disappear into the darkness, walk and walk along those country roads, beg for my bread, ask charitable folk to give me houseroom. Dear God, how I wept! I felt bitterly sorry for myself. I could picture it all so clearly, my worn-out shoes, my dirty, tear-stained face, my crusts of bread and fingers blue with cold. I felt to the very bottom of my heart that I had neither father nor mother, that I was all alone in the big wide world, and I ignored the fact that it was by my own obstinate actions I had put myself in this situation.

Had my rebellious heart hushed itself for one single moment, it might perhaps have been encircled by tiny shadows telling me what children had once suffered in this fertile region – trudging silently, doggedly along the country roads in the worst hunger years*, to finally bear witness with their emaciated little dead bodies, like cut flowers at the edge of the road, to undeserved affliction on this earth. If I had felt their spirits near me, felt the slightest breath of the sorrow-stricken soul of my native land, I would probably have been ashamed of my tears, resolutely picked up my suitcase and readied myself for something less arduous than the martyrdom haunting my overheated brain. But my heart was far from hushed and not at all inclined to hear frail spirit voices among the buzz and hum of that summer's day. It was shouting so loud that it should indeed have carried right up to the throne of the Almighty – its defiance, its longing, its insistence on life.

It took several significant coughs on Uncle Eberhard's part before I became aware of his presence through my extravagant snivelling. I looked up with a hiccup and a sob to see a lanky figure in a strange, snuff-brown frock coat, standing there watching me in the depths of my humiliation. He was hatless and his matted grey hair stood out like a sturdy sheepskin cap round his small head, which bobbed to and fro like that of some comical bird, his great aquiline nose cleaving the air. I had never seen such a sight in my life! I stared fixedly at him as for decency's sake I blew my own nose and wiped my eyes.

'Might this by any chance be young Vega?' said the mystifying apparition with a courtly bow.

His reedy falsetto voice confused me as much as his imposing figure. I nodded energetically, but could not get a word out of my mouth. To my intense surprise he ran his hand thoughtfully over his face several times, blinked his eyes in

67

a meaningful way and politely offered me his right arm, casually picking up my case with his left hand. Then arm in arm we processed along the platform, into the station house and out the other side, in dignified and solemn silence.

This made a deep impression on me. I was so bowled over by Uncle Eberhard's appearance that I instantly forgot my great sorrow and disappointment and did not spare a thought for the fact that the chaise into which I climbed was rickety and covered in dirt. I had to balance my case on my knees and there was such a clutter of other items that I could barely squeeze my little body in. It wasn't exactly what I had envisaged, but it was still more exciting than anything I could have dreamt of. Indescribable smells of horse and soggy leaves and old, sun-dried horse droppings tickled my nose, the hay under the seat scratched my legs and my heart chirruped like a bird: O Vega, this is the free life!

Uncle Eberhard stood beside the chaise, regarding me pensively.

'I believe you were crying, my girl,' he said.

And then I remembered all my humiliation, the fact that I had blubbed just like one of the womenfolk, and what would Uncle Eberhard think of me? I was utterly mortified that I, Vega Maria Eleonora Dreary, had proved so pitiful just when I had completed my heroic feat and was on the threshold of showing the world who I really was. I felt a disquieting lump in my throat, but I clenched my fists and opened my eyes wide, and with great effort forced out an angry mumble: 'Oh no I wasn't!'

Uncle Eberhard seemed satisfied, grinned and nodded his head repeatedly and earnestly.

'Well done, my girl,' he said. 'No, of course you weren't, no indeed!'

He said no more, but I understood that he would not reveal my shameful secret to anyone. At that moment, Uncle Eberhard became my friend for life. And when, after many loud exhortations, he induced the shaggy little horse to move and gave a triumphant wave of his whip, my heart jumped for joy in my breast, my back straightened and I felt I was seated in the finest carriage in the world.

We jolted along the country road, sending up glorious clouds of dust, past fields and meadows and the sweetest little cottages with staring, flaxen-haired children and cackling chickens by the front steps. We drove through pastures dotted with clumps of birches, where the sheep ran around bleating with little white lambs at their heels, and all the leaves gleamed and the trunks shimmered in the afternoon sun. Then suddenly we were in murmuring spruce forest with magical green hiding places, deep shade and cool air, and a pungent fragrance of conifers, marsh flowers and damp moss. My wonderful land opened its arms to me and let me experience its scents and enchantments, let me feel the play of its light and shadow as stabs of delight in my own blood. With all my senses I absorbed the soul of the country, taking in its taste and smell and squirreling them away inside me. We turned down jolly little side roads, bumpy and potholed as such happy byways are, strained our way up stony hills and coasted victoriously down the other side. Time and again we were brought to a halt by gates, and that was perhaps the greatest fun of all. There was always a scrum of youngsters waiting, dirty and bare-legged, and they would throw themselves at the gate like a horde of shrieking savages and then line up on either side of the road, baring their teeth in wolf-like grins. This would greatly agitate and discomfit Uncle Eberhard each and every time, and he would dig about in his empty pockets, look sheepishly at the urchins, stand up in the chaise and shake his coattails as if hoping a few coins would unexpectedly tumble out of them, then finally resume his seat with a thoroughly miserable expression – all to the youngsters' unspeakable joy. They knew very well that Uncle Eberhard never had any money, but this did nothing to detract from their entertainment. Before resolving to move on he would clear his throat portentously, raise his nose in the air and stare straight ahead as he said with great gravitas:

'There will be more next time.'

I simply had to laugh out loud every time he said it. What amused me most of all was the fact that he said it as solemnly and seriously as if making a genuine promise. Nor did he show any signs of realising what it was that caused me to chuckle. He sat there for the most part absorbed in deep thought and I did so wonder what on earth he could be pondering. Sometimes he gave me a genial look and I would think: He's going to say something, but the comical thing was that he never did. We enjoyed one other's company enormously, Uncle Eberhard and I. And just when the enjoyment was at its peak, we unexpectedly turned into a tree-lined driveway and I could tell we had arrived. Sure enough, there on the steps stood a real-life Father Christmas, huge and alarming, with a vast, snowy beard and the rosiest of cheeks. He took me in his arms and planted kisses here and there on my face with his peculiar, soft, toothless mouth, and I knew this must be my grandfather.

'Ah yes, dearie me, welcome!' said the old man, giving me a pat on the bottom.

Naturally I then expected to go inside and drop a curtsey to Grandmother and other old ladies and sit down on a chair and be offered coffee and asked how things were at home and what my plans were for the future and all those things that are part of the standard ritual when womenfolk are gathered together. But there was never any question of that! I was allowed to go with Uncle Eberhard to the stables – oh heavenly splendours! – which were crowded with horses, conveyances and yelling stable hands, and allowed to help unhitch the horse, learn the intricate tricks of dealing with harnesses, pins and straps, and before I knew it, Uncle Eberhard was lifting me up onto the creature and slapping its hind-quarters and off it set at a trot, with me on its back! It was terribly bumpy and I was thrown violently up and down, like a sack, but I held on desperately to its mane. I closed my eyes in terror and thought: I'm going to fall off – but I would not for the life of me show Uncle Eberhard and the stable hands that I was petrified. No I jolly well wouldn't! I pressed the upper part of my body to its withers and my hands clung to the lifesaving, flowing horsehair, and I boldly opened my eyes. To my surprise I was still on its back, and so the horse and I reached our destination, which was evidently the shore. That was where we stopped, anyway, proudly awaiting Uncle Eberhard's arrival.

Nor was this by any means the end of the sensations. The horse was going for a swim. Uncle Eberhard pushed the boat out and started to row, with me on board hanging onto the horse's halter strap, and off we went. The lake was lovely, as smooth as a mirror, and the horse plunged in with much splashing and whinnying. He swam like some prehistoric animal, giving strange, uncanny grunts that seemed to rise from his belly, his nostrils flaring wildly as the water streamed and fizzed about them. Cold shivers of excitement and fear ran down my spine – our boat seemed to me a seashell that this snorting monster could tip over at any moment. But contrary to my expectations all went well and I was the triumphant one as we ambled serenely to the paddock, Uncle Eberhard, the horse and I.

Before I went in that evening I had made the acquaintance of the stable hands, ridden down to the beach again, this time in the company of all the others, and watched with cries of delight as the lads rode intrepidly out into the water and executed great circles in the lake on the backs of their swimming horses. Back on the beach they set off at a gallop and I could see the horses' white hind-quarters gleaming and the muscles rippling in the tanned bodies of the lads, stripped to the waist – a reckless and brilliant cavalcade in which health, youth and physical beauty combined in a summertime ride across the world.

Thus was I caught up from the very first moment in the rhythm of free life – the rhythm of hotly pulsating blood and eagerly panting breath – and it held me so utterly captive as those summer weeks at Kangais flew by that my thoughts did not turn for a moment to my parental home or my previous existence. They simply had no time to do so! All those new impressions were washing over me and irresistibly swirling me along like a spring flood as it splinters the old landing stages. My hands, which had been the prisoners of books and needlework, suddenly flew up like birds out of their captivity and took possession of a world. They grew strong, nimble and sore as they handled tools and kit, fishing tackle, shotguns, tar buckets, pitchforks, knives and scythes, as they dug in the soil, played with dogs, fed pigs and chickens, reined in horses crossing open countryside and caught fish from still waters at dawn. My senses fraternised with the elements – with air and sun and earth and water and all that is in them. Like a field rapidly ploughed, my whole being was readied for future growth. My limbs trembled and ached, my skin burned and my bare feet stung – it was Mother Earth giving me her first powerful caresses. Through all my distortion and madness, deep inside I have never forgotten her rough embraces, never so completely broken the ties between us that after periods of godforsaken emptiness I was unable to recover my strength at her breast, nourished by her cosmic milk.

Naturally I played at leading the free-roving outdoor life with a rapture beyond all description. I dressed in breeches found for me by Uncle Eberhard, my tireless partner in all those boyish pranks, took furtive smokes behind outbuildings and woodpiles in the company of grinning farm lads, and learnt to spit and swear as befits a free soul and a man's man. I would like to have seen the person who dared say to me: That's not appropriate for a girl, or: A girl can't do that! From concealed humiliation, the need grew in me to assert my full, free human worth at any price – and of course it shimmered gloriously and brilliantly behind every fence and barrier I encountered on my road to selfhood! If I so much as glimpsed a 'No Entry' sign – and heaven knows a young girl's path is lined with those – I was instantly ready to jump the hurdle! Had anyone told me that these transgressions were insignificant, I would have laughed with scorn. And who knows, perhaps that scornful laugh would not have been misplaced. From all those oaths and crafty smokes, those splendid breeches stiff with dirt, those sharp knives I found behind the fence and those wild rides into prohibited territory, I drew some essence that enhanced my own selfhood and imperceptibly influenced the state of my will, distilling my goals and my means of achieving them out of the chaos of existence. With every passing day I felt freer, bolder, more vital – and before I knew it, the irrevocable decision had matured within me that I would at any cost steer my course round the submerged rocks of womanhood, round office and housekeeping and other stagnant waters, out towards the freedom of the coast where a human being, one element against the elements, can seize her own fate in her hands.

Indoor life at Kangais was equally well designed to fill me with loathing and contempt for the position of my own sex. Entering Grandfather's room was like stepping straight into paradise. The long, low room with the dark old furniture received me so gently and kindly, and its cosy and comforting smells of snuff, spices and ingrained tobacco gave me a deep sense of security. Its essence of menfolk, openness, zest for life and generosity could be scented from afar! And did I ever come in without the old man throwing wide his arms to enfold me? He was very fond of having something soft and warm in his arms and never missed an opportunity to pat my somewhat stubby person. Then, with the patting duly done, I was encouraged to go to the pipe rack and select one of the long pipes hung with beads and tassels. I would often linger over this magnificent display, fingering the showy trimmings, running my hands over the intricate pipe bowls and relishing the pungent scent that rose from inside them. These were playthings to my taste – racy, cheerful objects with a glint of men's secret collusion in the corner of their eye! Once I had chosen that day's pipe I would fill it carefully with fragrant tobacco and then perch back on Grandfather's knee to light it. The long pipe seethed and bubbled so comically as the old man puffed on it, giving us both a special little kick of pleasure. It was a bonus for a spirited and red-cheeked old fellow to have his pipe lit by a soft female hand, and as for me, I keenly inhaled the singular scents of the male being.

When Grandfather was in a really good mood he would open his desk drawer with a genial smile, take out a gold coin and put it into my hands. It was dazzling! Never in my whole life had I seen gold coins, still less been given any. The coins were kept loose in the drawer and the old man handed them out like toys. I suppose it was his deep distrust of paper money that had originally made him demand the banks supply him with gold coins – now he played with them like a child. We have an eye for all that shimmers and shines, we who bear the name of Dreary.

Grandmother's room, by contrast, was like the grave! You could not enter without feeling your soul contract, congeal and shrivel. There was no question of going in there just as you were, dirty, exhilarated and still in your breeches. You were expected to be dressed primly, with a freshly pressed apron, tidy hair and eyes modestly lowered. You gave a gentle knock at the door, tiptoed in and dropped a neat little curtsey. Grandmother was ill, and spent most of her time in bed or in her rocking chair; she could tolerate no noise, no sudden movement or raised voices. The child in its selfishness has no sense of sickness and suffering. No sooner had I entered the room than I was thinking of how to get out again. The pious talk was unendurable, the Biblical quotations on the walls were intimidating and I would stand there like a cat on hot bricks, thinking blasphemous thoughts. When the pallid, emaciated, birdlike face was turned pitifully towards me I did not think for a moment of how it resembled my beloved Uncle Eberhard's and little suspected that it was from her he had his intrinsic serenity and goodness, thinking only of all this wretchedness, these restrictions, anguish and mortal dread that were so intimately and detestably womanish. I did not puzzle over what it was that had brought all these women I knew – Aunt Mili, Aunt Emma, my mother and my grandmother – to this pass, made them so pathetic, so small, so fearful, pale and shrivelled. I merely placed myself instinctively in opposition to them, ready to fight to the end for my own liberation. Bitterly I turned away from the sad lives led by these poor creatures and directed my gaze instead towards the gentlemen's dashing, free and sinful ways.

Grandfather would occasionally let drop some comment that injured my female pride and momentarily made me feel something which could perhaps be called solidarity with my sex. This was heightened one day to a smarting sting. I was leafing through Grandfather's diary, where he noted down the weather, the wind direction, the barometer reading and the most memorable events of the day – a calf being born, a sow having a litter, a farm hand hurting his leg – but also any thoughts and ideas that occurred to him. As I was amusing myself by reading through the scrawled jottings of his shaking hand, I suddenly caught sight of the following entry: 'M. was the misfortune of my life'. This sent an awful pang through my breast, for I understood at once that M. was my grandmother Matilde. So many thoughts ran through my mind at that moment: the relationship between my father and my mother, the peasant woman I saw being beaten by her husband one day out in the yard in full view of the whole village, the taunts of the drunks in the village streets, the grey and forbearing females of the species, doomed to suffer and wither, doomed to second-hand life. 'Was the misfortune of my life.' My throat constricted, I pressed my balled fists to my temples and realised with a sudden stab of pain that I belonged to them, to the women, utterly and mysteriously, and that I would one day fall prey to their common destiny, see my life ebb away and run into the sand, unable to move either hand or foot, burnt-out, consumed in the fire of unsatisfied hunger for happiness.

But this bitter, semi-conscious premonition vanished as fast as it had come, like a breeze that suddenly stirs in a still forest and has no sooner set the leaves trembling slightly than it is gone. When the old man came stumping over to pat me on the head there was not a trace of rancour in my heart, in fact just the opposite: I was willing to forgive him anything. He was so splendid and handsome, Grandfather, with his towering height, his majestic mane of white hair, his droll whiskers from which mouth and red cheeks peeped like jaunty fruits on the tree of life! One could well understand that in his prime he had felt the need of motion, space, peril and passion! I felt proud of the old man and thought to myself: I'm a chip off the old block.

The person who took my ill-defined and seething contrariness and gave all those conflicting thoughts a settled direction was none other than Uncle Eberhard, poor, lost, rootless Uncle Eberhard. Without my really being aware of how it happened, he took a firm grip on the rudder of my boat and set my ambition on a course I myself had deeply despised until then. He roamed this world so footloose and free, Uncle Eberhard, his mind so unhampered and his thoughts so independent that he was actually capable of finding his way to a solitary heart that otherwise nursed a deep, well-founded suspicion of those around it. When his pale blue eyes turned their watery, transparent gaze on me I felt as though he could see who I truly was and what would happen to me. I could see, of course, that there was something not right about him, that he lived on charity in his father's house, as company for the old man and as errand boy to them all, even the dairymaids. He was everyone's servant, but the strange thing was that no one – not even the old man – was his master. In some way, I instantly understood this and was therefore very proud of the distinct friendship he showed me. I developed a deep and unshakeable trust in him. Initially we exchanged no confidences, but I was at his heel like an eager puppy. He had lots of things to do but no specific duties, and that was precisely what was so enjoyable. Something unexpected always turned up. One moment there was a sudden trip to be made into town, the next an urgent visit to be paid to the mill, and the next I was roused from my pleasant morning slumbers to go with him on a fishing trip or clamber aboard the clattering milk cart.

Sometimes it was grandly announced that we were going out hunting. I do not even know what kind of hunt it was meant to be, but the preparations were magnificent. The evening before, all the guns in the house were taken out, inspected and painstakingly cleaned. Once we had rubbed away for dear life and thoroughly covered ourselves – especially in my case – in grease, Uncle Eberhard would pull himself up to his full height and majestically raise one gun barrel after another to his eye.

'Splendid,' he would say, fixing me with a look as if we already had our quarry in our hands.

That was certainly how his elderly bitch Hupi seemed to see it. Every time he uttered his momentous 'Splendid', she gave a howling bark and her old body quivered with eagerness for the hunt. Two blazing pairs of eyes, hers and mine, would be trained on Uncle Eberhard, king of the forest.

At some early-morning hour we would set off with murderous looks, equipped with all the hunting gear one could imagine. I proudly shouldered my weapon – a dainty saloon rifle, basically little more than a toy – and Uncle Eberhard girded himself with an immense shotgun, a hunting bag crammed with food, a handsome sheath knife and other items of potential use to men of the forest on their expeditions. The bitch ran to and fro on ploys of her own, repeatedly setting up a loud bark that echoed through the quiet woodland. A lively accompaniment was provided by my own prattle, my monotonous chants that grew louder and louder, the further we penetrated the forest – halloo, halloo, tally ho! – and my furious egging on of her baser instincts – go for 'em Hupi, go for 'em! You could not blame the timid creatures of the forest for keeping out of the way and taking care not to cross this hunting party's path. Periodically Uncle Eberhard would stop, hold up his hand and say: Shhh. We stood still, holding our breath and spying in all directions, along the ground, into the bushes, up to the treetops.

'Can you see anything?' Uncle Eberhard whispered.

'I thought I saw something,' I replied, trembling with excitement.

'So did I,' Uncle Eberhard said.

The bitch, having watched our stealthy expressions, gave a series of furious barks and rushed in among the trees. We followed, of course, puffing and panting and tripping over tussocks and low scrubby bushes. We found her under a tree in a positive paroxysm of barking. As we approached, a crow rose lazily into the air from the top of the spruce.

There was no disappointment to be read on Uncle Eberhard's face. He took off his cap and mopped the sweat from his brow. Then he fell into quiet contemplation. For me, this made the forest a place of great solemnity. I sat myself down at the foot of the tree and put all my effort into staying so quiet that I would not disturb him. The ants crawling up my legs did not trouble me, the rustle all around me did not reach my ears, and had an elk emerged close by I do not think I would have noticed him. Nor would the elk have felt the need to flee – creatures so quiet and absorbed could not possibly be humans! However shy the genius of the morning forest may be, he could safely have alighted on Uncle Eberhard's astonished nose or my quivering, half-closed eyelids once his delicate wing beats had carried him over the antlers of the listening elk.

At such moments, Uncle Eberhard and I felt very close.

Others might well think it curious for Uncle Eberhard just to stand there like that with his face upturned and his eyes not seeing anything in particular but appearing to rest on everything, in the bright blue bounds of space. But to me it had such reverence to it. Greater reverence than anything I have ever experienced in all my life.

The first step of the fakir is to abandon thought,
and raise his head above all his rivals –

says the Persian poet*. When Uncle Eberhard sank into his contemplation it felt to me that he was raising his head above all rivals, majestic and liberated, allowing Some Other to take care of his thoughts.

Without shifting position he suddenly started to blink, as you do if you get something in your eye or are fighting back tears. It was a sure sign something had occurred to him that he wanted to convey to me.

'Be sure not to abandon your books, Vega,' he said from his great height. 'Love them more than anything else, my child. They are where you will find light.'

If it were possible to be more still than I was already, it happened now. It was not a liberating stillness, however, but an agonised one. I became acutely aware of how heavily I was lying on the ground, felled by Uncle Eberhard's words. I saw in my mind the hateful schoolbooks that had tormented and terrorised me all these years, while I longed for freedom and life. 'Love them more than anything else' – how could Uncle Eberhard say that? Did he want me to go back to them again – voluntarily allow myself to be imprisoned, submit to the yoke, shackle my free spirit?

'You've never had to go to school,' I croaked as the tears rose in my throat.

'I shall have to do it in my next life,' said Uncle Eberhard with a cheerful nod. 'It's too late now, you see.'

This so engaged my interest that I entirely forgot my dismay. Was Uncle Eberhard going to live an extra life?

'We all are, you too,' said Uncle Eberhard. 'There's so much we don't have time for in this one, after all. And I'm sure you realise we can't just part as we do, no, everything has to have an orderly ending.'

'Huh,' I said, 'you just mean Heaven and all that!'

He didn't know what I meant and had no comment.

'I believe it will be here,' he said serenely. 'I mean, we know everything so well here. But remember what I tell you girl, we have to commit it all to memory, everything we see and hear.'

It was a dizzying mental proposition. It struck me like a flash of lightning. In some way it coincided with my own most ardent desire – the big chance, the last trump card that would one day be slapped down on the table – but I instantly grasped that this line of thought turned everything on its head and gave me a different point of departure. A succession of extraordinary questions presented themselves and I could feel them surrounding me, stepping forward from the darkness and invading me from all directions. My thoughts grew more and more entangled – in this new and apparently endless thread that had evidently wound its way into the skein of my experiences without my knowledge. 'We must commit it all to our memory, everything we see and hear' – this was the most mysterious thing of all! Perhaps it was at that moment – as I stared in dumb astonishment at Uncle Eberhard, the oracle – that the first rays of light reached my inner eye and consciousness dawned in me of the deep secret of learning.

Inspired by this new concept but incapable of mastering it myself, I ran over and threw myself into the arms of Uncle Eberhard as he stood there at the post at which inspiration had put him, as tall and immovable as a fir tree.

'How do you know that, Uncle Eberhard,' I shouted, shaking him.

Then Uncle Eberhard solemnly raised a long, thin, tobacco-stained finger, as if to indicate that his lips were sealed. My impatient question died away into the forest.

But in my heart it did not die.

Then a splendid wilderness repast was swiftly assembled. Kindling was gathered, the coffee pan set to boil, and it was a delight to cut off huge slices of bread and smoked ham with the glinting sheath knife. The sun was high in the sky, the pine needles and green leaves released their wafts of invigorating scent, and a wise old man, a seasoned dog and a foolish girl savoured the bounties of nature. But the fire lit for the practical purpose of making coffee blazed like some alien element in the midst of that safe little group – a campfire, a fire signalling departure.

Uncle Eberhard tended the fire diligently, and as our eyes followed the licking play of its flames he opened his heart to me. He told me of his own burning desire to study, read, enquire, find out about things, but the old man had merely laughed at the notion. This had made him so heavy-hearted that he was unable to do anything else properly, either. From time to time he would be seized by such restlessness that his feet simply had to take him away from home. The first time the feeling descended on him he was taken unawares and found it very curious. He happened to be standing out on the road when he felt the urge simply to keep walking, just walk and walk and never turn back. He found it very odd – where in the world was he supposed to go? – but some inner force propelled him and he had no choice but to set off then and there, in the clothes he stood up in. He was gone for several months, getting along by begging and doing occasional casual jobs. But as surely as he felt driven to wander, so he was also impelled to return home one day. Everyone knew now that this was the way he was, and no one was surprised when he took to the road, not even he himself. But he was the only one who knew that he would soon leave and never return.

'Where will you go, Uncle Eberhard?' I asked anxiously.

'I don't know yet,' said Uncle Eberhard. 'But I shall find out before long.'

The alien fire burned so merrily among us.

'Now you,' he said to me, pointing his finger, 'must make sure the same thing does not happen to you. Do not abandon your books, I tell you! Do not think you will find any peace if you do!'

As I sat poring over works of philosophy in later years, wrestling with diverse thought systems and world views, the All-seeing Eye could doubtless have detected Uncle Eberhard's trembling finger in front of my nose.

From then on we would often speak of these things, whenever we had an uninterrupted moment. The closer we grew, the more we wanted to be alone with one another, seeking out places suitable for the exchange of calm, profound thoughts. We particularly loved retreating to the dusky comfort of the cowshed, where at this time of year only the occasional newborn calf or gnawing rat disturbed the deep peace, or to the hayloft where the swallows darted to and fro, the faint vibrations of their wings an accompaniment to our metaphysical topics. Casting my mind to the violet-scented musical academy on Lesbos*, I truly do not know if I would wish to substitute it for Kangais and the hayloft above the stables or the deserted cowshed. In these academies the scent was admittedly not so exquisite – it was as sharp as my country and my people – but a good teacher, a free spirit, implanted in my soul a love of light, of inner *enlightenment**, which has become my beacon in a life prey to the squalls of changing moods.

'Every book you read,' said Uncle Eberhard, 'will open a new eye within you. And everything will grow brighter within you, you'll see. It is all the blind eyes that torment me so much. They crave the light as the heart craves the water of the brook. It is terrible living with darkness deep in your gut, you see, that's the nature of human beings.'

It was the ideal of the free individual that Uncle Eberhard laid out for me in our discussions, and it was not his fault that I, with my sense of offended human dignity, understood it as a means and not an end – a means of defying those around me and raising myself above my feminine fate. The position I adopted gave me instead the unshakable power of one primed for battle. As if in the intoxication of victory I vowed not to let myself be ensnared in the circle of triviality that Mr Dreary had so cold-bloodedly marked out, but rather to insist with courage and resolution on my right to continue my studies, matriculate, go to university and consequently 'become something' in this world. This decision appealed to all my heroic instincts. I could already visualise myself standing before Mr Dreary, firm and implacable, my head held high, and saying: 'My road is a different one from yours!' Naturally I anticipated that he would yield to my intellectual and moral superiority, realising with profound shame exactly who it was he had treated like any ordinary girl.

As I stepped aboard the train in Tavastehus I was once again a proud princess, more self-assured than ever, armed with new and surprising insight into her opportunities, but with no sense of the heavy responsibility inherent in them, no suspicion of the acute dangers they posed.

I returned home to my first disappointment: no one took any notice of me. Mr Dreary was caught up in some grand new project and had long since forgotten that I had made my trip against his express orders. My mother had been deeply drawn into a new preacher's sphere of interest. But I tried to get their hackles up nonetheless, and proclaimed in an unnaturally loud voice and with an exaggeratedly self-confident demeanour that I planned to study for university entrance.

'Ah hah,' said Mr Dreary, and that was the only response he afforded me.

My mother nodded distractedly. I felt quite deflated.

Sunday in Gräsviksgatan

Sunday mornings tended to be the time when the collective indignation of the Dreary family discharged itself in a purifying storm. When this occurred, our little apartment would creak at the joints like a ship in raging seas. On this particular morning, the discharge had been so violent that it was a miracle anything in the house was left whole. Mr Dreary had played god of storms and anger with terrifying brio, the lightning had flashed, the thunder had crashed and the mountains had been rent asunder. Now I was finally alone at the scene of the battle. Like some unhappy spirit I wandered through the little rooms. The atmosphere was still charged, reeking of sulphur and gunsmoke in every corner. The doorposts buckled under the internal strain, the pieces of furniture were as sullen and irascible as veterans of the Thirty Years' War and all the more delicate items – girls' hearts, vases, china – were nervous wrecks and chinked in anger at anyone's approach.

Was this an environment for an elevated mind to dwell in?

I could not have been more ready for a *tabula rasa*. My present situation did not correspond in any way to the expectations which that heroic moment of mine had raised. My first 'new' year at school was over and what had it brought me other than disappointment? Lessons had been as laborious as before and never for an instant had I felt I was fighting for some great purpose. One just had to sit and listen, sit still and study hard, the whole world had to sit still and nothing ever changed! No, if one wanted to know anything, to discover the magnificent thoughts of the world, one had to look elsewhere.

And I had done so. I had informed my mind through works that took a broad perspective, embracing everything – even the mystery of creation itself – and I had completely seen through the worthlessness of contemporary civilisation and the fatal limitations of so-called scholarship. In libraries and auction rooms an unerring instinct had led me to my true soulmates – mainly bulky German tomes like *Über das Geistige in der Natur* or *Aus der Chemie des Ungreifbaren**, deeply attractive to me with their indescribable mixture of precise scholarship and metaphysical drivel. I had also pounced fearlessly on abstract German philosophers – the more incomprehensible the better – and with infinite patience and a feeling of secret triumph copied out the heavy, intricately constructed sentences, underlined certain passages, annotated the margins with NB! and Consider this! and Good! The very fact that there was so much – long sentences and whole pages – of which I did not understand a word gave me the sense that the mysteries of the universe were, so to speak, hanging right in front of my nose. Popular handbooks in chemistry, astrology, Esperanto, and guides *zur Steigerung der menschlichen Intelligenz* kept easy company with philosophical speculations, with Faust and Marcus Aurelius and Viktor Rydberg*. From this curiously chaotic muddle of science, speculation and humbug I ascended with infinite pains, without any supervision whatsoever, millimetre by millimetre towards the light of learning that dimly presented itself before my ignorance and intellectual isolation.

I thought nothing of resorting to the most shameful tricks and dissimulations where satisfying my thirst for knowledge was concerned. My mother was on Argus-eyed guard against any deviations in my choice of book – everything that was not homework was summarily dismissed as 'reading novels', a variation on card playing which served only to foster indolence, disinclination and sinfulness. How often I was obliged to hide my mystically alluring books beneath the protective cover of some hateful piece of sewing! My predicament was highly regrettable. It was unworthy in every way of a soul that had become alive to its own opportunities and beheld the dizzying perspectives that open up to the individual when she has achieved mastery of the secret forces of nature, developed her finer ethereal senses and freed her spiritual self from the demeaning shackles of the material world.

And there lay the offensive essay! My examination essay – the most splendid thing I had ever written! Degraded, defaced, dragged through the dirt by a petty teacher's contemptible comments. I had deliberately chosen that particular topic – 'Keep faith with small things'. I knew I could mock the subject, spring a fiendish surprise, write in a spirit completely different from what the unimaginative teacher had intended. And I had succeeded within its scope in brilliantly exposing the present degenerate state of religion, philosophy, science and art. In vain the thirsting soul sought an oasis in this desert! Science had run aground on 'the sunken rocks of experimentation', religion dissected dogmas, art poked around in details. Everywhere people kept faith with small things, nowhere could they rise to the seething world of ideas.

Lovingly I unfolded the sheet of paper and reread the magnificent closing lines:

'Keep faith with small things, humankind! Keep faith with small things, and you shall perpetually crawl like a worm on this earth, excavating dark tunnels where you can dwell in darkness and suffocation. You shall never experience the exultant emotions of the eagle as he rises towards the deep blue expanses of the unknown, as he sees his own radiant beauty mirrored in the rays of the sun and strives ceaselessly to draw closer to the source of the light.'

I thought it all sounded very fine. But I was never able to enjoy it in peace; my eyes had barely scanned the final line before they were irritated by the impertinent red ink beneath. There the teacher, that pedant, had written the following: 'And yet! If we do not nurture the insignificant, all remains merely hypothesis, without a foothold in the real world, merely vague figments of the imagination, words, plans and dreams.' Vague figments of the imagination – how dare he! I considered this a deadly insult to me personally. And as for that vile 'and yet!',

I could never read it without an overwhelming sense of inner tumult.

In a fit of bitter rage I seized my pen and struck thick black lines through the red text.

Today, unfolding the yellowing paper – defiantly preserved – I can detect in my own bombastic phrases and in the violence of those rebellious black strokes the passionate craving of a forgotten era for a more thrilling existence, bigger stakes, bigger profits and losses. With a pang of envy, a melancholy sense of having lost forever that great faith which so pluckily and prophetically apostrophises 'humankind', I listen to the confused and therefore all the more touching echo of the words which at that strangely ominous turn of the century, in that decade poised on the threshold of world war, generated such ferment in arrogant minds:

Behold, I bring you the superman!*

In our land, where culture has never been able to progress in any other way than by hurling itself from one extreme to the other, this was a time when every elementary-school teacher, every post-office clerk was a superman. All the questing, dissatisfied young people were supermen. The cities swarmed with them – recognisable by their long hair, their free and informal attire, their burning eyes, their proudly held heads – but even in the countryside, eccentric individuals started to appear, rebelliously raising their foreheads from the dust and speaking mysteriously of the destined time.

The most honourable and appealing of these supermen was my friend Fridolf. His mother was a widow and he had been obliged to sell his soul to the Post Office. He was a postman, plain and simple. With his eager, upturned nose, his healthy, freckled face, morose expression and his springy hair standing up on his head, with his whole angular and obstinate person he was the incarnation of the Finnish superman of those days – a peculiar hybrid, a cross between social utopian and God-defying unbeliever. In order to read Nietzsche he taught himself German, without a teacher and with the sole aid of a dictionary and a grammar book. *Also sprach Zarathustra* was the book by which he lived his life, but that did not prevent

Henry George* and Tolstoy from being his prophets, too. It was Fridolf who alerted me to the existence of a 'social question' – in school we knew nothing of such things.

'*Why* are some born to bottomless misery, others to excess?' he cried, fixing me with his gaze.

This made a harrowing impression on me.

'Why' was a word permanently on Fridolf's lips. He sat in daily judgement on life – severely, uncompromisingly. He took all problems in deadly earnest and laughed extremely rarely, and certainly never at himself or his life. Naturally he was an atheist. He was a real atheist, Fridolf, the defiantly fervent kind who cannot cope without God, the presumed tyrannical ruler. His bristly hair stood on end and his hand was raised ominously heavenwards as he declaimed in his halting German:

Ich dich ehren? Wofür!
Hast du die Schmerzen gelindert
Je des Beladenen?
Hast du die Tränen gestillet
Je des Geängsteten?*

At such moments Fridolf's simple person acquired a heroic glow. I would grasp his hand and as he squeezed mine hard in return we would both look menacingly up at the ceiling.

Fridolf was my soulmate, my spiritual support. How often we sat in Mr Dreary's lilac bower, pressed close together on the narrow, rickety seat, and surrendered ourselves to prophetic visions, dreams of the time of light, beauty and strength that was indubitably at hand! Our eyes gleamed like those of the beautiful young creatures of the forest, our chests swelled with the glorious pressure of our blood, but in our earnest, unyielding hearts we had sworn a monastic allegiance to our ideal which prevented our even thinking of anything resembling a kiss. We thought instead of humanity.

What could be keeping him today? I looked anxiously at the clock. One of my parents could be home at any moment and that would ruin everything. Fridolf and I met on

Sundays. During the week we exchanged postcards of mutual encouragement as a reminder of our lofty aim in life. On Saturday morning I had received a card from him that seemed to herald something particular. Its content was as follows: 'Please note! Character means never giving in and never losing your composure, whatever happens. Important news tomorrow. Your friend Fridolf.' Whatever kind of message was that? I slowly repeated the words 'whatever happens' to myself – and a flame was kindled in my eyes.

I stood up impatiently. It was unbearable sitting still in these rooms where the air quivered with pent-up tension, just sitting still and waiting. I paused for a moment in front of the mirror and looked with horror at my own image, my own face, my own gaze. In an unguarded instant I caught sight of myself from the outside, and was seized by the dark terror of intrusive exposure to my own individuality. My conscious thoughts were: Who are you, Vega Dreary? Where have you come from and where are you going? But it was more than this suddenly forcing itself upon me, something dark, greedy and passionate that made my face turn pale and my head spin. I turned in deep dismay from my reflection and the outline of my future fate I had dimly glimpsed behind it. I instinctively threw open the window to feel the crystal-clear air around my forehead and the sun on my face, my breast, my closed eyes.

My city is a city on the sea, all its streets lead to the sea – that element, proud and free, plays its mad game with the city, its people and their fates. I did not need to breathe its air for long before I felt liberated from the pressure within me, from the earth, from the suffocation of fruitless waiting. My chest expanded serenely and a triumphant smile spread across my face.

I took the book Fridolf had lent me under my arm and went out into the garden – a small patch at the back of the old wooden house – to concentrate on profound thoughts and steel my mind against the corrupting influence of everyday life. It was a lovely early-summer's day, light and ethereal, with the scent of bird cherry in the air and a haze of delicate, pale-green foliage around the earth, a celestial dancer's chaste attire. A few merry rays of sun found their way in among the lilac bushes and played occasionally on the book over which I was bent. The many lively sounds in the leaves and on the ground joined in the game as well, the birds twittering, the insects and other busy little creatures scurrying on their cheerful expeditions. But all this was too near at hand and far too insignificant to merit my attention. My thoughts were revolving around the farthest secrets of the universe.

Never in my life had I read anything so magnificent, so designed to fire my imagination, as this book! From the first moment I was mysteriously drawn to the mystical name of Etidorpha* – I literally tore the book from Fridolf before he had even looked inside. And the content exceeded my expectations in its great learning and depth of thought. The work was studded with the most stupendous phrases, like 'the earth-creating principle', 'the central energy sphere', 'absolute movement', 'the only permanent expression of omnipotence' – expressions which in themselves opened vast expanses to the thoughtful soul. With prophetic power and cogent argument the author revealed that the time of the white elixir, long prophesied by the authorities of the alchemical school such as Raymond Lully, Paracelsus and Arnold of Villanova, was now at hand and that humankind now stood face to face with a sphinx – the great unknown. How intensely I felt the truth of it! Had I not myself discovered the sphinx within me and seen glimpses of his inscrutable stone smile behind the curtain of my destiny?

Enlarging on the subject of 'the great unknown', the learned author entered into a dizzying succession of *whys* which truly proved that science dared not try to explain the causes of even the most simple things. At times I was aware of a vague confusion in my brain, but fought it down as ridiculous weakness. I strained my powers of reasoning to the limit and read on:

'Why does one bird hop while the other walks? Why does the tree frog change colour? Why do the nerves of the tongue convey taste, while those of the nose convey smell? Why is quicksilver liquid and not solid at room temperature? Why is common salt white, when coal is black? Why do bread and morphine possess such different qualities, although they both consist of the same basic elements? Why...? This why underlies all phenomena and all deep research ends in this question. Human beings can extend their superficial enquiries out into boundless space, but when the roving rays of light from the most remote of worlds reach their eyes they must cover their faces and let their thoughts dwell on this implacable, never answered: why.'

I leapt to my feet in complete rapture. With this book in my hand I was ready to defy a whole host of pedants and everyday souls with their petty 'and yet!' How magnificent this was! I gazed intently into the bright blue expanse of the skies and read the last, splendid line in my most majestic voice – read it to the astounded lilacs, the quaking caterpillars, the terror-stricken ants and the dumbfounded birds.

Standing at a discreet distance was another involuntary listener: Fridolf. When my last *why* had died away, he gave a cough. I was painfully aware of my simple, earthbound situation and felt an unpleasant blushing sensation. An invisible wall was raised between me and Fridolf – he had been given insight into something he was not supposed to see.

'Here you are at last,' I said irritably. He suddenly cut a rather awkward figure in my eyes.

He made a great show of looking all round and asked if we were quite alone. I nodded vigorously and all at once I was aglow with curiosity. Solemnly, he took a seat on the bench beside me. It was plain he had something of great import weighing on him.

'Vega,' he said portentously. 'The life we are living now is not in accordance with nature's intentions.'

My heart leapt. I moved closer to Fridolf.

'Not even in our higher aims,' he added meditatively. 'We must extract ourselves from all this.'

'I've known that for a long time,' came my hard and unwavering reply. 'We can't go on living like this!'

As if in awful confirmation of my words, a series of highly disharmonious sounds issued from the open window of the

Dreary family drawing room. I had no difficulty whatsoever in interpreting the meaning of those sounds – they were all too familiar to me. My parents had clearly arrived home at roughly the same time, both fully charged with fresh electricity.

'Right, that's enough,' thundered Mr Dreary. 'How many times do I have to tell you I am born for higher things than to stand here listening to women's babble!'

'He is the Antichrist himself!' insisted a shrill voice. 'Everyone knows he keeps company with the Devil, reads the Black Bible and summons up spirits.'

'And this is the person I have been married to for twenty years!' cried Mr Dreary pointedly.

'Does he dress like a decent Christian then, eh?' the other voice retaliated. 'He's got long hair like the heathens, he's simply appalling, eats grass and turnips like the pigs and cures sickness with water and the laying on of hands. He's driven lots of people to madness and now he's turned *your* head, Dreary.'

'Silence, woman!' yelled Mr Dreary, cocksure as ever.

'Yes, I'll be silent, Dreary! I have no say in this house, after all. Swindlers and heathens are the masters here. I shall suffer in silence. If it weren't for your daughter, I would have left long ago.'

'Get out and take your daughter with you!' shouted Mr Dreary in a frenzy of rage. 'I want peace in my house!'

The window was slammed shut. I assumed that my mother had realised in the midst of her agitation that it would be prudent to close it. I could not help involuntarily bracing myself – I expected Mr Dreary to throw it open again out of sheer cussedness. But nothing happened. The house remained silent and sealed. Instead all the windows and doors in my heart were thrown wide, strident exchanges issued forth, embittered voices hurled words of accusation, censure and defiance. A crimson tide stained my cheeks, exposing my shame to the whole world. I had heard that expression 'your daughter' a thousand times before, an insignificant phrase, a trick in the convoluted marital game. Now, suddenly, its dagger stabbed my heart and I abandoned myself unresistingly to the mood of secret antipathy that had imperceptibly been working its way to the surface all day.

Filled with animosity, I observed Fridolf's behaviour. Rather than throwing himself down on his knees at my feet or lifting me in his arms, vowing to be faithful to me and saying: 'Trust me!', he strode around as if I did not exist, kicking at everything that got in his way and intermittently uttering strange sounds that expressed anything but compassion for me or sympathy for my situation. He stopped with a jolt, looked up into the air and gave a foolish laugh. Nothing at that moment could have felt more insulting to me than such a naive expression of joy on his part.

'It can't be anyone else! It must be the doctor!'

These were astonishing words for him to be directing at me, just as I felt most profoundly aware of how dispossessed I was in life.

With a cold heart and an affronted look, I listened to his explanation. He was on the track of a wonderful man, a fine mind, a prophet. This man was called simply the doctor, everyone knew who the doctor was. From America, from England, from Japan, people came flocking to him, but here at home we were oblivious! He had cured people with water cures somewhere in the wilds of Karelia where he ran a little sanatorium. And this had made him famous! But it was just something he did on the side, while he was busy thinking. He realised you couldn't genuinely cure people without curing society. That was what he really wanted to do. Now he had come to Helsinki, to assemble a group of people interested in setting up a colony with him, a new community, built on the brotherhood of man. No private ownership would be allowed, everything would be held in common. They would live a simple, natural life, without God or laws or institutions or any of those things that stop people living as creation intended. They would work the soil together, meat and alcoholic stimulants would be banned, and all disputes would be settled by the doctor. As soon as Fridolf heard about the idea he realised it was just what he had been yearning for. He had been about to tell me so when we were interrupted by the Dreary family quarrel.

'And just listen to this,' said Fridolf. 'He is the self-same doctor your mother was talking about! Mr Dreary is clearly in contact with him, and possibly intending to join the colony. Then we would be comrades, Mr Dreary and I. Isn't that funny?'

'So you're planning to join this, too,' I said icily, but inside me I was rent by contradictory feelings that hounded one another, shrieking and baring their teeth. They are going to be comrades, I thought, the men –

'Of course,' said Fridolf. 'You don't think I would miss an opportunity to live a life of freedom and human dignity like this, do you, Vega?'

'And what about me?'

My question plainly put Fridolf in an awkward situation. It instantly dawned on me that he had been dreading such a question all along, but had been pretending it did not exist. I was seized by inexplicable horror and felt myself plunging down and down into the depths of an abyss as cold waves closed over my head. Was I to be shut out of everything, were there to be no opportunities for me, was my soulmate, my comrade in faith and hope, going to desert me?

With great effort and many florid and unaccustomed phrases, Fridolf started to explain – and there is nothing so terrible as people starting to explain when what you want is a single word, just a single one. The thing was that, at least to start with, no women would be allowed to go with them, for it would only sow discord and dissent, the doctor said, and initially exception could be made only for the doctor's own female patients, but once things had settled down and got properly underway, maybe in a couple of years or so, then a different arrangement for the women could be considered, and those who wished to could set up home and so on, and at that point he, Fridolf, had thought that...

I did not hear him to the end. The waves closed over me, a dreadful, sinking emptiness filled my whole being. From the emptiness surged forth those terrifying chimeras that self-pity generates, wounded pride's cruel and voluptuous dreams of crushing revenge. I saw myself floating as a corpse in an unknown river that ran through murmuring wilderness, beautiful animals clustered in mute sorrow along its banks, with water lilies and other fantastical and lovely water plants entwining themselves in my hair and a smile on my rigid lips. I saw myself, at the moment of my death, in a shockingly contorted position that struck the hearts of those present with horror and dismay. I saw myself, pale, solemn and as white as marble, whispering my final words of forgiveness to those who had wronged me. My eyes were stung by tears, as bitter and sweet as impotent revenge will always be.

'You see, Vega,' said Fridolf, 'I have been thinking of you all the time. It is only at the start that things will be difficult to organise. Later, in a few years –'

His face brightened as only the face of a genuinely credulous and committed young man can brighten. 'We shall have our own allotment,' he said, 'honey, bees and glorious freedom.'

'But for those first hard years, we men alone will fight our way through,' he said proudly.

Then the laughter erupted from me. Possibly the first self-confident female laughter that had ever rung out in Gräsviksgatan. I could feel the anger slowly rising in me. Was it me, Vega Dreary, he was addressing in that manner? Hadn't I arms and fists of my own with which to make my way, hadn't I strength with which to battle through the hard years? Was I to sit like the maiden in the tower and wait, simply wait for the knight who was away engaging in noble combat? Oho, we would see about that! 'A different arrangement for the women' – this expression suddenly seemed to me so inordinately comical. I threw my head back and roared with laughter. There must have been something wild and mad in my laugh, for I could see that it frightened the more measured Fridolf. A female gaze altogether too mature was directed on him through my narrowed eyes. I saw that Fridolf was a ridiculous, childish boy, the sort of person one need not take seriously, and in a strangely playful moment of rage I was struck by how like Mr Dreary he was, and that Mr Dreary himself was a childish boy, the sort of person one need not take seriously –.

As Fridolf stared at me with panic-stricken and wholly uncomprehending eyes, the fury within me gathered itself, curling up under my breast like a soft, quiet, purring ball. Clear-eyed and self-controlled, I stood up and left him without a word – and from my swinging hips, the elastic pliancy of my steps, a new rhythm pervaded my consciousness.

Just as I opened the door to my father's house, I heard an anxious cry of alarm from behind me:

'Vega!'

Was it Fridolf, or was it the forgotten days of my earlier youth calling me back? I hesitated for a moment, poised uncertainly between two worlds. I gently closed the door behind me, with an intense awareness of the mysterious allure of my destiny.

Fanfare for a dead soul

No no no, he will not set me free! This night lies ahead of me, so dark and menacing – shall I ever get through it? Sealed, black as sable, it surrounds me implacably like a coffin. Within it lies a lifeless Vega Dreary with a withered wreath of spring flowers on her breast. Why was she not left to lie like this, mute and unmoving, listening to the timeless dark swell of the night? Why was the unquiet fire reignited in a breast already turned to stone? Why didn't you turn your head away, Ta? Why did you send that lightning flash from the past passion of your eyes?

You turned as pale as death, I saw it! Your face tensed into a desperate, frozen expression and you pressed yourself to the wall as if you were trying to escape. But your eyes were like flaming bonfires – your gentle eyes, Ta! Paralysed, I stopped in the middle of the room, in the midst of all the people, and stared in terror into your face – your beloved, harsh, appalling face, Ta! You did not take your eyes off me, but held me captive as the Lord God holds the soul captive at the Last Judgement, forcing me in a single second to tear open all my old wounds right to the last, the deepest, that can never heal: my love.

'The interval is over,' says one of the ladies in the buffet.

Then I register that I am standing alone in the middle of the Opera House foyer. Like a sleepwalker I go mechanically up the steps and pick my way to my place in the auditorium. The music strikes up, the drama on stage continues to unfold and the elegant black man* sitting beside me shows his white teeth in delight.

'Une très belle mort,' he whispers to me as the performance continues.

I have seen and heard nothing of the opera, but I perceive these words of the stranger beside me with terrible clarity: A very beautiful death. I close my eyes and feel a sense of life rushing past me, somewhere close by, I hear rhythmic steps marching, marching, to unknown destinations, I hear voices, the murmur of the crowd, cries of excitement, the crack of wind-whipped banners, music, fanfares. As for me, I am lying somewhere aside from it all, so close that I am sensible to everything, but incapable of moving or giving the slightest sign to the others. Someone bends over me, smiling at the dead woman. I hear them dragging the stones, the heavy stones that will block the entrance to my grave. The gravel rasps beneath the weight, but they carry on dragging and pulling, coming ever closer, to lay the stones over my grave. The fire within me flares up in a consuming flame, it burns in my breast, it ignites in my eyes, burning as it steals beneath my eyelids: I am not dead! I want to live!*

With a convulsive wrench I tore myself free from the spell and a keening sound forced its way faintly from my lips. The dinner-jacketed black gentleman beside me turned his head and said with an encouraging smile:

'N'oubliez pas, mademoiselle, que ce n'est qu'un spectacle.'*

And at that instant the curtain fell and I realised it was a question of life and death. I leapt to my feet and elbowed my way past the other people, pushed through the throng to the cloakroom, collected my things and rushed out. At the entrance, shaking, I positioned myself where I could watch for the man who had condemned me to death.

How could it surprise you so, Ta, that I clutched your arm out there in the street? Or was it fear that made you recoil? You averted your eyes and tried to hurry past me. But I would not let you go. I had spent so many years just waiting, looking down into the flowing water, watching the birds fly, the people come and go as I waited for you. I crushed myself fiercely against you, felt the heat of your breath on my cheek, wrapped my arms around you, pressed my head to your chest and gave way to violent sobbing. My whole body shook convulsively in

*spasms that were deep and brutal. Life was trying to force its
way into someone already dead.*

*This did not provoke you to anger or violence, Ta. You
merely pushed me aside with quiet restraint and began to
walk down the road. Whining gusts of wind swept across
the Boulevard and the rain whipped us in the face as if
attempting to drive us back to the sinister past. I did not let
go of your arm; sobbing and stumbling, I walked beside you
along the pavement as people hurried by, shivering. I thought
of only one thing: not getting left behind, not losing my grip on
your arm.*

*When we had walked for a while and the crowds around
us had begun to thin out and disperse, you turned to me and
said:*

'What do you want of me, Vega?'

*I stopped as if bewitched when I heard you say my name.
All at once I could hear it in a thousand subtle variations, in
all the modulations and tones in which I had heard it from
your lips over those happy years with you...*

*Fresh as the morning dew, as it was when you said it for the
very first time, clearly and frankly, a new person's new name:*

'Vega!'

*Tender, deep and dark as a nocturnal siren call, a
mysterious **let there be**:*

'Vega, my Vega...'

Empty, flat and treacherous as you said it for the last time:

'Farewell then, Vega.'

*The mere fact of once more hearing it from your lips,
knowing that you were standing, breathing and alive beside
me, saying 'Vega', released everything that was dammed
up inside me and hurled me with great force into the raging
torrent that was the sensation of being alive. Whatever else
you said, your question, your impatient embarrassment – I
was oblivious to it all at that moment and could hear only that
it was you, Ta, saying my name. For me it was as if He who
wakens the dead had said to me: 'Rise, take up thy bed and
walk!' The old, deranged joy welled up in my breast again,
the deep, secret joy in my arrogant life: everything is still*

possible, nothing has been definitively and irretrievably lost! Unbounded presumption seized hold of me, the recklessness of a gambler, and I laughed at the storm, at the rain, at my own dead years. I laughed like someone starved to the point of hallucination. Were you not walking beside me, just as I had dreamt it over and over again in my bitter sense of loss! Did I not hear your voice, which I had loved and fervently responded to, as to no one else! Did I not hear you saying my name as no one else could say it, the name that belonged to you, the name you had shaped and given life, and which was a part of you!

How can you expect me to have seen what was going on inside you? Like someone intoxicated, I stepped into your path when you wanted to pass, forced my way right up to you, laughing to the point of tears in that crazy, exhilarated way we sometimes used to.

'Come!' I said.

A fleeting smile passed across your face. I thought I recognised it as that old smile of yours, wilful and endearing, and my heart was close to bursting with happiness. I tugged eagerly at your arm and said:

'Don't wait, come tonight!'

You instantly thrust me aside with a cruel, hard hand, knocking me to the ground in the street and leaving me lying there, barely conscious. A gentleman I did not know came rushing over, a car stopped and the driver got out. I sat up, weeping quietly to myself, and did not answer their questions. More people gathered, a ring of curious bystanders forming around me. I registered it all and could see by their expressions what they thought of me. But I was so terribly far away. When the kindly man touched my arm to help me up, I hit out at him, got to my feet and began to run pointlessly along the street. Behind me I could hear the taunts and jeers, ahead of me lay emptiness, silence and death.

You were gone, Ta.

Now I have nothing to wait for, nothing whatsoever to protect myself with. I am completely at the mercy of my own heart's accusations.

Oh how I hated your mother, from the very first moment. I felt instinctively that any danger would come from her. She wanted to keep you for herself, to drag you back to her circle. She hated everything that parted her from you – your father, your scientific studies, your love for me. Yes, I know your father shouldn't have treated her like that! I understand it all, the fact that you didn't want to carry on living with your father and enjoying the advantages it brought you once you had found out who your mother was and how she lived, like a poor working woman. Don't you think I understood that? I loved you for it, Ta! But you know as well as I do that it was her pride which prevented her accepting anything from your father. He would so gladly have supported her and she could have lived a life free from care, if she had so wished. But she didn't! She wanted vengeance and she wanted to snatch you away from him. Oh, I know women, better than you do! Their love is malicious. The neediness of her situation allowed her to appeal to your generosity and gave her greater power over you than if she had possessed all the riches in the world. The fact that you abandoned your studies, your research and your scientific career – this simply delighted her! It made you all the more definitively hers, entirely her own. Seeing you separated from your friends, your circle of acquaintances, your social setting – that was a victory for her. You would be wholly dependent on her and her alone, your cast-off mother! At heart it is only lost sons that mothers love – they remain dependent, unable to leave and take their own free road.

No, no, you don't want to hear this, Ta, I'm well aware of that! I was never to say a word about your mother. But now, you see, I must testify everything I know, there can be no evasion. My own heart is trying to condemn me to death.

Your best friend, the only one you still have, said to me: 'Save him for science, if you can!' He told me how much people had expected of you, how brilliant and able you were, how senseless it was for you to throw yourself away like that. He promised to help me and you know yourself, Ta, how much he did for us, letting us have the room that he loved best, that funny little room up under the roof, and smoothing the path *for you in that other country, far away from your father, your shame, your past. And don't tell me we weren't happy there. Didn't a new life lie ahead of us, untouched, waiting only for us to mould it? But letters went back and forth and evil tidings came streaming into the little sanctuary of our future life. Your mother here at home found a powerful ally in the surging wave of revolution*. The cause of the poor and of the working people! Your heart clung fast to it in passionate defiance. Long before the revolt erupted, its disquiet had invaded your mind. You could think of nothing and speak of nothing except what was being fomented here at home. I know it was then that you started to distrust me – because I didn't share your enthusiasm. But how could I? I knew as well as I do now that had it not been for the behaviour of your father – that distinguished old professor who lived his egotistical life for science, as the saying went, for his insects, his collections, his growing renown, taking no interest in the lives of other people, even those closest to him, your mother and you – if that had been otherwise, you would not have been as readily fired up as you were, nor have believed so blindly in a new mankind, in justice and brotherhood. I knew as well as I do now that you were heading towards your own destruction. Impractical and awkward as you were in all worldly matters – what chance did you have in a battle that involved firm will, resolve and ruthlessness above all else! I knew so well that you would be the first to be betrayed and delivered up for crucifixion.*

Did I in fact know, even at that early stage? Were my motives so pure? Was it truly in order to save you that I turned to your friend, persuaded you to move to Stockholm, and tried with all my might to stop you being part of the insurrection?

How is it that I thought so differently when I saw Fridolf's dead body, his poor face that the Reds* had cut to pieces? I felt a strange sense of disappointment and thought: Why did you fight them? Weren't they children of the same spirit as us, a fresh version of our impatience, our burning indignation, our dream of the freeborn individual? With a sense of having watched those in the vanguard fail I saw you, Fridolf, and so many of the insurgents from those idyllic days go over to

101

the other side. But you, Tancred – you weren't allowed to get mixed up in all that! For me you were in a class of your own, belonging to neither one side nor the other. You were mine, Ta!

Shouldn't I have understood you in this, too, realised that you were a person who had to act in a certain way, and followed you in that, as well? Was it my own arrogance that made me do battle for you? Was it your mother I was fighting the whole time, her influence, her power over you?

This is a thought I can't think through to its conclusion. Don't force me to do it, don't avert your eyes from me, Ta! I've been orbiting this thought all night, going round in a circle and never emerging on the far side. This night has no end. There is nothing but this night, no morning, no awakening and no life on the other side. As I listen out into the night that lies over my country I can hear so many feet pacing up and down, fruitlessly, hopelessly, like my own. There are many of us sitting here attempting to come to terms with the past – those of us who merely looked on and were too intelligent to sacrifice ourselves for anything, those of us who tried to 'save' the others, the poor, straying souls. We wrestle with the ghosts and spectres in our own proud hearts – while life slips past us.

And is gone!

Just a short time ago I was lying on my bed as if dead. I wanted to be dead, I felt dead, I was dead. I lay in my black coffin with the lid closed over me. Then I heard an urgent knocking on the lid, the rhythmic knocking of a living hand. It sounded like a fanfare. I thought: That's Ta knocking. He wants me to wake up.

'Aren't you angry with me any more?' I asked.

'Hurry up, Vega,' he said.

'Will it be morning soon?' I asked.

'We're going to settle the account,' he said. 'Come on, we'll go **together**!'

Then night silently and majestically lifted its lid, I breathed again, opened my eyes and looked around the room. But there was no one there.

The beautiful wild canaries

Say what you like about the good old days before the war, they were not as monotonous, slow or tame as has been claimed. In this country, at least, minds and spirits were in a great hurry! The stream of events was standing still, it is true, but it was the brooding stillness of an impending storm. Everything was waiting for the explosion. People sensed the pressure and scanned the skies to the east and the west, trying to interpret signs and wonders. Mr Dreary went about with a conspiratorial look, letting slip vague remarks about an imminent and major change of circumstances for the world in general and the Dreary family in particular. At school, none of us girls could quite shake off the dim and unsettling sense that a signal might sound in the world at any moment – upon which school books would be hurled against the wall, everyone would rush out into the street and great things would be afoot. We had a faint memory of goings-on in streets and squares at the time of the general strike* and we had heard tell of the 'Russian revolution' that everyone was secretly waiting for. A revolution – that meant barricades and fluttering banners! We instinctively envisaged the great transformation that would take place on the street with clamour and commotion. For us – children of a confined era, growing up in stuffy rooms crammed with dusty draperies, little china dogs, plaster ornaments and the first monstrous, wind-up gramophones – there was a strong and vivid impression that the new freedom would drag us all out into the streets, old and young, helter-skelter into the raucous crowds.

There was no question of anything else – Vega Dreary was ready to hurl her books against the wall at any moment and rush to the top of a barricade! She thought, like all young people in quiet times, that when 'events' finally erupted it would be with grandeur and majesty, sweeping everything clean at a single stroke. Then all one had to do was breathe out and live as a free human being under clear skies. At least that was what most people thought when the war broke out.

Mr Dreary's thoughts were not quite as chaotic as his daughter's but were equally or even more intently focused on change. His home soon turned into a veritable headquarters for the curious movement whose high priest and leading light was that controversial figure, the notorious doctor. It became a haunt of the most singular thinkers from all parts of this slowly wakening land – this pioneering land, as it proudly proclaimed itself at the time. And what these thinkers brooded over was nothing less than the great and universal transformation of lives that was approaching.

The world had ceased to be stable.

The new age dawned with a proud roar across the forests of heroic Väinämöinen*, across the sacred groves where the fires of paganism defied Christianity through the centuries, across the hunger grounds and the tarn-black waters which for centuries safeguarded their spiritual power with words of sorcery and protective curses in runic inscriptions. The great world transformation cast its flame-hued shadow over the virginal land that was suddenly swamped with agitators, miracle-mongers and prophets of every kind. The soul of the people was like a parched field waiting for the rain from the storm clouds massing in the distance. It greedily soaked up every drop of prophetic preaching and welcomed every breath of wind from invisible centres of dissent. The new-fangled agitators with their red neckerchiefs, burning eyes and flowing locks were bathed in an apocalyptic aura. Movements that were part prophetic, part revolutionary were gaining ground, prompting unrest and questions in the most distant crofts and cottages. Fresh light was kindled in dim eyes that had long been fixed only on the turf. A new tone crept into the wistful songs of the girls on summer nights. Every young lad knew that something big was brewing and the world would one day look different from the way it did now.

If anyone had put their ear to the ground at this time, they would undoubtedly have heard the Finnish granite being shaken by the great words being proclaimed to the most far-flung reaches of the land: Hey there, here comes a people of the future, marching into history!

In detention in Kakola prison* at that time, and perhaps to this day, was a quiet, mild-mannered and courteous man, a tailor, who had drunk deeply from the well of wisdom. He was a Christian man who had studied the Bible and been much impressed by its prophesies of the millennium and the anticipation of Christ's second coming; he had studied the mysteries of Kalevala with equal enthusiasm, mulling over the elevation of the Pohjola people* and the enigma of the fortune bringer Sampo*. But he was also a man of his own time who had heard the agitators' account of a new society in which there would be no injustice, no wailing and gnashing of teeth, and heard their exhortations to arise from the night of oppression. In his prophetic mind, all this wisdom had merged into one big vision, a great, overarching vision of the world-historical nature of the Finnish people's task. With the Book of Revelations in one hand and Kalevala in the other – and his gaze unflinchingly fixed on the sacred brotherhood – he had preached in the district that the millennium was imminent and that the place where that kingdom would come was none other than the land of Suomi*. Here the new light would dawn, towards which all people on Earth would eventually turn their eyes. He attracted many followers and his teachings spread to many parishes. The only person to scorn him openly was his own elderly father – a man in the mould of the peasant Paavo*, he had grown up in the belief that the words of the song were true: 'Our land is poor, and shall so be', etc.* The old man laughed in his face, convinced his son had lost his mind. He should not have done that. For the tailor this was a sacred cause and he spent many nights brooding on his father's contemptuous words. One morning he got up and killed his father, in the same quiet, mild-mannered yet emphatic way he did everything else.

He had many kindred spirits in his own country, the tailor, many more than he knew. Among the prophets in Mr Dreary's drawing room, among the apostles of temperance and clean living, among the inmates of the prisons and perhaps even the asylums, there lurked the first ecstatic forerunners of this primitive nationalism – coloured by heathen blood mysticism and Christian advent mysticism, with vivid extra hues of hate-filled and fervent class struggle – that the post-war period was granted the privilege of bringing forth.

There was no question but that this land and this people had been called to occupy a dazzling position as the sun rose on the future. This was where the new society would be built, this was where the new, noble, naturally healthy human being would be born. And to this end there would be reform here! There would be dreams, grandiose and high-flown dreams of global proportions! There would be prophets working overtime! There was no time to lose, it was vital to be at the head of this surge to the future. The people hurried to pull on their seven-league boots – and reforms and 'movements' swarmed around their booted legs. Lofty-minded idealists hastened from their forests, in the clothes they stood up in, and made their laborious ways towards the light of the new age. Line by line they picked their way through labyrinths of the printed word, their stiff index fingers unused to being extended so far. Bearded, free-born and fanatical, they walked from village to village with their knapsacks on their backs, in their skiing boots and rough homespun, aglow with their passion for freedom, natural medicine and democracy.

These individuals followed in the doctor's footsteps to Mr Dreary's house. And where better for Mr Dreary to feel in his element than in this general 'movement'! Admittedly he, like all members of the petty bourgeoisie, felt a deeply rooted mistrust of socialism per se. It had long been the scapegoat for all the evil that happened in the world, all the increasing insolence and disrespect of the inferior masses – formerly so biddable and God-fearing. But he would not have been Mr

Dreary if he had not sooner or later acted directly counter to all his earlier opinions and allowed himself to be enthused by ideas he had previously condemned in the most sulphurous terms. All it took was for an idea to be diluted with a sufficient element of the fantastical for him to embrace it with open arms. And the doctor, you see, had this down to a fine art! He was a real wizard when it came to conjuring up fantastical utopias. He made a deep impression on Mr Dreary. I tend to believe that, from the word go, Mr Dreary saw in him a man of destiny – the man he had been waiting for all his life. He assumed a specially solemn expression whenever he spoke of the doctor, lowered his voice, knitted his brow and raised his eyes, the way he did in any of those moments when he was taking himself profoundly seriously.

'That man is the genius of the century,' he would say, fixing his eyes on all those present to see if they would show any sign of doubt or opposition.

He was indubitably a remarkable man, the doctor. It was impossible to tell whether he was a dreamer or a conscious deceiver. The first time I saw him step inside Mr Dreary's humble abode I really did go weak at the knees. Blithely unsuspecting, I ran to open the door at the ring of the bell, and who did I see but Christ himself, just as he appeared in all the much-loved pictures – with his broad cloak, high, smooth forehead, and neat beard, and the flowing hair of a man of God. I drew back in dismay, as if I had seen a vision. Then he held out both hands and turned his great, burning eyes on me. For all my education and reading, I trembled like an aspen leaf, and in my agitation and deep confusion I might have fallen at his feet and kissed the hem of his robe, had not Mr Dreary suddenly appeared and taken charge of him with much bowing and scraping. They went into the drawing room, where the minor prophets were already assembled, and I had to stay outside, as befitted womenfolk. But in my heart the flame of my hero worship was burning brightly. I loitered in the hall for a while, surrendering myself in solitude to the wondrous and shocking sensations awoken in me by this man, this demi-god.

From that day on I waited with jealous anticipation for the drawing-room meetings. I burned with a single desire – to see him again, meet his eyes and hear a word from his lips. At nights I lay awake and fantasised about him, something I would never have permitted myself as long as I was in an upright position. How it would feel if he took my hand, if he put his arm around me and I rested my head on his breast. Every time the bell rang I rushed to the door – not even Mr Dreary's rebuffs and rebukes could stop me – and to my mother's particular surprise I suddenly became very interested in taking the coffee tray in to the gentlemen.

But it was a long time before I caught a glimpse of my idol. He seldom came and when he did it was unexpectedly, without his disciples' foreknowledge. He well understood how to maintain his position as *père suprême* – by a degree of stealth, a degree of enigmatic incognito that not even his most trusted apostles were able to penetrate. I had ample opportunity to study his flock of followers. Sometimes it sent shivers down my spine when I entered the room unannounced with my innocent coffee tray and saw some long-haired individual in muddy boots and clothes of coarse grey homespun, collarless, bare-chested, standing in the middle of the room with his arm raised in some wild gesture worthy of the Old Testament, his eyes burning like hot coals set deep in his bearded face, white with unaccustomed and over-intense brainwork, as a stream of menacing prophetic words issued from his lips. The tray shook in my hands, but I stepped bravely forward, firmly resolved to defy the spirits of the abyss itself for the doctor's sake.

However alluring, however mystical all this was, a deep contempt for these characters took root in my head. On the one hand, they frightened me – their ponderous Biblical language, peppered with violent expressions loaned from the class war, their dress, their smell, their whole attitude of mind, revealing the primitive force of unchristianised heathendom. No power in the world could have made me believe these were the people called to bring forth the new age of freedom! On the other hand, I still felt a sting in my heart, a sense of wounded female pride, which kept my distrust alive and made me feel excluded from these exclusively male proceedings. Only a few years earlier, before Mr Dreary's betrayal, and yes, perhaps before Fridolf's shameful proposition, I would have stood behind the closed doors, quivering with eagerness as I tried to catch the odd word to give me a hint of the mystery unfolding within. I would have besieged Mr Dreary, offering my services, my strong arms, my belief, my spirit of self-sacrifice. I would have gone around feeling immensely proud of my papa, who was preparing for great things and would one day show the world who Dreary was.

Now everything was entirely different. Whatever those fellows were busy discussing in there, it was of not the slightest interest to me. I found that colony project simply ridiculous; in all probability Fridolf had in his foolishness misunderstood the whole thing. At any rate, he was not permitted to show himself here! So he was not among the select few! The doctor had doubtless not taken him seriously – if Fridolf had actually dared to go and speak to him after the two of us fell out! I laughed inwardly. Self-confidently, I raised my head higher and looked down with contemptuous indulgence on the doings of these immature men. I already sensed that my route to freedom would be another, completely different one, internal and imperceptible. Intellectual arrogance had set its stamp on my brow and shown me a secret way – the secret, revolutionary way of all classes, castes and individuals restricted in their freedom of movement.

But it took no more than the sight of the doctor – that stately, godlike figure! – for me to give in and be gripped by the most ludicrous exhilaration. What power in his eyes! What fervour in my limbs! The merest glimpse of him put me in a state of excruciating happiness for the rest of the day, a sort of agonising ecstasy that made me blind and sent me off to bump into doorposts, collide with chairs and table edges, break china and create general havoc. To serve such a man, to give one's life for him – what bliss! Why was life so infinitely cramped and trivial – a narrow little track that only ran between school and Gräsviksgatan, a pale, thin ring around a few uninteresting people and trifling events? Why were there no wide-open spaces to romp in, no inaccessible ravines to stir my pride, no oceans to enrapture me? Such a man as the doctor – all I could do was go and look at him. He had no need of me! He did not come up to me and say: 'Oh there you are Vega – finally!' He barely noticed me! He sat in there philosophising with those old fools, while I, Vega Dreary, possessed of the truly grand ideas and a burning desire for the struggle and the fight, had to make do with the absurd obscurity of existence as a daughter still living in Mr Dreary's house. I hated that old crew, I hated Mr Dreary and Fridolf and everyone who had, or might be imagined to have, anything in common with the doctor – I hated them with the bitterly concealed cunning of inflamed jealousy. I told myself that this circle was unworthy of the doctor and took pleasure in picturing in my mind's eye the day he would catch them all out by leaving them and vanishing. After all, it was plain that their plans were getting nowhere. Their philosophical discussions had been going on for months and looked likely to continue until doomsday. No, that kind of undertaking took people with guts, pluck, determination and belief!

One day I met the doctor in the street. I saw him from a distance – he was a head taller than anyone else. He strode along hatless, his grey homespun cape flapping in the wind. It was instantly plain that this was a prophet. And sure enough, people turned round and stared after him – such visions were not usually available on our streets. My breath caught in my throat and I felt my face turn blood red. At the last moment I almost slipped away across the street, for the tension was almost unbearable. Before I had time to calm myself he was right in front of me; I made a deep curtsey and the ground seemed to shrink from under my foot. But he did not see me. He went gliding by, lost in lofty reflections. In my crazed confusion I started running after him. Thoughts chased each other through my head. Could I run past him and then turn to meet him anew? Perhaps that would make him notice me, stop, speak to me? I had to talk to him! Here, out in the freedom of the world, away from home, human being to human being.

If I could only address him he would instantly realise who I was. He would put his hand on my shoulder, look deep into my eyes and say: 'You are someone I can trust, Vega!' He would take me with him and we would go off together into the great unknown. Just the two of us, the doctor and I.

Hungry, rootless and homeless as I was, I invested all the burning surplus of my emotional strength in fantasies such as this.

But as I dithered I was confronted by reality in the shape of a beautiful lady of foreign extraction, who hailed the doctor and positively sucked him towards her with her alluring gaze. A sword plunged into me. At a single glance I understood that she was a dazzling creature from unknown regions, a woman of the world, something I could never be. Bleeding inside, with the tears stinging my eyes and all hope lost, I was obliged to walk on by and pretend not to see them. Her and the doctor.

Alas, it was not easy to be young in the good old days – and least of all to be a young woman. Where was 'the good fight', calling one to join its ranks, where was the banner being raised and the watchword being given? Emotion ran on through time, finely tuned senses felt the aching weight of impending destruction, purge and sacrifice, but no one organised the young people, made use of their intellectual power or their hungry will to reach their goal. Dissatisfied, narcissistic and affected, they stood out from the orderly and well-arranged futility of existence – consumed by a fire that had nothing to burn for.

The pressure of the coming change in our lives lay over Mr Dreary's house. It really was in need of some fresh sea breezes to cheer the spirits just then! Old Master Hard blew in that evening like some much-loved relation, welcomed by father and daughter alike. He arrived in the middle of one of the prophetic meetings, but was nonetheless received with effusive cordiality by Mr Dreary. It was probably a pleasant relief to take a little rest from all the strenuous formalities with the apostles. Variety was something Mr Dreary always valued, apparently now more than ever. They had been waiting in vain for the doctor of late, in fact he seemed to have abandoned his flock. And the fateful and decisive moment felt more uncertain than ever. Mr Dreary's expression darkened with every passing day. He was even to be heard making remarks such as: 'That doctor, who knows what sort of man he actually is...'. When old Master Hard unexpectedly stepped through the door it was a joy to see how Mr Dreary's face brightened. He skittered around with quicksilver in his body, just as he had done in days gone by, and even called for Mama, which sounded so strange to my ears, like an echo from the time of my childhood. He whispered eagerly in my ear that old Master Hard was to be served a toddy. I wasted no time in carrying out his order. As I bore the steaming drink into the drawing room it was clear to see that its sinful pungency caught in the prophets' noses and twisted their firmly principled souls into a bittersweet grimace. How it delighted me to see the outspoken and weather-beaten skipper among all those pale, bearded and landlocked barbarians!

And as for old Master Hard, he lifted me onto his knee, patted me on the bottom and declared that he would have been glad to have a daughter like me, but now it was too late. He was a confirmed old bachelor, Master Hard, and I liked him so much for it. He did not fall for women, not he, unlike certain other people. The sea is my bride, he said, his little screwed-up eyes glinting like pearls. He was a man after my own heart, free, frank and happy-go-lucky. He came and went as he pleased and could be gone for decades, only to appear on the threshold out of the blue, his pockets full of goodies and his heart full of the treasures supplied by a good memory.

Whenever Master Hard and Mr Dreary were reunited, they were sure to talk of Åland*, as night follows day. Åland was the land before all other lands in the world for Master Hard, the place where he was born and where he would die, were he not granted the privilege of dying at sea. He never tired of describing those fair islands, the paths worn smooth across the steep rocks, the women skipping across them like mountain goats despite the heavy yokes on their shoulders, the milk frothing in their pails, the echoing villages, where the songs of the girls and the clang of the cowbells were carried far and wide by a crystal-clear reverberation, where bird cherry, Swedish whitebeam and wild roses blossomed around smiling bays while the men were away on long sea trips and many a girl made her way to the tallest clifftop to scan the firth stretching away below her. It was so comical to hear Master Hard talk about Åland, for he would turn his rough skipper's tongue, more used to curses and ripe language, to the softest and most feminine of phrases, using 'fair' and 'bonny' and other romantic adjectives, speaking more of flowers, animals and birds, singing girls and the shearing of woolly sheep in the sunshine on outlying holms and islets than he did of men and rough seas and winter fishing and eyes on watch beside the decoy birds. If the ocean was the bride of his manhood, then the country set in the Sea of Åland was the sweetheart of his youth!

Once in his own youth, Mr Dreary had gone camping with Master Hard out on Klovskär island in the season when eider ducks make their mating calls, black-throated divers send out shrieking cries and long-tailed ducks sing their cheery farewell: *ow-owoolee*. You could wager that by the time these two excellent gentlemen had spent five minutes in one another's company, thoughts of that spring would descend on them like the Holy Spirit at Pentecost, and whatever other topics were discussed, they would revert in an instant to Klovskär, Mangrundet and Skrakanhara and God knows what other names they had, those blessed islets and skerries.

'I always remember...' Mr Dreary would begin, crossing one leg over the other as he always did when he felt really genial and disposed to tell a story.

'Heh heh,' Hard would chuckle before the first syllable had even been uttered.

Gentlemen of mature years have the capacity to laugh immoderately at stories they have told so often and so persistently that even their most distant relations have known them off by heart for decades, and these fine fellows were no exception. The Dreary drawing room, so recently stifled by fateful prognoses, was suddenly resounding with candid, boyish laughter that seemed to knock holes in the wall and open up a glittering sea-green horizon behind the backs of those mulish, homespun greybeards.

My heart rejoiced. I positively luxuriated in the good old sun. Not only did it feel natural to me to stay in the room, which never happened otherwise, but I also became, in a sense, the focal point of the group. Both Hard and Dreary liked an audience – not for nothing was there an element of the performer in both of them, though their appeals on such subjects were hopelessly lost on the prophets. I, on the other hand, was a willing listener and laughed lustily at their well-rehearsed punchlines. Mr Dreary leapt about in front of me, waving his arms just like old times, and winked at me pointedly whenever Master Hard laid it on too thick. I was engrossed, enjoying it all, but at the same time I observed those two cronies as an older person might observe a couple of children. It amused me to see how unalike they were. All Mr Dreary's stories were about people. He knew little of nature, of the sea or the birdlife. All that was pure decoration to him, theatrical scenery, framing the stage on which the astonishing human drama played out. With concealed tenderness I found myself identifying with that trait in him and thought: That's the kind of folk we are, those of us who go by the name of Dreary. Master Hard, by contrast, revelled in descriptions of nature, painting a vivid and dramatic picture of juniper bushes, wild pansies and the steely blue whistle of a northerly gale in the night. In his majestic world, human beings played a subordinate role. Imitating bird calls was his party piece. All his love for the wild freedom and beauty of that life were invested in this art. With him in the room, you could really see the sun rise over the ocean, the clouds blossom into flame and the firths cast their fiery colours up toward the black shores as the eider called its *ah-ooh, ah-ooh.*

He suddenly turned to the unsuspecting prophets, whose indifferent attitude clearly irritated him, and said with calm dignity:

'Åland, now there's a country for you. They have canaries there, too.'

Mr Dreary gave me a big wink. The old men sat there as silent as a wall. Finally one of them cleared his throat, spat with great skill in the direction of the tiled stove and said:

'Well, there are canaries everywhere, you know.'

'But on Åland there are wild canaries,' said Hard with his most earnest natural scientist look. 'Out in the forest, in the freedom of our Lord's natural world. By God, they are magnificent birds, too, and how they sing! Like choirs of angels, there's no better way of describing it.'

Mr Dreary thought this well said. He leapt to his feet, patted Master Hard on the shoulder and said:

'We hunted canaries, you and I, back then.'

'And our aim was first-rate,' beamed Master Hard.

Well well, lads, I thought, you have not changed as much as you think. I had scarcely completed the thought before I jumped up as if stabbed by a dagger. It was a ring at the doorbell, I heard it plainly, but I would not for the life of me go out there and open it. I stood as if paralysed in the middle of the room. Mr Dreary looked up, listened and glanced involuntarily at me, as if he knew I was thinking the same as him. The same fire ignited in both of us, flashing across our eyes like lightning and holding us captive in a momentary magic spell. Everything is possible, nothing is lost!

It was the doctor.

And now, of course, the apostles were suddenly alert and animated! They looked up at the doctor in naive delight, the way human beings will look at the person who has been capable of converting them from their old self and giving them faith in that much-coveted new life, the one thing they needed. Their eyes grew as tender as those of young girls in love, and they stroked their beards and picked their noses out of sheer bashfulness. They had cast themselves adrift from house and home and wife and children, but they doted on the doctor like old nannies. More than anything they would have liked to worship him and wash his feet and not fall asleep and desert him like certain other disciples, that was plain to see. Mr Dreary behaved like an infatuated fool, not knowing how to bow or where to put himself to please the doctor. I observed all this with a growing sense of resentment. I was burning with the same fever as everyone else in that little room in Gräsviksgatan, and like everyone else in this humble little time that so badly wanted to be great, chosen and prophetic. And my eyes were directed like everyone else's at the doctor, the man to fulfil our expectations. But I was a woman; I wanted him for myself! I wanted to fight at his side, be his right-hand man! He was to direct his looks at me, notice me, choose me from among all the others! I could not bear to watch the rest of them fawning over him and ingratiating themselves. I found them ridiculous. I withdrew to a corner and hastily considered how I could most suitably make my exit with head held high, curling my lip in pride, so that every one of them would be aware of Vega Dreary's departure from the room. The surprised doctor would watch me leave and ask himself how it was that he had not noticed my person any sooner.

As I stood there weighing up my options behind the safe back of old Master Hard, Mr Dreary came mincing over, jabbed me in the side and told me to bring more coffee, the way men do to womenfolk and unobtrusive servants, people who have no other task to perform or think about. As a blush of shame rose in my cheeks, I tossed my head and looked Mr Dreary straight in the eye, not moving from the spot. I was dreadfully scared and thought for a moment he was going to hit me, but had firmly resolved not to budge an inch. No, that was not the way I wanted to leave! Mr Dreary made an impatient gesture and I turned red and white by turns, but I did not want to depart in that fashion. Not for the life of me would I carry in coffee trays for gentlemen! With terror-filled delight I felt the doctor's gaze resting on me, his powerful, magnetic gaze that pierced my very marrow, and a fierce feeling of triumph suffused me. Mr Dreary melted hazily away, I no longer felt the floor beneath my feet, time and wretched existence vanished from my consciousness and I sensed the sun of destiny rising for me.

'You have a very distinctive appearance, Miss Dreary,' said the doctor. 'It would interest me to know when you were born.'

The room fell completely silent, so silent that you could hear the wingbeats of fate. Everyone's eyes were turned on me. All at once I felt completely calm, the way great generals do before a crucial battle or ordinary people after a car crash or some other sudden and overwhelming event. I met the doctor's eyes and made sure that mine contained the superior calm of my equal merit.

'I dabble a little in the astrological sciences,' he added with the ostensibly self-deprecating yet inexhaustibly vain smile of the seasoned seducer.

How many times I had been on the verge of writing to an English astrologer who advertised horoscopes in the newspapers! How covetously I had listened to the tales of certain sibyls' and chiromancers' fabled interpretations of peoples' characters and fortunes! I had even gone with my girlfriends right out to Vallgård where there lived a horrible, sinister witch. They had come away pale-faced and shaken; she knew everything, down to the tiniest detail, and had foretold for them remarkable fates with a dark man that individuals of their character could not escape. I had a fervent desire to behold what was written in the book of my fate – but I did not go to the fortune-tellers and I did not write to the world-famous astrologer. All of that frightened me in some dark, exciting way and I dared not play with it. From my childhood onwards I had had such a strong sense of my fate hanging over me, something inescapable that would happen one day, once and for all, seizing hold of me and hurling me forward to my destiny – I did not dare to approach it prematurely, to wake the sleeping bear.

Now I felt the moment had come for me to be granted sight of the book of my fate. Bewitched, I looked into the doctor's eyes as if into some source of power over life and death and solemnly told him the day and hour of my birth. I did this as if I were a witness in an important case concerning a certain Vega Dreary, a person whose dark outline I had barely glimpsed in the confusing multiplicity of events gliding slowly and secretly towards a specific goal.

'Ah,' said the doctor momentously. 'So three is your number. I would have guessed as much.'

He sank into a state of inward reflection that made a deep impression on us all.

'This constellation is unique,' he said eventually.

In such a fateful situation, Mr Dreary and I could not help exchanging looks. Our gazes were irresistibly drawn to the surprised enchantment at the prospect of a boundless horizon that we could only find in one another's eyes, in those hungry, restless, expectant eyes of the Dreary clan. It was comical the way we looked at each other, like two Roman augurs chancing to meet out there in the throng, each well aware of the other's acts of deception, but nonetheless captivated by their common secret. We both knew, after all, that there was something special about us, however far we had drifted apart. It was no longer a question of discord and insubordination – the cabin enfolded us both and the sails of the conquistadors went gliding by across the shining sea. *Trinidad! Concepcion! Victoria!*

We merely gave one another a nod, Mr Dreary and I, when the doctor announced, loud and clear:

'I can tell you right away, Miss Dreary, that an unusual fate has been bestowed on you. Whether for good or ill, I do not wish to say at this point.'

It was almost uncanny how glorious it was to hear it expressed. Finally expressed outright! By a man whom fate itself, through no doing of mine, had put in my path! I now felt that the chain of events that had befallen me and entered my consciousness must have been set in motion by some mighty hand. For good or ill, it made no difference, because now at least I was underway!

'Vega!' my heart yelled in triumph. Never in my life, before or since, has the significance of my own name, my controversial but secretly beloved name, been so evident to me as in the strangely ambiguous state of awareness I felt at that moment.

Perhaps much of my life would have turned out differently if this prediction not been made, confirming me at a crucial moment in my rash belief in a fate greater than the human being who will shape and sustain it. Perhaps I would have husbanded my resources more carefully and been gentler and more understanding in my handling of life's chance events. What do I know... Perhaps I would also have been more easily crushed, more ready to lose faith in any sense of meaning to my life. For at least a year, it must have been – I accepted the prophecy and hid it in the least accessible crevices of my heart. I have never been so beaten, so cowed that those innermost crevices, those solitary places of refuge, have yielded up their spoils.

'What care you for our condition, you who have never tasted sorrow?

As you sit at the river's edge, what know you of the devastating power of thirst?'*

How I got out of the room I shall never know, but I simply had to escape, out into the stormy solitude of the late autumn night. Among columbines, crown imperials and greater burnet long dead and decayed, among what remained of the last frost-damaged wild stocks and daisies, I walked up and down the miniature paths of my childhood garden as the raw, damp air cooled my burning cheeks and dazzling tropical birds sang out the yearning of the northlands in the leafless trees.

The mysterious rose

Knowing yourself chosen, but only in such general terms, with no idea of what you have been chosen for, or which direction it will take, is not as much fun as might be imagined. One moment you have the promise of a brilliant future held out to you, the next you are falling into dark despair at yourself, your weakness, your inconstancy, your vacillation. In my own case, I was intensely interested in two things, one of which was 'life' and the other myself. And both of these were equally unfathomable. How terrifying 'life' was! It was not at all the same impersonal, scholarly concept that Fridolf and I had so successfully pondered to solve all its problems – this was something alive and dreadful that I could feel right up close to me, panting its hot breath virtually into my eyes, lying at my side, immediate and intimate, purring and growling like a lion. The most terrible thing of all was that I did not know what it was!

I lived in an age very willing to keep me supplied with literature on the subject. The more the shadow of approaching world war darkened over the quiet years, the more intent that era grew on knowing what life was and how it should be managed to live it in the right way. World-famous authors, mostly of Anglo-Saxon descent, wrote popular handbooks in the art of getting the most out of life, the art of seizing the moment, of dividing up the twenty-four hours of the day to make them as profitable as possible. They were sent round the world in mass-produced editions and some of these found their way to Gräsviksgatan. There they were pored over passionately with the aid of a dictionary and a pencil.

And that pencil most certainly knew how life should be lived! If I found myself reading in private anguish about how most people squander their day by being sleepy in the mornings or how they fail, from pure lethargy, to start dividing up their day the new way, a crucial step for those not wanting to see their vital energy wasted, the pencil would leap into action, scoring its firm and determined lines under the most striking sentences, the really incontrovertible truths. Such as: 'Most people sleep themselves stupid' or 'Dear sir, you simply begin.'* It was so surprisingly simple, so strikingly true! But good grief, everyone knows what happens in cases like that. It proves impossible to have the book permanently open in front of you and the pencil poised! You put the book aside, lose track of it, somewhere out of reach, under other books or in some unlikely place in the bookshelf, and that is when the trouble starts. You cannot see the wise book, so you forget it, and the treacherous hours slip through your hands toward some unknown destination.

I often had a ghastly sensation of the hours, days and even months slipping through my hands. Of course I achieved a few things in the meantime, but they did not in any sense match up to the inexhaustible riches I suspected lay within me. I had a sense of flitting back and forth, burning and cooling, swirled constantly between feelings of hunger and of disgust, which I could not remedy with the best will in world. One day I would be reading Strindberg's *Getting Married** in rancorous indignation, sharpening my pen for a crushing retort that would find a response across the world and spark mass protest from women proud and free. The next I would be sinking with Ellen Key into sentimental rapture over the Brownings' perfect life together* and dreaming of the beautiful mystery of a marriage of noble souls.

My whole being was aroused, a dark and oppressive arousal that could find no outlet anywhere. The blood would rush gratuitously to my head and then sink back again, like a spent wave, leaving behind it a feeling of distaste and lassitude. I started avoiding people; there were certain gestures and moves I could not bear to see made by anyone, man or woman.

But I greedily devoured everything that quasi-scientific books had to tell me about sex. The naked scientific terms brought me a certain release; the pictures seared themselves into my imagination. Afterwards I would despise myself profoundly, beyond words. I made desperate efforts to jolt myself out of my degradation and get a grip on that strange life lying there at my side, panting and growling and purring, as the days flew by, those precious days that were supposed to bring me closer to my exceptional fate.

My mother sent occasional enquiring looks in my direction, the way mothers do when their girls start to barricade their internal lives with great secretiveness. I do not know how much or how little she suspected, but she said nothing to me. I once heard her complaining about me to one of her closest female friends. She said that I was by temperament hard and uncommunicative and that my misanthropy was simply unnatural. I brooded on her words for a long time and thought vindictively of what she would say if she knew who I really was.

That was my other great and exciting theme – *who I really was!* I would often sit in my cubbyhole off the kitchen, as motionless as a fakir, mirror in hand, deeply absorbed in self-observation. But let no one believe it was my own generally inoffensive and trivial appearance I was contemplating. I was tediously familiar with that and considered it a shameful mask behind which scornful fate had forced my spirit to conceal itself. I was engaged in solving the riddle of the sphinx. Hadn't the doctor shown that people with vision could see through the mask to the other face, the secret mark of my genius? 'You have a very distinctive appearance,' he had said. It was *the face the doctor saw*, the face of the chosen one, decreed by fate, that I, in fear and trepidation, was seeking in my own reflection. I tried to pin down the living gaze, the eternity, the riddle, in my own eyes. I saw what all who seek answers in mirrors see – the cruel and malevolent darkness in the dead pupil of the reflected image and around it an iris, horribly alive, contracting and expanding like some mottled, slug-like creature! Hypnotised by the terror within me, I closed my eyes and let the mirror fall. It was good that way, closed eyes felt nice. In a solemn chant, as if intoning the words of a ritual, I spoke my own name, Vega Maria Eleonora. Over and over again I repeated this chance combination of sounds, for me so pregnant with meaning, as I listened blissfully to the inspiring melody that wells from the breast of a human being in the process of attaining selfhood.

But I feared the mirror, the mirror and the urgent, incessant and lacerating question: What does Vega Maria Eleonora *mean?*

Of course the world was small and well-ordered in those days, the universe benevolent, existence clear, transparent and suitably arranged. On the table with its floral oilcloth my books, my blue exercise books, were stacked in a neat pile. My homework was done for the following day, my reading task completed, my essays written. On the shelf stood the alarm clock, ticking indefatigably – tick-tock, tick-tock – crumbling cosmic time into tame, tidy, foreseeable little units. My school timetable was neatly written out: History, Geography, Mathematics, everything divided up into subjects, invulnerable to disorder and uncertainty. To make quite sure, this passe-partout of education was carefully fixed to the wall with four drawing pins, one in each corner. But something was in profound disorder, all the same; somewhere, ominous chaos reigned. A certain Vega Maria Eleonora was groping her way forward in dark depression, straight through a pitch-black pupil into an unknown eye, towards the natural destiny of her being.

Whither do you journey
   through the ice and snow
across the angry seas,
   where will you lead us?
– Homewards!*

Like a peculiar echo of my own metaphysical anxiety, the sound of my mother's favourite hymn reached me from the adjoining room, where the sisters in faith had assembled around aid for God's children, while the hopeful homespun acolytes in the drawing room defied God and the world order.

My lip curled in disdain. I had no faith in that 'homewards', I belonged to no such congregation, no such community of believers. I had only myself, my chasms, my terrifying, magnificent life, my isolation! There was nothing I was more proud of than my isolation. I guarded it avidly. It infused me with a vertiginous sense of standing infinitely high above my surroundings and raised me higher and still higher with each passing day.

God knows how high I would have risen in the end, how inscrutable and profoundly abstract life would have become to me – an immature child of profoundly abstract Nordic educational circles – if my calling had not suddenly struck me like a flash of lightning, igniting the accumulated emotional force, allowing it release, granting inner escape. One evening I went to the theatre, to all intents and purposes the same Dreary girl as ever, bewildered by a thousand contradictory impulses bubbling from the restlessness of my blood and mind, and I came away as one who knows her mission in life, a hero and liberator, a young Napoleon.

I had taken a big decision.

I went, as everyone else did, to see the great Ida Aalberg in the role of Nora* – I tried as best I could to keep up with the more notable events of cultural life. But what did I see if not a revelation! My own mutinous longing embodied in a radiant female vision. I could scarcely sit still, so excruciatingly did I suffer at seeing her tighten the noose round her own neck. My eyes were fixed on her as if my very life depended on it. Way up in the gallery where I had my seat, I could feel how ghastly that home was, detestable, claustrophobic, poisoned. I quivered with indignation and could not comprehend why she wavered. Couldn't she see through that man, see how egotistical and ridiculous he was, entirely and utterly unworthy of a woman like her? And the children were the same, of course! I clenched my fists in impotent rage, I clawed at the velvet of the barrier in front of me and in my rash passion whispered proud cues to my heroine.

And look, a miracle has happened! Here she comes in her simple skirt suit – serious, reserved and as unassailable as a fortress. That is how a woman should look!

I must stand entirely alone if I'm to get an understanding of myself and everything outside. That's why I can't stay with you any longer.

My heart is thumping with furious joy, my eyes flash like lightning. Of course that low villain of a husband makes his cloying comments about her most sacred duties, about her husband and children and what people will say.

I have other equally sacred duties ... duties to myself.

My heart laughs with delight. Isn't it wonderful of her to say that! Myself! Just say it straight out, calmly and majestically, as such things should be said. Who can touch her when she says something like that? Yet who thinks it will be enough to silence that popinjay? You might think he'd had as much as he could take, but no! He just keeps parroting his words about wife and mother. Wife and mother above all else, have you ever heard anything like it! I start rising from my seat, muttering my protests, and hear shushing from behind me, but I lean forward in irresistible ecstasy, right out over the railing as if to catch the fervently anticipated closing line in mid-air:

I don't believe that any more. I believe I am first and foremost a human being.

Did you all hear that? First and foremost a human being! I am to think things through for myself and learn all about them! People, can you see now what is at stake here? If no one else can, Vega Dreary certainly does. The moment I hear the door slam shut behind Nora, the door through which she breaks out of her home, I sense that the curtain is rising on a great drama in which I myself have been selected to play a part.

I was ignorant and conceited, I knew nothing of the real state of affairs, but I found myself fired by the same inspiration that ran through the world of women in those years, driving the suffragettes into battle, impelling high-born ladies to throw stones through shop windows and pour acid through letterboxes, to climb into ministerial cars and shout their 'Votes for women, Mr Asquith' into the face of a statesman fearing for his life. I was totally unaware that such things were going on in the world; perhaps I did not even know that the women of my own country had recently, before the women of all other countries, been gifted the right to vote. I had never heard of the existence of that venerable institution the Finnish Women's Association*, still less dwelt on its mission to promote the intellectual prowess of women and improve their economic and civic status. All those small sewing circles* in Limingo, Suojärvi, Kangasala, Finby and Pargas, in the most remote rural areas and the largest towns in all corners of our land, were working away entirely without my knowledge, sewing and dabbling and organising their little projects to support poor mothers and children, provide work for destitute women, maintain children's homes, workhouses, weaving schools and libraries. If I had known anything about them, I would have despised them from the bottom of my heart, those sewing circles. I knew nothing of the women in my country who worked in quarries, copper mines or brickworks, in match factories, sawmills, at wood grinders or paper works, in spinning mills, bakeries, flour mills and tobacco factories, who supported themselves by cooking, lacemaking, sewing, taking in laundry, ironing, copying work, bookbinding or as stevedores. If I had known them, too, and seen their bent backs, their tired, worn hands, I would not have had any idea that these were the women, the least legally protected and most scorned of them all, who by their hard, underpaid work, their double labour, in society and in the home, had laid the foundations for women's freedom and made it possible for a few Noras to open their front doors and say: I am first and foremost a human being!

I had no understanding of what was really going on and did not see the wider context or realise the extent of the revolution that was taking place, sometimes silently and covertly, sometimes with shouts and banners and hallelujahs, and least of all did I realise that labour, the secret freedom of labour, was at the core of this revolution as of all others. But I did grasp one thing, all the same, instinctively sensing this to be an appeal, an exhortation to march, a battle fanfare. I was familiar with the spirit speaking through Nora's lines, recognising it as my own *fighting spirit*. This united me with all those of whom I knew nothing, my sisters, my scattered and irresolute legionaries the world over.

Ida Aalberg was feted like a queen that evening. She was such a great star of her time that she was making only a guest appearance at our National Theatre, between her triumphs in St Petersburg and on the Continent. Crowds packed the square in front of the theatre, lining her path to the hotel where she was staying, cheering, crying and worshipping her. And the person forcing their way right to the front was me! Tears were coursing down my cheeks as I shouted and cheered at the top of my voice. My coat was flapping open despite the biting winter chill and it would not even have occurred to me to cover my head in the presence of this great tragedienne, the first woman I had seen in my life who held her head high. What good fortune that I at least had a fur cap to press passionately to my breast!

Standing there in such a fashion I must have been quite a curious sight, and it was hardly surprising that the great diva noticed me as she passed slowly by. Perhaps she was also touched to see such naive and conspicuous youthful rapture. She stopped right in front of me, took a rose from the armful she was carrying, handed it to me with a radiant smile and said: 'Thank you for coming, dear child!'

I stood there transfixed with the rose in my hand, the sacred rose of the chosen one. There was a buzz of people talking all around me as the crowd pushed and shoved and trampled on my toes. I stood calmly, looking at my rose. I was no longer shouting or cheering or weeping, nor was I swimming in a sea of supreme happiness. The great and solemn thing that had happened to me suffused me with a feeling that was pure, exalted, austere, a sense of responsibility, an urgent certainty requiring me to summon all the strength within me. In my eyes it was not the celebrated actress who had presented me with the rose and picked me out from all the others. It was Nora, the Nora my passionate heart had conjured forth and experienced to the utmost drop of its red blood, she was the one who had given me the rose with the words: 'Never say die, Vega!' In one glittering second of inner vision that chance gesture revealed to me the secret direction of my contradictory sensations and experiences, the jealously hidden goal of my proud, irrepressible dreams.

It was then I decided to become the knight, the champion, of the proud, free woman! Rose in hand, I made a solemn promise never to fail that cause. Never in my life would I marry, never would I succumb to the inducements of a man! Free, pure and unperturbed, I would bear the women's standard and carry it to victory. Activity, long curbed and suppressed, burned once more with a glorious flame in my breast, militancy in my very being, and the contradiction in my name claimed its due. Atahualpa's avenger raised herself from her degradation in my soul, swords clanged, armies prepared for battle. What music in my ears! What bliss in my breast! I would show them all, show Mr Dreary and Fridolf and everyone who had classed me as womenfolk and pushed me aside from the freedom and danger that was life, exactly what a woman could achieve in this world. To think no one had realised this before! It was beyond my comprehension. I was convinced I was going to create a worldwide movement. Women could surely not voluntarily allow themselves to be locked up like that, as Nora had, for example, to become dependent and be pampered like children all their lives? All it would take was for one woman to be bold and lead the way, and then all the rest would follow. And that bold woman, that was me, Vega Maria Eleonora Dreary!

In the beautiful glitter of the clear, starlit winter's night I walked home to Gräsviksgatan with my rose, my delicate flower, tucked close to my own breast to protect it from the cold of a merciless universe.

Since receiving the rose I was no longer the same person. Something had brushed my very soul, as lightly and fleetingly as a breath of wind, like the scent of a rose, but with the power of those enigmatic, silent messages that seem to lend our lives meaning and give us the strength to endure the cruellest of losses. I felt the change the moment I went into my room. As I stepped through the door with the rose in my hand, grave, composed, deeply affected, I felt the room expand, growing to the size of a church. On the table I could see my books and exercise books, just as I had left them a few hours before, but to me it felt such a long time since I had been slaving away at that table. With brisk and decisive hands I cleared them all away – like another von Döbeln* on the eve of battle, sweeping from his desk the medicaments he took for his infirmity – and set the rose in solitary majesty on the table, as the symbol of my new life. I stood there for a long time, my clenched right hand resting on the table top as I contemplated the rose, the room and the solemnity of existence.

In those moments, the foundation must surely have been laid for something indomitable in my being, something quiet, collected and indestructible that would persist even after defeat, when great words have turned to dust and one's personal fate has been dealt a hammer blow.

The next morning I was cast headlong into turbulent waters! Alarm clocks, the twenty-four hours of the day and how best to spend them were no longer important. Mirrors and other metaphysical trappings were no longer required. Deeds and action burned bright in my breast! My hubris knew no bounds! Had I not been clearly and manifestly singled out by fate? Was there not an immense project of liberation waiting to be ignited by the spark of my unique personality? How the whole thing would happen, precisely where and in what circumstances I would raise the flag of rebellion, I naturally as yet had no idea, but that did not matter at all. What I knew was that I had a specific mission in life, and that infused me with a sense of inexhaustible riches. A shaft had opened inwards, a cover had been lifted outwards; my head felt so light and free, my thoughts so young.

Cosmic life streamed towards me from invisible sources*. My ability to receive, digest and usefully absorb was incredibly heightened. I read so much and so widely that winter, consuming more reading matter than I have since been able to get through in ten years. And I not only read, I also tried to penetrate areas of education and culture that had been completely closed to me until that point: music, theatre, the fine arts. I copied out analyses from histories of art, attempting with their help to develop some idea of the greatness in the classical works I saw in the collections of the Ateneum.* I prepared myself scrupulously for each theatre or concert visit, read reviews, speeches and polemics and brooded over references I did not understand but behind which I detected knowledge beyond price. The fact that there was so much I did not comprehend and so much that I missed was absolute torture to me. Though I was not strictly aware of it, that crucial line pealed tirelessly and clearly throughout the drama of my awakening, like a silver bell within me: *First and foremost a human being –*

By what process I cannot say, but my inner self was somehow reshaped under the influence of various circles of light and my soul was drawn imperceptibly into the diffuse sphere of secret life that surrounds the actual facts of knowledge. The rose I had been given had already withered – I had gathered its petals in a little box – but its scent suffused my being. I lived in a state of expectant enchantment.

At school everyone could see the change in me, of course. The mystifying thing about it was that it happened so fast, so unexpectedly, virtually overnight. I suddenly revealed myself to be an outstanding student – I, the disinclined, recalcitrant, dozy Dreary girl! Suddenly everything was so easy for me, like a game, and no task was difficult enough to satisfy me. I, too, was astonished at the change and observed my own attainments with admiration. I particularly impressed myself in mathematics, previously my Achilles heel. I genuinely loved those problems and equations, the more complex the better. The maths teacher was the only one I truly esteemed, his strict and demanding nature commanding my respect. He was a man with ambition and he pushed us hard. I liked that! I liked experiencing in his hands that pleasurable litheness and lightness of the essence of intelligence, of the delicate precision in my own thoughts. Once when I had acquitted myself well in a test, he turned to the whole class and said it was rare for girls to achieve that sort of thing in mathematics, and my pride knew no bounds. But like all great minds, I did not let it show. I smiled inwardly, thinking: This is nothing. Just you wait and see!

Every personality in the making is without a doubt a world conqueror in miniature; perhaps I was more aware of it than the rest. Not for nothing had I had a teacher such as Mr Dreary, not for nothing were the little bark boats I played with carved to imitate grand, full-rigged ships like *Trinidad*, *Concepcion* and *Victoria*. It afforded me immense pleasure to read about the stumbling, uncertain and thoroughly humiliating youthful years of great men. The way they lived apart, misunderstood by those around them, randomly reading everything they could lay their hands on, impelled by a vague hunger for knowledge, and the way they were subsequently able in some miraculous manner to capitalise on all this as they set about accomplishing their life's work. I was particularly enchanted to read of young Lieutenant Bonaparte on Corsica, that figure of immortal youth, who prepared himself by his unmethodical studies and was still dreaming of Corsican liberation as the thunder of the French Revolution rolled in. I loved the young lieutenant, loved him as my brother.

It was no surprise that the Dreary home felt cramped, given the towering personalities Mr Dreary and I had become. Personalities are difficult within the confines of a home, they need such an immense amount of air under their wings. Take Mr Dreary, for instance! Once he had properly grasped socialism in its true, apostolic form, the form innocently interpreted in this land until the uprising as a great and noble spiritual movement with unlimited credit in the millennium, he grew so expansive that even rooms larger than ours in Gräsviksgatan could scarcely have contained him. He, too, became something of a *père suprême*, a living law! His chest expanded, his coat-tails flapped freely in the brisk winds and he climbed intrepidly to the heights of his life, from which he could see humanity at his feet.

One can't blame him for feeling frustrated with the burden that a family constitutes in such circumstances. Didn't it limit his freedom of movement? Didn't it demand of him clothes, food and maintenance? Hadn't the whole of society conspired to keep him in these ignominious shackles! In the face of the momentous decision now closing in on him he could clearly feel how low he had sunk, how insignificant and deeply degrading his life had been. He had allowed himself to be ensnared in cares for the morrow, in setbacks and sheer trifles. Cowardice had made him shrink from every crucial action for fear of what people would say, out of consideration for his family. A man of his intellectual resources, reduced to a weak, pitiful, passive figure!

To set down a clear marker that he was aware of that fact, he had his bed moved into the drawing room. This arrangement made it plain to all concerned that he derived no use or pleasure whatsoever from his family and also helped him see it more plainly himself. The drawing room became a sacred space, the first victory trophy, the first stage on the path to the great and definitive transformation of life. No one was allowed to enter it uninvited. The room was no longer part of the Dreary home; it had been snatched from the paralysing grip of the old life.

When I saw my mother's eyes red from weeping, her frightened and bewildered look, I thought: She doesn't know any better, poor thing. She's afraid Mr Dreary is going to leave her. How comical! Surely she should be glad to be rid of him! An independent life, on one's own, was the most sublime and wonderful thing I knew and I failed to see why my mother and all other women did not realise it. Such petty details as economic circumstance were naturally not a matter with which I concerned myself. And as for love, that was something one nursed in deepest secrecy for some inaccessible, remote and glorious individual. There, too, being free and independent was a priceless advantage. It was only a matter of briskly setting one's mind to it. It seemed simply incomprehensible that no one had thought of this before. But women were so peculiar. The more I thought about it, the more clearly I saw that the problem with them was that they were so fearful. Fearful of any kind of change and terribly fearful of being left alone. How lucky it was that at least there was one woman born who was not fearful! In me, the world would behold a woman who stood as firm as a pillar!

Wholly unexpectedly, as springtime came around I found an ally in my fighting spirit of feminism. It was Miss Mildred Jonsson, my resolute defender at the christening. I instantly realised I had always privately admired her. And in any case, one had only to see Miss Jonsson come sailing into a room to be reminded what a remarkable character she was, a person not to be trifled with, particularly if you were a weak little man. Her imposing figure, her ample bosom, adorned with quivering butterflies and fantastical silk flowers, and above all her loud voice and bold speech all announced that she had status and did not need to ask anyone but herself for money. Her unconstrained manner, often injected with a streak of humorous, outspoken impudence, seemed to underline that she had fought hard for that status and was in no mind to let its fruits slip through her fingers.

Miss Jonsson owned a fashionable dress shop in Fredriksgatan and was in every respect an adornment to our social circle. She had been in Paris and knew how things were done in the big wide world. She wore powder, perfume and lipstick and mixed with artists and students. In those days, no respectable person on our block or in fact anywhere along Gräsviksgatan wore make-up; they had heard it was a practice favoured by 'whores'. My mother felt a sense of moral indignation every time she saw Miss Jonsson take out her powder puff and lipstick in front of the spartan mirror in our hall; but, after all, dear Mildred was in other ways such a very kind-hearted person! I would hang back in my mother's shadow, subdued and silent, but my blue eyes, accustomed to mirages and castles in the air, would be intently focused on Miss Jonsson's mysterious operations.

That evening she made her customary sweeping entry in a cloud of sinful fragrances that took possession of our unsophisticated home and lent my stern, puritanical eyes a belladonna-like gleam. She seemed somewhat surprised at the sight of me – it was quite a while since she had last been to visit us.

'The girl has looks on her side,' she said. 'It's a pity she's chosen the studious route. Girls who read a great deal are fit for nothing but marriage.'

Miss Jonsson was deeply contemptuous of marriage. 'It is not a respectable profession,' she would say. When minxes and lazy sluts were wed, she thought it served them right, but if a fellow came along and took a clever and capable girl, a really good, honest worker, she blazed with anger.

She gave a sudden toss of the head and declared with a vigour and a vehemence that neither I nor my mother understood:

'If the girl had been put in my charge she would have been a skilled modiste by now. As it is, there'll be nothing for it but to marry her off.'

I could no longer control myself. In my mother's presence I was in the habit of never revealing my innermost thoughts, which explains, incidentally, why Miss Jonsson and I did not find one another sooner, but this was my most sensitive spot and I felt deeply hurt by her offensive 'marry me off'. As if I were some mere species of womenfolk! My face flushed a fiery red and I looked Miss Jonsson straight in the eye, my words almost falling over themselves as I blurted out:

'I shall never get married!'

You should have seen Mildred Jonsson then! She lurched out of the chair where she had installed herself, opened her strong arms and pressed me to her mighty, motherly maiden's breast, beaming with joy as she said:

'Well damn me, so you're never getting married! You can rely on Mildred Jonsson, you know!'

Bright tears of emotion coursed down her incipiently sagging but cheerfully and optimistically restored cheeks.

'The young are made of sterner stuff than we are,' she said, blowing her nose loudly on the delicate fabric of her perfumed, lace-edged handkerchief.

With no softening preamble she turned to my mother and asked:

'What are you going to do now, Agda dear? I hear Dreary is flying the nest this spring.'

'I don't know anything about that,' said my mother, instantly stiffening. She looked at me with the wide and frozen eyes behind which she was concealing her distress and her shame.

Miss Jonsson gave a rusty witch's cackle. So my mother was oblivious to what the whole world knew! Perhaps Dreary hadn't mentioned it? So she would just twiddle her thumbs and wait for Dreary to deign to say something! And how did she intend to get by financially afterwards? And did she believe it was as innocent as it sounded, anyway? She, Mildred Jonsson, would be willing to swear there was another woman in the picture. A man doesn't leave his wife and child otherwise.

'You're old, Agda my dear,' she ended her breathless tirade. 'Don't forget that!'

'Dreary isn't like that,' said my mother with dignity. 'No one understands him. His is a great soul.'

It was with immense surprise and not without admiration that I heard my mother utter those words. But to someone as hardened by life's storms as Miss Jonsson they were like water off a duck's back.

'All men are swine,' she said emphatically, in a way that made one suspect it was a maxim that drew on her whole life's bitter experience. 'There isn't a single exception!'

Well, I realised at once that it was Miss Jonsson who had truth on her side and that my mother was like a child. In an instant the whole ignominy of our plight really came home to me. Mr Dreary was intending to leave us, it was as simple as that! We would be poor, abandoned women, my mother and I. People would laugh at us, offer their sanctimonious expressions of regret whilst inwardly despising us. My cheeks grew warm and my ears reddened as I thought of it. Should I, the champion of the proud, free woman, silently submit to such treatment? Was there no way to salvage our honour, to show the world which of us was being stung here? Wild projects swarmed into my overheated brain as I strode up and down the room, where the solitary bed told its own eloquent story of our predicament.

My female pride was faced with its first serious conflict.

'We won't stay here a minute longer,' I exclaimed. 'We'll move out of here this very evening! Then we'll see what Papa says when he comes home.'

The others stared at me, speechless with astonishment. This was a bit extreme even for Miss Jonsson. But I was suddenly sure it was the only thing for us to do.

'We must be the ones to leave him, not the other way round,' I declared. 'Don't you both see that? Why should women always have to sit and wait? It's just ridiculous!'

'That girl will go far, you mark my words,' said Miss Jonsson, full of admiration. 'She's not your average fledgling.'

From that moment on, I had a very high opinion of Miss Jonsson. We exchanged looks the way people do when they learn to appreciate to one another. It took me some time to notice that my mother was sitting in a corner of the sofa, crying.

She was crying so quietly and unobtrusively that the tears running down her pale, sunken cheeks were the only detectable sign. She had managed to hide her dreadful apprehensions, kept her anxiety to herself and proudly repudiated Miss Jonsson's insinuations. But when there was talk of leaving her home, the furniture she had dusted and seen gradually succumb to wear and tear, the rugs she had woven, the beautiful palm she had nurtured as the apple of her eye, her pelargoniums, her mind-your-own-business and her beloved blue passion flower which was as beautiful as the one her mother had when she herself was a child – when there was talk of her leaving all this, all at once and with no time to prepare, it was simply too much for her and she cried like a child.

Never before in my life had I noticed how small my mother was! She looked so tiny, huddled in the corner of the sofa, so frail, so touchingly helpless. I felt a lump rise in my throat, my breathing was painful in my chest and I could not stop myself running over to kneel down in front of her and say 'Mama,

Mama,' as I stroked her hand, feeling an overwhelming urge
to rest my head in her lap and weep with her.

'Now now, girls, don't take on so,' said Miss Jonsson soberly.

At that I felt ashamed of my weakness and stood up,
determined not to let emotion get the upper hand. Perish the
thought of my being as childish as my mother! If I were, who
was to take this family in hand and sort out the question of
women's rights in the world in general? Whoever did it would
have to be as hard as steel, as steadfast and brave as a soldier!
Was this not a classic case of it being better to choose death
than a life of degradation? I was about to say something really
calm and superior in that vein when the doorbell rang and
prevented all further discussion.

I gave a start. It felt like such a pregnant moment every
time the doorbell rang in those days. I was always anticipating
that something would happen, though I had no idea what.

When I opened the door an unfamiliar young man was
standing there, looking terribly embarrassed. He gave a
nervous bow and an odd, shy smile crossed his lips as he asked
if Miss Jonsson happened to be there. I heard very clearly that
he was asking for Miss Jonsson, of course I did, and his question
rang like a bell in my ears, Miss Jonsson, Miss Jonsson. But
instead of answering like a polite and well-mannered person
and inviting him in, I stood there staring at him as if he were
speaking Hebrew! I gave a completely gratuitous laugh and
watched in fascination as his face went through every stage
of awkwardness and embarrassment. What an odd face he had
– as mobile, open and naive as a child's, but still so nervy and
dangerous in some way, all too pliable and yet so manly! My
God, what a lot of interesting people there are, I thought.

'Please could you deliver a message to Miss Jonsson,' he
insisted.

I was roused from my foolish mental distraction and
rushed to my mother's room, cheeks glowing. In a whisper,
as if it were a matter of something remarkable and exciting,
I told Miss Jonsson that a gentleman was looking for her. I felt
strangely bitter to see how readily she leapt to her feet and
hurried out to the hall. I was on tenterhooks, eager to catch

the odd word of what the two of them were discussing in whispers out there. I thought I heard him mention the name Valdemar, but even that I could not be sure of. What in the world could it mean – Valdemar? Who was Valdemar? But if he really had said Valdemar, he could hardly be referring to himself. No, it couldn't be him, of course! He had definitely said Valdemar, I clearly heard him say it. And just now he had said that he had a message. From Valdemar, naturally! I rubbed my hands with delight. I felt as if I was flying.

'Shouldn't we invite that gentleman in?' I heard myself say to my mother.

'Do you think so?' my mother replied wearily.

Mama was always so impossible! I could not understand this indifference in such an exciting situation. *He* was out there in our hall, talking to Miss Jonsson!

Then she comes sweeping in, of course, very red in the face, her eyes darting about as her fingers scrabble nervously for her powder compact in her magnificent, pearl-studded silk bag.

'It was a message from home,' she says. 'Important business, I have to go right away. The best thing will be for Vega to come to my house tomorrow evening so we can have a serious talk about things. And you, Agda dear, are not to sit here grieving. We shall clear this up, you'll see. You can trust Mildred Jonsson not to leave her old friends in the lurch!'

And with that, she was gone. I didn't have time to put in a single word. The door closed on the two of them and they went off together. He didn't even bother coming in to say goodbye to me.

A feeling of emptiness and disappointment descended on me. I was brought reluctantly back to reality, to the impoverished little room, to my semi-abandoned, mournful mother, to my own silent amazement at what had happened to me. I did not know why I suddenly felt so hopelessly dejected. It was as if everything had simply lost its sheen: life, the battle, the whole show.

There is of course a text that says anyone who wants to live shall die...*

Alas, my rose, my rose!

My spring!

I was inordinately proud and self-assured as I went to negotiate with Miss Jonsson the next evening. I had a distinct feeling that I was now the head of the family. Mr Dreary's role was at an end. He was a capricious character, a fantasist, a child who could only be made to see reason with firmness and unbending resolve. It was hilarious to think that I was now going off to conspire against such a mighty figure as him.

Laughing under my breath, I made my way along the road in high spirits. I could picture so vividly how he, having been so thoroughly humbled, would have to take the road to Canossa, that is, to me, and make peace. Because Papa could not get by without us, that much was crystal clear! A week or two of living alone and abandoned would certainly soften him up. No food on the table when he got home, no one to put the blame on, no one to alarm and terrorise! An altogether dismal picture. And then there would be the dirty washing, the socks with holes, the hot shaving water and all those other things! He was extremely helpless all round and needed constant supervision. And this was the fellow who thought he could found a colony, if you please! With only men as far as the eye could see and not a soul to wait on them!

With every step I took, it became clearer to me that my first impulse had been the right one. We would walk out, Mama and I! That was the only way to open his eyes and in doing so we would deprive him of the frisson of leaving *us*. At any event, a man is very dependent, I reflected. He is like a child, requiring care and attention. He is quite easy to control, if you put your mind to it. For my part, I intended to suggest to Miss Jonsson that she, kind as she was and keen to show solidarity with her own sex, might let us stay with her for the short time it would take to soften up Mr Dreary and knock the fancy for independent living out of his head.

It was hugely exciting to sort things out by myself! I felt responsible, I was taking decisions and pulling my weight in the world. I was a full-grown human being, an individual. With the unruffled bearing of a serious and determined human being I stepped into Miss Mildred Jonsson's genteel hall, where the bracket lamps shone on either side of the gorgeous mirror and a soft carpet pleasantly muted one's purposeful footsteps.

The maid who opened the door looked oddly puzzled.

'Is the young lady expected?' she asked.

I found this strange and, what was more, rather impolite. But I replied with quiet dignity:

'Miss Jonsson is expecting me this evening.'

She instantly vanished and was gone for a long time. I found it slightly unnerving to be left like that and did not know whether to take off my coat and just go in, or how in the world to proceed. It's the way things are done in grand houses like this, I told myself. Like a hazy memory of some novel, the concept 'visiting card' came into my mind and I uneasily wondered if it was *de rigueur* to arrive bearing some sort of card when one came to visit. A flush of embarrassment spread over my face as the thought occurred to me. How mortifying not to know how one was expected to behave! Miss Jonsson simply could not conceive of my having no visiting card.

But look, here comes Miss Jonsson herself, advancing across the hall with a resounding welcome, inviting me to 'Come in, come in', and all is as it should be. I resume my previous dignified bearing and expression. Perhaps I am not quite as sure of myself as I was a few minutes ago and I am taken aback to see a number of young men gathered in Miss Jonsson's drawing room. In an instant I take in their self-conscious looks, the small, half-empty glasses and coffee cups scattered around on tables and realise how unfortunately timed my arrival is. Did Miss Jonsson simply forget I was coming this evening? It seems unimaginable!

'This is Miss Dreary,' she says to the gentlemen, I bid a good evening to each of them in turn and they tell me their names. My head is spinning and contains just one thought: how I can extricate myself from this with my dignity intact? But I can find no solution and am consequently obliged to sit down on a chair. Sitting down on a chair is terrible in situations such as this! I feel as if it is sucking me in, paralysing my powers of reasoning, my willpower, preventing me from moving. Here I sit, marooned! And the other guests, those who were genuinely expected, exchange looks and cough and don't know what to say to me.

'Well this is jolly,' says Miss Jonsson in a slightly forced way. 'We ought to make a proper party of it tonight, the unplanned kind are always the best.'

Not a word of the serious topic I had come to discuss, not a word of explanation, not the slightest hint. My mouth is a thin line and my whole body grows cold and rigid.

'Vega, you could do with some cheering up. We all could, for that matter. We are children of joy, not of sorrow, said the man who was about to hang himself.'

'Well hello!' twitters one of the gentlemen, raising his glass.

I squirm in my luckless seat, working out that I will say I've a lot of work to do and can't stay very long, besides which, for various reasons, my mother is waiting rather impatiently for me to get home. But I find it impossible to utter a single word. Miss Jonsson talks all the time and seems in unnaturally high spirits; I've never seen her like this before. You wouldn't think she was the same person. And the others are all talking at the same time, too, and suddenly there seems to be a great commotion. Someone sets the tinny gramophone going, someone else sings a snatch of a tune and some of the others laugh uproariously, at nothing at all as far as I can tell. There's no chance of saying a single sensible word in that company.

One of the strange gentlemen seems terribly conceited and won't leave Miss Jonsson alone for a moment. Milly this and Milly that, the whole time, and Miss Jonsson obeys the slightest wave of his hand, as if he were the master of the house. Milly – it sounds really comical. I think Miss Jonsson is rather ridiculous. Just then I hear her calling him Valdemar and everything falls into place. He was the one who sent her the message yesterday evening, of course, making her dash off like a scalded cat. Important business indeed. She's in love with him, of course, perhaps he is her lover? How ludicrous! Just like all the other women! And she's supposedly taking up arms for the women's cause and pretending to despise women who get married! I'm starting to feel that *I* despise Miss Jonsson.

Telephone calls are made to all and sundry. Valdemar wants more girls, and there's to be dancing and a party mood. I am in agonies. The very mention of the word dance fills me with anxiety and makes my legs freeze. I hear my mother's shrill voice saying: no dancing or card playing for you as long as I'm still alive! I so much want to dance, of course I do, but I know I can't. I have tried many times, at school, with the girls, they taught me the steps and I learnt them, I still know them. But when I dance, everything seems to go wrong – the instant I begin, I lose both the beat and my balance in sudden confusion. I shall never forget my mother's face when she once caught Mr Dreary and me in the midst of a merry polka – we were gleeful about some imaginary exploit, I can't remember which. I was scared out of my wits and both Mr Dreary and I felt the shame of what we had done when she walked in on us and just stood there, looking.

So what am I to do when the dancing starts here? I am caught in a painful dilemma, the sweat beading my brow. I fear dancing as something terrifying and forbidden that is secretly my heart's desire – as sin itself! I want to get away, to hide my shame, to disappear. But the chair has me in its implacable grip; here I sit as if I have been paid to do so. How could I get up and go? What would I say, what expression would I assume and what movements would I make? It is horribly complicated. And now we have the arrival of some amazing ladies, with bare arms, falsetto voices and insolent, velvety eyes that run over me as if I were air. I shrink beneath their gazes, aware of my inferiority, my ungainliness, my thoroughly gawky and clumsy presence. The painful realisation dawns on me that my book learning, my brains, my character will cut no ice here. Everything in this room hinges on things I am not used to counting as assets. In the face of these splendidly sexual apparitions, Vega Maria Eleonora Dreary is quite simply a ridiculous figure, a nobody.

Spirits rise and the flirting starts in earnest. I try Miss Jonsson's sweet liqueur. For the first time in my life I taste an alcoholic drink. My cheeks glow and the sensuous, liquid atmosphere in the room seeps slowly into me like a poison. An intermittent sense of suffocation makes me yearn for clear water and fresh air.

I dare not even look at Miss Jonsson, it all feels so horribly demeaning. There she sits on the lap of that Valdemar, though she is large and plump and the fellow as spindly as they come, a pipsqueak not yet dry behind the ears. Then she gets to her feet with a clucking laugh, lifts her skirt above her knees and does some silly pirouettes in the middle of the floor, raising one leg after the other and swinging round. The gentlemen snigger and applaud, praising the elegance of her legs. She does actually have quite nice legs, unusually slim for someone of her ample proportions, with a beautiful line to the ankle and knee. She is inordinately proud of them and blithely unaware that the young men are making fun of her, poor thing. My sense of shame is bottomless. I have no idea where to look. What would Mama say if she knew about this? Just think how Miss Jonsson has pulled the wool so completely over all our eyes! But then we have only ever seen her in the mornings, at ordinary coffee parties. Look at her now, frantically kicking aside the costly carpet in her urge to dance! Her body demands space for movement, her senses demand rhythm and life! She throws herself at the gramophone beside me, and as she winds it up I come into her line of vision. She nods at me and smiles as broadly as a witch scenting child flesh:

'In Hell they go rowing in a tray, because there's no turning round there, hee hee.'

This completely incomprehensible pronouncement fills me with unspeakable horror and I stare at her as if at some spirit from the infernal depths. She must have lost her mind. There is red flickering before my eyes and the room begins to sway. Through a mist I see a man standing before me, wearing a red neckerchief tied Apache style* and grinning at me with white teeth and moist red lips. I realise he is inviting me to dance. I close my eyes and shake my head vigorously. It is all I can do.

'Are you unwell, young lady?' he asks. 'Shall I get you a glass of water?'

'Thank you, there's no need,' I answer dismissively.

His nose put out of joint, the youth vanishes with a shrug of the shoulders and my mind sinks into a state of profound insensibility. The music pounds on, heady, seductive, drawing me in. Every now and then I glimpse Miss Jonsson's full breasts in the whirl of the dance as a magnetic stream of rhythmically gliding bodies envelops me in its sensual caress. But I sit so motionless in my seat, so far away, excluded from life's clamorous fiesta. The blood music rises from within me and I listen to the sigh of rising and falling rhythms in my internal organs. Merciful darkness closes in, even in the middle of this dazzlingly illuminated room, isolating me from everything that is going on around me.

Are you never to feel the fire of passion, you solitary heart?

All at once my eyes open wide at the sound of a piercing cry. Miss Jonsson is lying on the floor; she slowly pulls herself up to a sitting position. A trickle of blood runs from her mouth, soiling her beautiful dress and all the splendid decoration on her chest. She sits staring straight ahead, saucer-eyed and vacant. What she sees is not those of us in the same room, but the debasement of her own life. What she sees is that she is old, she is out of the game, and it has all been for nothing.

Valdemar, that youth on whose lap she was sitting, had suddenly struck her in the mouth and thrown her aside. Now he sits calmly on the sofa, smoking a cigarette. I look at him as if at my mortal enemy, hatred flashing in my eyes. I have forgotten in an instant that I despised Miss Jonsson and considered her conduct inappropriate. I see before me my natural enemy, the man who treats a woman however he chooses, with caresses or with blows. The full measure of degradation and shame I have experienced all evening wells up inside me. I know it is entirely this man's fault. He is the personification of everything I have instinctively rebelled against all my life – the embodiment of ownership and entitlement, the debaser of my sex!

'You should be ashamed, you lunatic,' I yell, beside myself with anger and resentment.

It seems outrageous that the others are just standing there, looking on, rather than grabbing him by the collar and throwing him out. I stamp on the floor and choke back tears as I hurl a 'Cowards!' in the faces of the timid beaux.

Valdemar regards me with a look of amusement and says:

'Well look at that, the minx has a temper!'

I turn my back on him in contempt. As I do so, I see that a new arrival has appeared in the doorway. I stop, spellbound, our eyes meet and a thrill runs through me. It's him! It's him! A sense of unutterable calm descends on me and my inner tensions miraculously dissolve. All is as it should be. It does not concern me in the slightest what Miss Jonsson and that young man are up to. He has come, the stranger, and I realise that he is the one I have been waiting for all along, that he is the reason I am here this evening and he is why I could not leave but had to hold out to the end. Unconsciously I somehow knew – that he would come. It could not end like that, I just knew it. We had to meet, the two of us!

He is barely through the door, Tancred, before he does what seems entirely natural, though no one else has thought to do it. He goes over to Miss Jonsson, wipes away the blood with his handkerchief and helps her up.

'It's easy to slip on this floor,' he tells her, though he understands full well how it happened and was also witness to my outburst.

'Yes, I'm damned if I know how I slipped,' says Miss Jonsson, rallying to cheery vitality again. A moment later she appears to believe it herself. She sits down beside Valdemar, talking brightly to him as if nothing has happened. Valdemar looks at me and laughs.

'You'll turn out well, given time,' he has the cheek to say to me.

I find it insolent, incredibly insolent, but by now I am in such high and foolish spirits myself that nothing can touch me. I just laugh at him, my mortal enemy, debaser of my sex. What happened to my female dignity, my fighting spirit and righteous indignation? I well know that this is a disgraceful game and what we really need here is a proper reckoning, home truths and prompt reproaches. Of course I do, but my God I am so infinitely happy, more senselessly and idiotically happy than I have ever been in my entire life! Isn't it odd, his voice, so tense, so childishly eager, and occasionally even breaking! He is unlike anyone else I have ever seen. He does not move like other people, does not talk like other people, does not laugh like other people. I can't take my eyes off him. I look at him with the same astonished, touched, insatiable curiosity as a father seeing his newborn child. For me, as for the father, that child seems to come falling out of nowhere, external to myself, yet still be mine in some profound and mysterious way, my own child, part of me.

Here he is, stepping forward and introducing himself to me in a courtly fashion. Isn't it comical of him to introduce himself like that? When we are such good friends that no two people have ever been such good friends! It's like some funny sort of game.

'That was a fine thing you did,' he says, looking at me with obvious admiration. 'Pay no heed to them making fun of you like that. Never pay heed to such things, just say what you think!'

It fills me with happiness to hear him say such words. I beam with joy; in a single second my heart bursts into bloom, like a rose.

'I esteem women very highly,' he says. 'I have my mother to thank for that.'

Who has ever heard a man speak in such a way? I understand that he must be an unusually noble man, an unselfish, truly cultivated individual. My heart's inextinguishable capacity for hero worship gathers itself instantly round his person.

'You are an unusual man,' I say with feeling and conviction. 'I am glad to have met you.'

Then he takes my hand, squeezes it firmly and confidingly and says:

'I can see we have a great deal to talk about, we two. I realised it as soon as I saw you act so courageously. I wish you and my mother could meet.'

It is a case of mutual admiration; the fateful creation of idealised images has begun. I find what he says about his mother particularly touching and beautiful. I visualise a distinguished old lady, as gentle and serene as a madonna, and I can already see her radiant eyes turned on me, the woman her son has chosen, and her hand extended in caress and blessing.

'I would so much like to meet your mother,' I say, my cheeks aflame.

At that, the last traces of cautious reserve in his manner melt away. He is boyishly high-spirited, talking and laughing as if we have known one another since childhood. He tells me with disarming honesty that his father is a low, mean man with whom he wants no dealings, that he has an implacable hatred of all brutality and any sort of tyranny, and that he feels contempt for people who seek only their own advantage and have no ideals beyond a comfortable life, a large income and all manner of outward success. He scorns anything like that. He dreams of a life of complete freedom and independence, and that can only be achieved by keeping one's needs to the bare minimum. He admires Tolstoy precisely because the writer saw so clearly that he had to set himself free from Mammon. No man can serve two masters and that is the truth! But whoever has found truth must fundamentally transform his life. And this he had done. Having abandoned all worldly cares, he now felt so glad and free. He wanted to live a completely natural life, like the savages, like the flowers, like the animals, delight in each day as it came and went, in the sun, the moon and the skies, in the wondrous truth and beauty of life in the natural world.

Every word he spoke was a revelation to me. His soul opened itself to me like a green meadow in the early morning, with a thousand glittering pearls. To think that a human being could be so rich!

'I like you so much for being so simply dressed,' he says, so simple and serious.

Then we talked a lot about poverty, how splendid it is, rendering a person genuine and free. The whole secret of life consists in just that, in the ability to be poor, to renounce everything, bind oneself to nothing. If you are poor, you never have to compromise! Owning nothing is the mark of real nobility of mind. To me this sounded magnificent, a majestic thought. What could be more glorious than two impoverished young people going through the world hand in hand, not dependent on anything or anyone!

'I am looking for the sort of girl who understands me on this subject,' he says. 'But most of them think only of how much money one has in one's pocket to spend on them, on dances and entertainments and so on. And then they expect marriage and children and there one is, tied for a lifetime.'

How well I understand him on that point! Surely a man like him would not go and get married and become a family breadwinner like everyone else, allowing his spirit to be shackled. That would be the death of him! I raise my head proudly and say from the bottom of my heart:

'I think marriage is demeaning to both parties. You never see those who are married developing intellectually, do you? On the contrary, they simply regress.'

And see how happy he looks, Tancred! His eyes rest on me as if I were an angel, a supernatural being, a vision in a dream. I know he thinks me a marvel and this incites me to add:

'For my own part, I intend never to get married. The one I love must be free, and so must my love. That's the only way to retain human dignity.'

He gives me a look, stranger than I have ever received before from anyone, any man. An eddy of heat grips hold of me, yearning and ardour swirl up from the depths, I tremble, I burn, I close my eyes in delight and consternation, feeling something incredible and wonderful happening to me. His arms lift me and he carries me round the room in mad triumph, shouldering aside the dancing couples and planting himself in the middle of the floor, raising me high in the air and laughing up at me. Everything we have said and discussed and so sagely set to rights dissolves into unreality, like vapour, like something that only existed so this could break through it, this liberation, this crushing happiness.

The gramophone is still pounding away in a room where everything else is suddenly deathly quiet. It is as if the whole company, rowdy and drink-befuddled the moment before, have stood aside for an imperative power, a truth dazzling in its nakedness, a passion, a flame. They spring to attention, every one of them. Tancred sets me down on the floor, puts his arm around me, clasps me to him softly, tenderly, and we skim slowly out across the floor and dance our first waltz. I dance with closed eyes, gliding gently in a deep, mysterious trance. I am dancing! I am dancing! The gramophone has stopped, someone has started whistling the tune, but I am oblivious to that. I am dancing! I am dancing with my beloved, my man, my unfathomable stranger. I am dancing into my life.

Happiness descended and overpowered me. Everything within me opened, just opened up as quietly and irresistibly as the bell of a flower opens to the sun. Shackles melted away within me, fetters broke and my foot barely touched the earth, so light had I become, so free, so young! A newborn being without name or destiny... Dazed, I looked around the room when the dance ended, as if tossed up on a foreign shore, tossed up from the surging sea that had brought me forth. I felt the swell of the waves in my blood, their swaying cradle, their soothing swing, the waves that rocked me into life. I laughed to my beloved. My hair, my eyelashes gleamed with pearls, my skin and my limbs glistened like a mermaid's.

'My bride,' Ta whispered to me, laughing.

Once I had parted from him at the front entrance to my home I could not bring myself to go in with my heart so trembling and full. I sought my solitude, my garden. The gate squeaked slightly as my hand touched it and a shudder ran through me. With that first kiss still burning on my lips I stood in the middle of the path in my father's nocturnal garden, holding my breath. A faint mistiness rose like a spirit from the ground, a first hint of breeze stirred in the trees, heralding morning and stormy weather. Shivering, I huddled into my coat and looked about me in surprise, so unfamiliar did it all seem, so curiously abandoned, as if I had returned home after a long trip to find that strangers had taken over my property, the places I knew, the sites of my immature dreams. I spared a glance for the bench where Fridolf and I used to sit; it hunched there damply in the morning mist, rickety and grey on the bare ground, in the mud, between the bare trees. As unrecognisable as my whole garden, my loneliness, my girlhood life.

*

Spring came upon us early, in April, inundating us with its heat and intensity. My city awoke in that headlong way she does in spring, the white queen of the still-frozen waters, her crown glistening with sun and cobalt. She asserted herself, she breathed, yet trembled in the debilitating grip of the sun, and the stretches of ice around her quaked. People went uneasily back and forth, stopping at street corners, looking out to sea, hungry for the first glimpse of blue, of sparkling, faraway blue. In Gräsviksgatan, windows and doors flew open in the rows of small wooden houses, old folk emerged from their winter lairs, sat on the benches in the little garden patches set out in rows in front of house after house, looked across to their neighbour's patch and asked if they would be growing the same flowers as last year, chatting to one another across the low fences, encouraged by the glorious weather. Birds came flying, the children ran to and fro, slamming the gates, digging in the soil, and all at once, every second boy was holding a magnifying glass, the wonderful cosmic toy that lets you burn holes in your new trousers and send blinding flashes of light to annoy those indoors. The spring was so blissfully lovely this year!

As for Ta and me, we would meet early in the mornings and late in the evenings. My window, the kitchen window, was the only one that looked out over the yard and the little patches of garden. I slept so lightly that spring, so lightly that the slightest scraping sound would wake me. I knew it was Ta, scratching at my window. In the early hours, as the sun rose in its silent, solemn beauty, Ta would come, finding it hard not to run as he made his way through the quiet streets, bare-headed and with sandals on his feet, and when I awoke from my light slumber he would be standing there, waving. I was up in a trice, knowing several glorious hours lay ahead of us before it was time for us to go to our respective work. We strolled along the quaysides, we walked in the forests, we watched nature coming back to life day by day, little buds bubbling up on bare branches, colour and sheen developing around us, the pussy willow catkins blooming, small insects emerging, butterflies spreading their wings. It was a pure miracle; never before in my life had I known so much to happen in just a few weeks. Ta could talk so engagingly about it all, tell me the stories of each animal, flower and tree, silent tragedies, wondrous destinies, celebrations of beauty and the intoxication of love, wild battles and treacherous deaths. He knew everything, my Ta! He had tales to tell me of distant lands, too, Australia, Tahiti, tropical oceans, and he never tired of describing the Canary Islands, 'the happy isles', their natural beauty, the life there, the delightful climate. All you need in the Canaries are a few breadfruit trees and you can lead a carefree life for the rest of your days, he said, a life in the sun, an act of worship held in the natural world. There's no need to toil for clothes and for solid walls for your house there, for pork and potatoes and rye bread! The sun gives it all to you for nothing!

The sun gives it all to you for nothing!

The sun shone down on me that spring as never before; my hair took on a new glossiness, my eyes a new sparkle. 'You're so beautiful,' said Ta, 'your hair gleams like gold and has the scent of new-mown hay. There is nothing so blue as your eyes!'

One hot morning I was hurrying along Stora Robertsgatan. The narrow pavement was clogged with people, the traffic clattered and rumbled, the air was pungent with dust, asphalt and human exhalations. A young worker with eyes like black coals in a face gleaming with sweat pushed close to me and gave me a squeeze as he passed, just below my left breast. A violent shiver ran through me and I instantly turned to see him laughing at me, his teeth glinting like young diamonds. Aroused to the point of feeling drained, I plunged into the shoal of people, sensible in that glorious second to the marvel that was my body, the ardour in my limbs.

The sun gives it all to you for nothing!

The following morning I went out alone. I woke at five, feeling hot and uneasy. I lay there and waited for a while, still dazed and with the exquisite intoxication of my dream lingering in my blood. I thought Ta was in the room. He had been lying at my side just now, hadn't he, with his head resting on my shoulder, leaving my arm a little stiff, and I felt happy as the pressure faded and vanished, like a memory. With eyes half-closed I lay there waiting for him to come back, lean over me, slip into me, into my mysterious depths. But nothing more happened in that quiet morning hour, except that I gradually became fully conscious and realised I was lying in my own bed, the same old bed where I had always slept, in my father's house. I sensed the morning outside, felt its clarity all around me, as if I had bathed in air and light. I got out of bed, took off my nightdress and contemplated my own body in wonder. To me it looked so beautiful, so taut, so pure, resplendent in its muted sheen, and I smiled as I thought of Ta: he is going to be happy.

Was I now to I wait for him until he came, an interminable hour, perhaps more, and sometimes he wouldn't come at all? I dressed in feverish haste, suddenly finding it unbearable to be indoors. I had to get out and breathe and experience my own happiness in a way I could only do alone with myself. I yearned to wander in solitude along our quaysides and see everything glittering at me. When Ta arrives the bird will have flown, I thought, laughing. It would be stupid of him to go home. He ought surely to come looking for me and guess where I would go on such a morning! It was a thrilling, entrancing game.

With my heart in my mouth I ran out of the apartment block and stopped short in the middle of the road, captivated by the streak of dizzying blue at the end of the street. People call Gräsviksgatan ugly, but I think it is as beautiful as a street can be, with its classic vista of one-storey wooden houses, the kind only to be found in my city, with fretwork flourishes around the windows, and then the gleam of the dazzling sea in the background. The view was currently further enhanced, dramatised as it were, by the funnel of a steamer right in the centre of the gap. My steps were irresistibly drawn towards that gleam, towards the sea.

I sat down on the edge of the quay, my feet dangling comically over the water and the sun shining right in my face. A few small cargo boats lay sleepily at anchor in the harbour. From a few spindly tin smokestacks, thin columns of blue smoke ran straight up into the air, spreading hints of sweetly aromatic morning coffee. Now and then a face looked out, a figure emerged from a cabin, went about its morning deck chores and vanished from view once more. A shaggy old ship's dog lay indolently by the rail, and I could not tell if he was asleep or gazing at the glittering surface as I was, with wide and shining eyes. The sea was as flat as a mirror. My eyes strayed to the horizon, just the way ships glide out and are gone, to destinations unknown.

'Lovely morr-ning,' said a voice behind me.

The fellow engaging me in conversation was a somewhat disreputably clad character. He sat down casually beside me, crossed one leg over the other, spat skilfully into the water and pulled a cigar stub out of his pocket.

'Why's a young lady like you sitting here all lonesome?' he said, slipping an amorous arm round my waist.

Now one might well imagine this would have petrified me! I ought at the very least to have risen in regal rage, shaken him off in disgust and told him what I thought of him. The strange thing was that I looked at him with amused curiosity, noting that he was unmistakably a young man, a free young man with glittering, adventure-loving eyes. The light touch of his arm was not at all disagreeable, in fact just the opposite. It was rather pleasant, a funny, exciting little contribution to my body's bright morning life. But I shifted cautiously away from him, even so. I had barely put a reassuring distance between us when he unexpectedly grabbed my arm and pulled me to him, squeezed my breasts and tried to kiss me. Ah, but I was not one to be trifled with! I struck him in the face, scratched him and would have bitten him if I got the chance. My body contracted, my muscles tensed and my eyes flashed with the blistering anger I felt. Even in my alarm I was laughing inside, laughing as I sensed my own strength and agility and the joy of battle.

'Bloody bitch, you are,' he said when he had finally freed himself from my claws. Out of breath but as proud as a scalp-hunter I watched him set off ignominiously back into town. He would certainly think twice, that fellow, before affronting a free woman again!

My morning peace had been shattered, even so, and I was about to get up and go when Ta's familiar whistling reached my ears. How happy that made me! He had come looking for me, and he had found me! It felt as though we had been parted for an eternity. I ran straight into his arms and pressed myself tempestuously to his breast.

'Do you love me, Ta?' was the first thing I asked.

'You little rascal,' he said, and kissed me.

We sat down on the quayside, a little way along from the scene of the drama. A breeze had sprung up and clouds were looming at the edge of the sky, gathering to create their ever-changing spectacle above our heads. One moment you saw a knight in full armour advance and point in a particular direction as if danger threatened there. The next you saw riders of the apocalypse make a charge on their snorting horses, circling one another like teasing spirits and then clashing together, clustering into a single, fantastical mass. Still heated after waging my own battle, my pulse racing and my senses glowing with the premonition of approaching fate, I watched in strange excitement as the celestial joust played out, as if I were the lady they were fighting over, as if mine were the colours worn by some of the cosmic horsemen.

I felt for Ta's hand and pressed it to my breast.

'Look, she's hoisting her sails, what madness,' said Ta, pointing to one of the ships riding at anchor. 'Surely she isn't venturing out in the storm?'

Then I saw all the riders falling back and being swallowed up by a mighty tower that advanced with overwhelming force, filling the world with its dark and menacing shape.

'This is what fate looks like!' The words escaped my lips as I stared wide-eyed at the spectre in the clouds.

Ta laughed. He thought I meant the ship setting out into the storm.

'We should have been aboard, you and I,' he said. 'She could be bound for our happy isles.'

I don't know why, but it sounded so awful, so ghastly, our happy isles, just as the bank of black cloud was towering above our heads and the demented ship was giving itself up to the Evil One. There was a first flash of lightning, a rumble of thunder, and my heart constricted with dread.

'She'll go down!' I cried.

Sails full, she ran before the wind as the waves frothed and the storm intensified. Shivering, I pressed myself to Ta, threw my arms around him and burrowed my body close to his.

'Are you afraid of the thunder, little Vega?' said Ta, cradling my head against his chest as if I were a child. 'Then it's best we go home.'

'No, no, not home!'

I was fighting for breath, my whole body was trembling with an unfathomable fear and my eyes were riveted to the ship as it headed straight into the impenetrable blackness. Was it the ship of my dreams slipping away, never to return?

'Never abandon me, Ta!'

My Ta laughed that funny laugh of his, childish, infectious and carefree. Tears ran down my cheeks and my heart was heavy, but I still had to laugh back.

'Look, it's starting to rain, we'd better hurry home,' he said.

'I don't want to go home,' I insisted, like a stubborn child.

At that, his face darkened and his mouth began to twitch. It was now raining heavily and we were soon soaked through, but neither of us took any notice. He looked at me with his big, burning eyes. A silent battle was being waged between us, and we both knew what it was about.

It had crept between us, this battle, without our noticing how or when. Our mornings were so free and happy, brimming with the joy of cosmic life, but our evenings were heated and uneasy, weighed down with conflicts we could not solve, overshadowed by dangers whose names we did not even know. We were both so inexperienced and did not know how we wanted things to be between us. He lived with his mother, in just one room, but however many rooms they had, it would make no difference. For her sake he had abandoned his father, his work, his research, and he loved her as you would love your own deepest sense of pride, for which you had sacrificed yourself. This peculiar, saintlike pride isolated him from the world. He had never had a relationship with a woman, despite his mature years; he lived as an ascetic, a dreamer. Neither of us really knew what we wanted of the other, strangely enough. But we were irresistibly drawn together and felt utterly wretched whenever we were apart. We could think of nothing but one another and hurried ardently and eagerly to our assignations. Once we were finally alone in a room together, we were timid with one other and extremely self-conscious. Our hands made passionate contact, he pulled me to him violently and kissed me, but then such a strange look came into his eyes, restlessness seized him, he got to his feet and began pacing the room.

I was crestfallen. I could only think that deep down inside he was distressed about abandoning his studies and grieving that he would not be able to make anything of himself in the way that now lay before him. But he had staked his pride on providing for his mother. He had forced her to give up her job and taken her into his care. Perhaps he had imagined he would be able to continue his studies even so, but it proved impossible of course, with all the private lessons he was obliged to give. They absorbed all his time and attention. His unique insect collection, his notes and his correspondence with foreign lands were now no more than clutter on a closet floor! I was never allowed to see them, and he could not tolerate my even mentioning them. God, how I loved those beetles! I loved them as foolishly and jealously as if they were my children, my own trapped, incarcerated children. I suffered terribly, considering it wholly unnatural for him to squander his talents like that. I was so proud of my Ta, my prodigy, my genius! I so much wanted him to shine for the world to see! I dreamt of extricating him from that terrible room with his mother and taking him out into the free arena where laurels are gained and victories won.

The battle between us was conducted silently, imperceptibly but unrelentingly. This wasn't freedom and independence, I thought. Freedom meant crushing all resistance, fighting through to a heroic achievement! All the proud exploits I had dreamt of for myself had suddenly, as if by magic, been transferred to Ta. My rose was forgotten, my interest in women's rights had cooled, Mr Dreary's sins of commission and omission faded from my mind and my burning ambition was for Ta alone. Had anyone told me that I was unconsciously pursuing my own aims and seeking a way to make him mine and bind him to me, I would not have understood what they meant. *I* was the one trying to set him free, wasn't I?

On that curious morning so unlike every other morning, charged with electricity and dark desire, terrifying in its fateful splendour, my blood surged restlessly as my sensations chased one another to the point of exhaustion and all my stifled anguish gathered itself for a cry, a demand, a challenge inside me.

'Come on now, don't be silly,' said Ta impatiently. 'You're going to be late for school. And I've got a lot of work to do today. I'm going home, anyway.'

That constant repetition of 'home' was like a slap in the face to me. I pulled away from him, leant backwards, supporting myself with my hands on the ground, and raised my head to look him scornfully in the eye.

'You!' I said through gritted teeth. 'That's all you can ever do, go home. To your mummy!'

I blanched even as I said it. God knows what evil spirit prompted me with those particular words, and I was well aware of how irreparably hurtful it must be for him to hear me say them. The very person who was supposed to be his friend!

His face froze into a mask. His mobile, sensitive, open face grew as dark and rigid as a menacing stranger's. He got to his feet without a word, lithe, silent and sealed. I leapt up in utter terror and covered my face with my hands so as not to see him leaving me. Then I felt his arms close around me as he swept me off the ground and bore me away. He spoke not a word, but his lips, his feverish lips, moved over my face, my neck, my breast, and he kissed me as he had never kissed me before. I felt so light lying there in his arms, eyes closed in the delightful numbness of released tension. Perhaps we met other people, perhaps they turned to watch us go, shaking their heads, but I know nothing of that. The gale howled around the city, the rain teemed down and the thunder cracked, but I basked in the ardour of Ta's face as he breathed me in through his mouth and took me as his own.

He stormed through the streets, propelled by anger and love, his lightweight burden in his arms. And he carried me, as if in a single breath, all the way to his home. He carried me up the stairs, straight in at the door, and laid me just as I was, in my wet clothes, on his bed. He stood there for a while, leaning over me, and I could hear how heavily he was breathing and feel his gaze on me through my closed eyelids.

'Now you're home,' he said.

The air resounded and effervesced around me: now you're home, now you're home, Vega. You've come home now! I just lay still and listened, smiling at my heart. I was distantly aware of someone else in the room, moving about, of an agitated, whispered exchange of words, a commotion, sudden movements, but I felt no anxiety. No thoughts troubled me, no clear appreciation of what was happening penetrated my consciousness. I lay there as if in the arms of the Holy Mother, beyond all danger, beyond everything that can deal out blows or commit murder.

And look, it was Ta, standing beside me and shaking me! He wanted me to take off my wet coat and warm myself by the stove while he made some coffee so we could get something inside us. I was exultant! I leapt up and started helping with various tasks as if I owned the place. We knew exactly how we wanted things, the two of us, and it all seemed so natural. Neither of us mentioned school and his work might as well not have existed, nor his mother. Ta was so eager and deft; no one would believe how endearing he was, going about his domestic chores. And as soon as we had had our coffee, he shot off to the closet where the beetles languished, dug out everything he kept there and arranged it all on chairs and tables, dusting, sorting, untying string, opening cases and boxes. I sat on my chair in breathless excitement, my expectant eyes gleaming like silent, secretive mice in their burrows.

For there he was, laying out the whole lot in front of me!

He produced his collections, displaying rare specimens which to me appeared unremarkable, but also shiny metallic beauties in fabulous emerald and sapphire colours. He revelled in dung beetles, scarlet lily beetles and scarab beetles, waxed lyrical about ladybirds, stag beetles, click beetles, deathwatch beetles, tumbling flower beetles and God knows what other names they had, those outlandish creepy-crawlies that had suddenly materialised in my life. He told me about all their diverse lives and livelihoods, expounded in baffling terms on the significance of secondary sexual characteristics, pointed to wing-cases, feelers, mandibles and compound eyes. Slightly stunned by all this new terminology, I saw a world of marvels opening up before my eyes. The astonishing functions of nature, the ingenious battle of the spirit silently waged in the hidden world of the soil and the ground, revealed itself to my imagination, and I could not grasp how all this had existed, playing out in front of my nose while I remained totally oblivious to it. Good grief, of course I had occasionally seen a beetle struggling on its back on a dusty road, but I had simply no idea the pathetic little creature led such an exciting existence!

Once Ta got going there was no stopping him. All his long-curbed enthusiasm flared up in an instant; he was trembling in his eagerness and his eyes were glinting as he surveyed the collection in all its glory. It was clear to me that he was absorbing it all and would not easily relinquish his booty. I was in a state of profound tension, my heart pounding; my life cried out for its consummation through a thousand mute and tiny insect mouths. It was festive, it was joyous! When he started bringing out his scholarly journals from abroad, I was at the peak of my excitement. They contained articles that he had written, my Ta, in both English and German. And now he was no longer attempting to conceal his pride. He showed me passages where world-famous experts mentioned him by name and cited his research. As I read he stood in front of me, legs planted wide apart like a captain on his ship, self-assured, nose in the air, and thumbs stuck in his waistcoat pockets with his fingers splaying out in all directions. Every time I looked up at him in admiration he pulled such silly faces that I was in gales of laughter.

But all at once he put a finger to his lips, assumed a mysterious expression and laid out in front of me some beetles that definitely did not look very remarkable. They were Sacred Scarabs, would you believe, *Scarabaeus sacer*, the legendary talisman of the Egyptians. Scientifically speaking it is nothing more than a dung beetle that lives on excrement, but there are no limits to what an imagination hungering for eternity has done with that beetle and her ball of dung! As Ta told me all about it my eyes widened, like a child listening to amazing fairytales as darkness falls, seeing the room peopled with beings from east of the sun and west of the moon. What is truth and what is imagination in this strange game? I could picture the beetle vividly as she made her intricate balls out of the dung she could find on cheerful, bustling thoroughfares and laid her eggs in them; I could see the cocooned chrysalis enclosed in the dung, seemingly dead and yet alive. But as Ta digressed into the realms of Egyptian legend, another beetle was conjured up in my mind's eye, a stone idol, a supernatural symbol through the ages – that of resurrection. The austere emblem of the mysteries of the eternal cycle, the enigma of birth and death, which the Egyptians tirelessly depicted in their monumental art, in their temples, on their consecrated talismans: the Sacred Scarab. Defying the wind, the sand and the assaults of the centuries it still bears witness today, like the Sphinx and the Pyramid, to a people's belief in eternal life.

What is truth and what is imagination in this strange game?

In my quailing mortal heart, an answer made itself heard as I sat there, bent over the small, shimmering black bodies of the dead insects and listening to Ta's tales of their ever-busy lives on the roads of Syracuse and Pompeii. A wordless answer with no clear meanings, an indistinct singing and humming, an ancient, invincible note of unknown suffering, a song of the birth-giving, death-bringing mystery of life. A women's song, a humming, cosmic *yes, yes* ...

But Ta, he had no time to linger over anything now. He was racing across his domains, restless and eager, with a freshly awakened urge to plough and sow and produce. He was already looking for something else to show me. As he rummaged through his jumble of possessions a book came to hand, and I could see at once that there was something special about it. With a deft turn he slipped it into my lap. *Catalogus Coleopterorum Scandinaviae* – a title which told me nothing, except perhaps that we were still on the subject of beetles. I opened the book somewhat abstractedly, caught up in my own fantasies. 'To Tancred on his twelfth birthday, from Papa,' I read on the first page. How strangely diffident Ta seemed in the presence of that book! He scarcely dared look at me as I leafed through it. And as for me, I had great difficulty holding back the tears. His twelfth birthday! That was when he had seriously embarked on his studies. That was when he had started making his notes, with a sense of long-term purpose. In a small, firm hand he had drawn up his future life's work. I felt contrite, overwhelmed – in my feminine inconstancy. Now I truly understood what a child prodigy he was, my Ta! It felt like a glimpse into how they had lived together, he and his father, in a world of their own, and the way his father had urged him on, helped him, driven him forward, and how proud he must have been of his son. And then his mother had come into the picture, a passionately personal element in this clear, objective, male world. How senselessly he had sacrificed everything for her, his rejected mother!

But was it senseless? Did I know what fires it took to mature his soul for its destiny? The book lay in my hand and I looked at it as if at a toy, and smiled to myself. For the first time I comprehended, gained a true vision of, how Ta loved his mother, how he loved me, and the mysteriously self-effacing way in which a man can love a woman.

Ta was kneeling on the floor with his back to me, pretending to be engrossed in something. I could see his back, his neck, his gleaming, silky-smooth hair standing out like a cloud round his head, and I experienced a tenderness unlike anything else. I instinctively started gently swaying, as if I had a baby in my arms, a suckling child. I rocked him in my arms, a man, eternal child of all mothers. Dim and sacred memories rose to the surface of my fleeting consciousness, memories of obscured women's lives over many centuries, and I was no longer the young, inexperienced girl with her anxiety and her excitement, her disguised wishes, I was as old as womankind, my face was grey, my eyes as blind as those of a seeress.

When Ta got up and came over to me, we both knew I would be his. My face shone towards him in the ecstasy of devotion, my body trembled in anticipation of the painful bliss that the Earth has allotted to those who give birth.

In the light night of early summer, as if after an annunciation, filled with a secret as clear as day, I walked home alone to my parents' house. My friend, he was still sleeping and, locked and barred within their houses, people were dreaming their dreams behind unfurrowed foreheads and closed eyelids. It was a long way to walk; my limbs were heavy with the melancholy of untimely maturity and my heated dreams had evaporated. Inside I felt as strangely empty and desolate as the waters on whose face the spirit of God moved before the Creation.

As I turned into Gräsviksgatan I saw a curious figure standing on our front steps. He was bareheaded and staring straight up into the air, into the ambiguous light between night and morning. In one hand he carried a comical little suitcase. I felt a sudden constriction in my chest and peered eagerly through my short-sighted eyes to get a better view. Goodness, it's Uncle Eberhard! I thought. He must have set off on his long journey. I increased my pace, almost breaking into a jog, so keen was I to meet Uncle Eberhard, look into his calm, clear eyes, hear a quiet word from his lips. Just think, he must want to meet me again, to tell me that now, Vega, Uncle Eberhard has left for the last time, just so you know! But as I got closer I saw that it was not Uncle Eberhard, who would have cut a much taller and lankier figure. So how was it that he somehow reminded me of Uncle Eberhard, his demeanour, his funny little suitcase, his whole appearance of a man *der seine Sache auf nichts gestellt**?

In fact it was Mr Dreary I encountered in the early dawn light of Gräsviksgatan. He had doubtless seen it was me long before I had convinced myself it was him, my father, the last person I expected to meet like that, in such a situation. He was walking towards me with an embarrassed smile and it was plain that he didn't know what to do. Had he been my father in the way he was before, he would have taken me to task, interrogated and rebuked me. Where had I been for so long and what sort of time was this for a schoolgirl to come home? But Mr Dreary had neither house nor home at that point, he was neither a father nor anything else, he was a gentleman passing by along the street, a universal figure, just anyone, a possibility. With the suitcase in one hand and his hat in the other, he passed me without looking at me, as one passes people one happens to meet in the street. He was en route to his new life. But there was a smile playing on his lips that I knew was for me, a smile that said: You and me, we have our ways.

Once he had passed I felt a painful twist in my heart. This was my father leaving, after all. I was forced to stop and turn round. He, too, turned round, and gave me a cheery wave. I waved back at my papa. Tears came into my eyes, the altogether disquieting uncertainty of life descended on me, the shadows of my own fate loomed in my path and I hardly know how I got through the door, stumbling through the phantoms that my heart had summoned up as it contracted in fear.

I went straight to my mother's room. She was asleep in bed. She looked like a child when she was sleeping. Her breathing was as light as a bird's, and she looked so peaceful and lovely lying there, oblivious to everything. I stood still for a long time, just looking at her, afraid of making the slightest sound that might wake her. What cause had she to wake, in actual fact? To look around her with her helpless, watery blue eyes, yet still not comprehend anything of the life she had entered inadvertently and quite without preparation? When I saw her like that in the white bed, her features smoothed out and her hands resting, childlike, on top of the quilt, it seemed so implausible that she had brought me into the world, that she was my mama. She seemed so immature and undeveloped, compared to me. How was it possible for her to have gone through all – that? Did she really know everything I knew? In a sudden, peculiar flash my mother appeared to me as a girl lying there, a little girl who had brought a baby into the world without knowing what was happening to her. And my papa out on the steps – what could he be trying to divine from the early morning light as he made up his mind whether to leave us? It was all as strange as in a dream I'd had long ago and had half forgotten, half remembered.

Just as I was about to withdraw so as not to disturb my little mama while she was sleeping, she suddenly opened her eyes, roused by some inner warning.

'Vega!' she cried in an anguished voice, holding out her hands.

'Yes, Mama,' I answered. It sounded so new and encouraging to my ears to hear Mama call me Vega; in the midst of all my agitation, I laughed as I turned to her.

'I thought you were never coming back,' she said in a feeble, reproachful tone.

'You only dreamt it,' I said.

Our eyes met and I think she realised at that instant how things stood with me and the deeps from which I had come. She stretched out her hand and pulled me to her. Without a word she held me close so my head was resting on her breast. She gently hummed some nonsensical old song and stroked my head. Lying there, I felt closer to her than I had ever been before. I realised that she knew everything, that her light, watery blue eyes patiently held their secrets and hid their loneliness like a colourless pearl on the sea bed. I felt the great, beautiful sense of calm in my mother's arms. I rested deep within the foundations of my own being.

'Papa has left us,' I told her very quietly. It felt quite natural, as if there were nothing special about it.

She made no reply. She leant back in the bed and closed her eyes. I never discovered what she was thinking, and it was likely she was not thinking anything in particular. More than anything she was probably relieved that the agonising uncertainty was finally over, so she could start being herself again.

Dialogue in the June night

I did not understand it until this very evening, this very night.

The whole time, I thought I was writing for myself, to get away from this state that is neither life nor death, but utter damnation. It came over me so intoxicatingly, the impulse to go back on my own tracks through the jungle. If I did that, I would be bound to find my way out! At some point, the free horizon would most certainly open before me, and bring peace to my spirit. After all, I had once lived in the cosmic light, like everyone else I had seen the sun, the moon and the stars and understood the signs in the skies. As soon as I made out the position of Mr Dreary's constellation it brought the scent of my childhood, the scent of the wild places. My tracking instinct was suddenly roused. The secret of the points of the compass was revealed to me and I realised all at once which way I was going, something I had not known since I lost myself. I saw all the funny, self-contained images of my life mysteriously merge together to form a whole.

Of course I got a fright when Ta appeared out of the blue – long before he was meant to be there, and in a completely different way. But nothing had the power to bring me to my senses. He could have hit me, but I would still not have awoken from my dream. Blinded by my own yearning, I knocked on the door of the past, fool that I was! Now the door has opened and I see there is no path behind it to lead me anywhere. The same jungle whichever way I go, tracks winding round and leading back to their starting point.

I saw Ta tonight, with a strange woman.

I saw them from behind, just as they were turning towards Kaisaniemi Park from Elisabet Square. They went down the stone steps, arm in arm, and just where they passed out of sight through the gap by the granite balustrade, I suddenly saw Ta's face. I stopped instantly, petrified, at the end of Elisabetgatan beneath the tall and terrible wall surrounding the hospital. It looked so gruesome, as if his face had torn itself free from his body and placed itself there to warn me. I was not to follow him!

I covered my face with my hands and pressed myself to the wall, but I could still see his face right in front of me, seared into my own heart for all eternity. And then it came to me that *I* was the one persecuting **him**! That I had gone into my past for him alone, to find him again. It was not myself I was looking for, my free horizon, it was him, always and only him, via a thousand deceptive and circuitous routes. I wanted to go as far back as I could in order to walk once more the path that led to him. He was there in the background when I started and I blissfully slipped into a state in which Ta did not yet exist but was still standing there ahead of me. So powerful was my yearning that it finally forced him to manifest himself bodily. I had him, yes, I had him back! As a shadow, a horrible phantom from a dead past.

There was no strength left in me for new life.

I wanted to hurry away from there to escape the fire that was at my heels, but my feet were as heavy as lead. The last trams clattered past, somewhere there was a glimmer of lights, and ship's lanterns, somewhere there was the murmur of people passing by. The wall breathed dampness and icy chill, a prison wall, a burial chamber. Nobody in the whole world could see me. There were no roads leading away from this place. Ta was entering into a life where I could not follow him, not even with my yearning. He went arm in arm with a strange woman. For me she was Death, come to take what was mine.

I have nothing left, not even my memories!

I felt someone touch my shoulder. I have often seen him in these parts before, the old Russian priest, but in my agitated state I was as alarmed as if I had seen Death himself in a black cassock. He said a few words that I did not catch, but through his wild, unkempt beard I could see his lips moving. The incomprehensibility of his words, of my whole situation, of everything closing in on me, surrounding me from all directions, struck terror into me. I ran from the place, driven by that nameless, occult horror that has lurked within us all since time immemorial, the shadow of death projected across the sunlit fields of our consciousness. I ran as if for my life through the deserted streets, down to the station, up Henriksgatan and right over to Tölö where my home lies. Can I still call it my home? Thud, thud, went my feet, echoing through the quiet night. Thud, thud, I heard them running after me, my own distressed steps. It's all over now, there'll be no more dreaming for you now, no more running round to the places you love, looking into the clear eyes, lifting the corners of the concealing veil. You shall never, ever look out across the ocean and see the ships come sailing towards you like proud birds, your dream ships. You shall never touch what happened between you and Ta, his tempestuous awakening, his relapse, then grief and disappointment and ultimate, brilliant redress. You shall never experience the voyage out and away, the morning when you stood alone on the deck and saw the beautiful foreign city rising from the water, a magnificent solitaire, set among the other jewels of the channel, with a faint mist around the heights of Söder*, like a vague sense of hope. Never shall you see any of this again! It will die and rot away, along with your love.

A cold and malevolent light has fallen over my whole life. Death is shining his lantern in my face.

When I saw the foliage of Hesperia Park standing out benignly against the desert of stone, I slowed my steps. As usual I took the route through the park, along the shores of Tölö Bay. As soon as my steps carried me beneath the trees, the tension within me eased and I came to a halt, transfixed by the secret nocturnal beauty of the scene. Stillness lay in the trees around me, their delicate catkins quivering in the light air; stillness lay in the water beneath the dome of pale blue, with the faint blush on the horizon and the high, thin crescent moon in the east; stillness lay in the mist above the damp grass along the shore. Everything was breathing, fragrant and alive, in thrall to the midnight light.

I sat down on a bench with my face turned to the water and the light and the dreamlike silhouette of the city on the other side of the bay. I could feel the chill at my back and knew Death was behind me, but he did not frighten me now. More calmly than ever before, my eyes scanned the water.

'I know it,' I told myself. 'I have no strength to start a new life. I have a fever in my body, shadows around me, and I am tired to death. I have no other wish, I know how everything stands and my gaze is clear-eyed. This is my final resistance.'

Then Death leant over me and engaged me in whispered conversation.

'You can see for yourself how it is, of course,' he said. 'You're not alone in being tired to death. If the strength to start a new life exists in your land, in your world, then presumably it also exists in you? Why do you think people are finding things so hard, why is it hurting their chests to breathe? What is weighing them down, do you suppose? It's sickness, fever, the blood-spattered shadows of the past. They are all rising up from their graves, haven't you seen?'

'But there are so many young people coming forward now,' I said, not wanting to believe him. 'Nations are rejuvenating themselves, beating down the shadows, finding their way back to a healthier, more primitive, more youthful existence, to vital wellsprings.'

'Back, like you!' replied Death. 'That's an illusion. Have you ever known life to move backward rather than forward?'

I felt stung, and realised what he meant. He meant that life is action and death is reaction. This time was Death's.

'Haven't you noticed that the young people coming forward now are marked by death?' he added reflectively. 'Or perhaps you have heard the leaders calling them to something else? I haven't heard that, and my hearing is pretty acute, I can tell you.'

'But so much enthusiasm, so much youthful courage!' I protested.

'Yes, they will lend beauty to the sacrifice,' he said in a flat voice.

A shudder ran through me. There was a fiery stripe on the horizon in the north, the new sun blending its colours with the suddenly evaporating lilac glow of sunset. The treacherous cold of the dawn hour crept into my body and I shivered.

There was still the pulse of hot red blood in my veins, and I was still sensitive to the chill! I scrambled to my feet and scurried away to escape the terrible cold. But run as I might, I could not generate any warmth. The chill closed around me, penetrating to my very marrow, and I was afflicted by shivering as severe as if I were suffering from a high fever. I realised that he was following me, Death, and that there was no point in running. When I opened the door to my home, the cold hit me. He had got there first.

The shivering still has not stopped, but the sun has come up. Its gleam is catching the house diagonally across the road and all the windows are aflame. I look out over the treetops to the south. There lies the sea and beyond the sea the great, restless continent. The horizon is blindingly bright. It is as bright as the consciousness that looks out of our eyes. But the ground beneath our feet is heavy with blood and memories, and with every step we stumble over graves that open and spew their coldness over us, their melancholy and their transience. Over there, so many men and women of good will are active, travelling from country to country, gathering their flocks and speaking rousingly of tomorrow, but at the crucial moment their voices are drowned out by the wild clamour of chaos, just as the human voices on the radio are intermittently drowned out by the metallic screech and roar of interference beyond our control.

Where is the fresh, unspoilt continent which people can traverse, light of step and looking to the future, as we do when life lies ahead of us?

My confession is at an end.

I am a witness who could not report anything to shed light on the puzzle that our era's sharp-witted detectives have been entrusted with solving, the puzzle of the person who wanted *new life – life! – and went back. She was found one morning, you see, having died by her own hand, and no one could fathom the reason why.*

I can hear my guest here in the room growing impatient. Well, that is fine by me!

The awakening

In the dark, agonising depths I wrestled with the snake. He coiled himself around me, crushed me to pulp, smashed in my chest cavity, making the blood spurt from my mouth and my eyes pop out of their sockets. I shuddered, I fought for breath, suffering excruciatingly in the grip of such a supernatural black force; my bones cracked, my limbs were torn from my body, and a wheezing gurgle issued from my throat. My poor life was locked in battle with Death.

I sat bolt upright in bed with a cry, my arms flailing wildly at thin air. A sudden gleam of light revealed a white figure bending over me and then I was gone again. Long spells of numb repose when the profoundest absence had eased, but just as I was about to regain consciousness fully, I felt a hard blow to the chest and was cast quaking into the inhuman wrestling match once more. It has been in progress ever since that night I myself challenged Death to single combat.

How ruthless he was, and what violent force lay in his assault. When I was still among the living I had been entirely unaware of the horribly fierce look of cunning in his eyes. I had felt the cold emanating from him, but it was not so bad as to prevent me having a discussion with him and calmly putting my affairs in order in his presence. I thought the finale would be just as simple and conducted in as dignified a fashion as the preparations, just a sober little act and it would all be over. I am sure all living people who speak of committing suicide think the same. They don't know what they are talking about, and have no inkling of the appalling struggle awaiting them at the end. The very moment I raised my hand to grasp the implement of death, the hissing monster was upon me, dread took me in its embrace, pressuring and battering me with stupefying force and my poor, palpitating body attempted to defend itself in its ultimate hour of need. My whole being cried Murder! Murder! And my eyes were wide with terror, my body drenched in the sweat of a fight to the death, by the time my semi-paralysed hand finally managed to carry out the execution. As life began its faint and flickering retreat from my veins I was obliged in the depths of my exhaustion to relive the dreadful struggle over and over again until my strength was utterly drained and I slipped away into the region where all creative ability stops, and with it the hallucinations.

Suddenly, as when a picture comes up on the cinema screen, I found myself wide awake. I'm dead now, ran my first quick thought, and the awful part is over. An immense and beautiful sense of calm descended on me, and sunny little thoughts were moving somewhere in the back of my conscious mind, but they never took shape, merely ran together in a sense of newly-won safety. With that feeling, I was roused to life. I saw I was lying in a sickroom and there was a nurse sitting by my bed. I did not reflect on this. Things were as they were.

'We're going to be well again very soon,' said the nurse and gave me something to swallow. Then I drifted off to sleep quietly and without any fuss, because nothing bad could happen to me.

The days and nights all merged for me into chiaroscuro, light and floating, an element expressly for all the silent beings that belong in the boundless kingdom of our guardian spirits. I simply had to laugh out loud, for it was so very nice to meet Uncle Eberhard again! All at once he was standing there at my bedside, apparently lost in thought, his head bobbing up and down. How very high up it was, his comical, birdlike head! Perched high on a thin pole.

'You're a proper scarecrow, you are,' I said with a little chuckle. No one could possibly know how merry it made me that Uncle Eberhard had come. He had left his little bundle on a chair by the door.

He made no reply to what I had said but I did not mind, for I knew one had to be patient with Uncle Eberhard. I must have dozed for a while, but just as I woke I heard him say:

'Now Vega, you must pay heed to this moment. These are important matters.'

His words fell with a tinkling sound into the great silence in my heart. They rang like bells in there, playing tunes full of premonition that I can still hear whenever I close my eyes. Ethereal creatures – perhaps they were angels, perhaps the same spirits who lulled me as I lay in my cradle – opened their mouths and sang my forgotten melodies in strangely ringing, high-pitched voices. Were these memories or intangible premonitions of what was to come?

'Now that you are so alone like this,' Uncle Eberhard went on, 'you must try to sing quietly to yourself so no one else can hear. Then your soul will return to you. She is the one who knows all and remembers all, but you yourself know nothing.'

He told me a great many more things, Uncle Eberhard, as he stood by my pillow, yet I somehow seemed not to hear the words themselves, but only their echo inside me. I felt so safe with him there. He was like a rock, like the truth. The memories he called up from my depths had no connection with the memories I had carried about with me; they did not lead me back to my dread and my night, but opened a gateway to a kingdom somewhere in the midst of my soul, at the crossroads of what had been and what was to come, the living kingdom. A feeble little song came welling from my lips, though only I could hear it. It was my own. Nothing in the world can make me as happy as that song. I own nothing at all as I sing it, neither a place of abode nor a place to rest my head nor anyone's love, but a thousand kindred spirits answer me through the air.

'The day of parting is done, the night of absent friends is over!'

I thought I heard a soft sound and opened my eyes. Uncle Eberhard had gone. He had taken his bundle and slipped out as unnoticed as when he arrived. And then it struck me that Uncle Eberhard is dead. One winter some men hauling logs in a forest way up north found him dead under the snow, and the little bundle was all he had with him by way of worldly goods on his final journey.

He is not dead, I thought. He had many friends beyond what is visible.

I am not dead! my heart cried in delight. I shall live!

This thought, this mysterious and impenetrable thought, opened itself up to me like a fissure opening in a rock face. Music came pouring forth. There was a mighty, thundering roar, like the sound of organs, and I thought I could see the person playing, a male figure, larger than life, with his face vanishing into cloud and only his hands brightly lit, the big, beautiful, creative hands playing on universal instruments. 'He is risen from the dead!' I could feel the power emitted by those hands, see the sparks flying all over the world, waking the dead, bringing them back to life, fortifying the weak, feeding the hungry and igniting the urge to take on the immense tasks awaiting those who are to create the world anew. A spark from his hands jumped across to me, and to me in my impotence it felt like fire in my veins. He is risen from the dead, the Son of Man. From out of our degradation we shall rise up! From out of our sickness we shall die!

As the organist played, the past fell away from me, just as sunburned skin peels off in flakes and is renewed. I saw the fresh new continent growing before my eyes, my Atlantis rising from the sea, beyond the horizon I perpetually scanned, we all perpetually scanned, Mr Dreary and Fridolf and Ta and I and the peculiar prophets, the proud and godless supermen from the idyllic era of my youth. It was emerging just where we had lost our gamble and tasted defeat, we, the great personalities.

Fridolf's deathly pale face with its horrifying gashes, the gaping wounds inflicted by a battle whose significance neither of us had understood. Ta's tortured face, his strained and harried expression as he spent days and nights contemplating the decisive step of a move to a foreign land, alone and without the support of the person closest to him, weighing his own life, his happiness, his future against the demands of his conscience to support the little people looking for a chance to raise themselves up to freedom and light. Mr Dreary's hunched back as he dejectedly made his way home one stormy autumn night after all his hopes had foundered and the one in whom he had placed all his trust had proved a traitor who put his own profit above others' welfare. From such faces, dead and living, such strained features, such hunched backs, the outlines of the new land emerged as if from a receding fog.

From the living reality of my own people, from all the aspects of its existence that were exciting, heterogeneous and tragically charged, my Atlantis grew. As never before I felt my sense of belonging to that people, of my fate being bound to its route through history, of my participation in its future. Lying there in my bed in a hospital that had received me without my knowing it, had extended invisible hands of human fellowship to pull me, the suicide, from death's claws, I felt myself rooted in existence, in a people, a people that was peculiar to me and through it a humanity, a universal life. Having stood aside from everything happening in reality, pursuing the phantom of my own happiness, I could now feel how a task and a belief can grow out of death and burning shame.

'I shall open up a path to the interior or perish.'

I distinctly heard a voice saying these words. I knew them of old, the words of the great Scotsman, which he carried through to the extreme. Emaciated beyond recognition, worn down by fever, privations and superhuman exertions, he was driven by an irresistible force to plunge deeper and deeper into the heart of the wild black continent. What was he seeking? The sources of the Nile? He died at Chitambo* without finding them. But from his death there issued forth a blinding light. The whole of that dark land saw it. Those savages who destroyed one another in civil wars and themselves became victims of the bloody hunt for slaves saw it and hailed him as a messenger of peace. His black servants saw it and loved his dead body more than their own lives, braving danger and death as they bore that body many hundreds of miles to reach the coast. The whole of humankind saw the light that shone out from his death.

Ah yes, I knew them well, David Livingstone's words. And yet it was as if I were hearing them for the first time, with a new meaning. I could so clearly hear the force that was uttering them. It was the love of humanity, which alone can open up the path to the interior.

The first thing I saw when I returned to my home and my life was the torn-out page with David Livingstone's picture on it, a page that had fallen from my hand in my moment of despondency, pointing to something which I had failed to understand until now. He sat there as he had sat through all the years I had known him, my old friend, his eyes fixed on some faraway goal and his hand ready to write down what he had found out. Freighted with love, his words came to me: 'the open sore of the world, the Africa of the black man'*. And I understood what kind of explorer he was, one of the greats, one of those who had devoted his life to relieving the curses visited on humankind. I was touched once more by the solemnity of this vision, but now he no longer seemed so distant that I could not reach him; he drew close to me, he was my brother, one of us. I might not have accomplished what I was intended to or found what I was looking for, but then nor had he found the sources of the Nile. I might not be called to open up the path to the interior of Africa, but there were dark continents* enough for me in my own land, hardship, darkness and night, enslavement and civil war. The great and exceptional thing he really did achieve with his life was his death in Chitambo! A true and beautiful death that sends out the light of love to illuminate the world. Death that does not tear apart or cut short but is a consummation: a mysterious seal.

I was crying with happiness that I had not had to die in my torment.

Chitambo! Chitambo!
Onward, comrade!

Notes

18   The little Corsican: Napoleon. In the chapter 'The mysterious rose', Vega refers to herself as 'a young Napoleon' (p. 124) and writes that in her studies of young men of genius and ambition she was enchanted to read of Bonaparte, adding: 'I loved the young lieutenant, loved him as my brother'.

22   This could be a reference to Luís Vaz de Camões's epic poem *Os Lusiadas* (The Lusiads, 1572), which describes Portuguese explorer Vasco da Gama going 'through seas never before sailed'.

24   'The Three Graves on Beechey Island' is an illustration of the last camp of Arctic explorer Sir John Franklin, from which he set out in 1846 to his death.

24   'The Death of Cook on 14 February 1779'. Captain James Cook died in an affray between his sailors and local residents of the Sandwich Islands (now Hawaii) on his third visit to the group of islands.

26   Alexander von Humboldt, a Prussian naturalist who became one of the pre-eminent scientists of his day, made an expedition through South America in 1799-1804, collecting data on many aspects of what he saw.
The source of the quotation (Man must will the good and the great, the rest is in the hands of fate; in the original German: 'Der Mensch muß das Gute und Große wollen, das Übrige hängt vom Schicksal ab') is a letter he wrote to Carl Freiesleben as he set sail on the voyage in 1799, first from Marseilles to Tenerife and then on to South America.

32   This chapter heading is in all probability a reference to the admonition of Alexander the Great's father: 'Seek another kingdom, my son, that may be worthy of thy abilities; for Macedonia is too small for thee.' The episode is reported by Plutarch in his *Lives*.

39   This is a quotation from Jon Sørensen's *Fridtjof Nansens Saga*. Jacob Dybwads Forlag, Oslo 1931.

40   The name Pip only occurs once and with no explanation, but it is, as George Schoolfield identified, the name of the little black cabin boy on board the *Pequod* in Herman Melville's 1851 novel *Moby Dick*.

46   Swedish-language poet Johan Ludvig Runeberg (1804-77) is known as the national poet of Finland. Inspired by Romantic nationalism, he wrote many works including the epic poem *Fänrik Ståls Sägner* (*The Tales of Ensign Stål*), which was published in two series, in 1848 and 1860.
May Day is the Labour Day holiday in Finland, and also seen as a chance to celebrate the arrival of spring, with numerous festive student traditions.

53   Tabor church meetings: The Tabor church is a free church and part of the Pentecostal movement.

60   This is the hymn version of a somewhat grisly wake-up call 'O syndig man' by poet Lasse Lucidor (Lars Johansson, 1638–74), which exists in several variants. The one used by Olsson has kindly been translated for this volume by John Irons, who has gone on to translate the full original poem and has made it available here:
johnirons.blogspot.com/2018/11/lucidor-o-syndig-man-wake-up-call-from.html

67   'Hunger years' is a reference to the famine of the 1860s, triggered by harvest failures and exacerbated by the severe frost of 1867. Some 200,000 Finns died during the famine.

78   'The first step of the fakir...': this is very probably a reference to, or quotation from, the vast epic poem *Schanameh*, The Book of Kings, written in the year 1010 by Abu al-Qasim

Ferdousi (sometimes transliterated as Ferdowsi), who is widely considered the national poet of Iran. The opening sections of *Schanameh* were translated from Persian into Swedish by Baron Eric A. Hermelin in 1931. Hagar Olsson made the translator's acquaintance through his niece Honorine Hermelin, while staying with her and working on Chitambo. The women first met at the Women Citizen's School at Fogelstad in Sweden, which Honorine had helped to found in 1925. Olsson later reviewed Eric Hermelin's Ferdousi translation in the Swedish literary magazine *Ord och bild*.

81   The island of Lesbos was where Sappho, teacher and lyrical poet born in Greece sometime around 615 B.C.E., ran an academy in the city of Mytilene for young, unmarried women.

81   The Scandinavian term *upplysning* is not quite 'enlightenment' in the French or Eastern sense, but central to cultural radicalism and the welfare society.

84   These German titles appear chosen to represent a certain type of literature. There is a work entitled *Aus der Chemie des Ungreifbaren* (From the Chemistry of the Intangible) by Paul Köthner, 1907. The other works mentioned here and a few lines below, which can be roughly translated as 'On the Intellect in Nature' and 'Towards the Enhancement of Human Intelligence', may or may not be genuine.

84   Viktor Rydberg (1828-95) was an influential Swedish writer of the Romantic school, whose areas of interest included paganism, Christianity and mythology. Among his most famous works are *Singoalla* (1857, rev. 1865) and *Dikter*, (Poems,1882).

86   Quotation from Friedrich Nietzsche, *Also sprach Zarathustra*, (Thus Spoke Zarathustra, 1883-85). Hagar Olsson goes on in this chapter to caricature very drily the appropriation and imitation of his ideas in Finland at this period by many a young man who fancied himself a superman or *Übermensch*, creating a 'peculiar hybrid' as Vega puts it.

181

87   Henry George (1839-97), US land reformer and economist. He
      argued that governments should finance all projects with
      proceeds from a single tax, on unimproved land. George's
      idea was largely borrowed from, among others, John Stuart
      Mill.

87   Lines from 'Prometheus' by Johann Wolfgang von Goethe.
      One English translation, by Richard Stokes, runs: 'I honour
      you? Why? / Did you ever soothe the anguish /That weighed
      me down? / Did you ever dry my tears / When I was
      terrified?' A work of the *Sturm und Drang* movement, it was
      written between 1772 and 1774 when Goethe was a rebellious
      young man, and first published anonymously in 1785.

89   *Etidorpha: Strange History of a Mysterious Being and an Incredible
      Journey Inside the Earth* was a work of utopian science fiction
      and pseudoscientific speculation written by Cincinnati
      pharmaceuticals manufacturer John Uri Lloyd and published
      in 1895.

96   In the original text, this is 'den eleganta negern'. Translating
      this as 'the elegant Negro' would have marked it as of its
      time, but here it seems merely descriptive rather than
      used with any intent to demean, so its use would not add
      anything to the work in English. See also the Translator's
      Afterword.

97   The only opera in the general repertoire that ends with
      a living burial is Verdi's *Aida*, first performed in 1871. Its
      heroine is an Ethiopian princess who has become a slave.

97   In English: 'Do not forget, Mademoiselle, that it is only a
      show.'

101   'Revolution' could refer here in part to the events of 1917 in
      Russia, when Finland was still part of the Empire and thus
      experienced the February Revolution, and also in part to the
      Finnish Civil War of 1917-18.

101   The Russian Revolution in 1917 left a power vacuum in
      Finland and a struggle, a civil war, ensued between the

conservative Whites who wanted independence from Soviet Russia and the socialist Reds who opposed the separation.

103   The Finnish general strike of October 1905.

104   Väinämöinen was the heroic central character of Finland's national epic *Kalevala*, compiled in the nineteenth century by researcher and poet Elias Lönnrot and based on Karelian oral folklore.

105   Imposing Kakola prison, high on a rock, was the central jail in the town of Turku (Åbo in Swedish) and was in use from the 1850s until the early twenty-first century.

105   In folklore, Pohjola is depicted as a mythical and inaccessible place in the perilous Far North, home to a prosperous people.

105   In the Finnish national epic *Kalevala*, the Sampo is a magical artefact or talisman that brought the Pohjola people wealth and good fortune.

105   Suomi is the Finnish name for Finland.

105   Paavo is a stoical peasant farmer who features in the poem 'Paavo of Saarijärvi' by Johan Ludvig Runeberg (see above), published in his *Dikter I* in 1830.

105   'Our land is poor and shall so be': words from the Finnish national anthem 'Vårt land' (Our Land; 'Maamme' in Finnish), written by Johan Ludvig Runeberg.

112   Åland is an autonomous, Swedish-speaking region of Finland comprising over 6,700 named islands in the Baltic Sea. Hagar Olsson's father was a clergyman who took up a living in the island parish of Föglö in the Åland archipelago soon after her birth. She and her three brothers were schooled on the mainland but went with their mother to spend their summers in the archipelago. Hagar Olsson's childhood memories inform this chapter of the novel.

119   Despite enquiring widely, I have been unable to identify
        the source of this quotation. In the original Swedish, it
        reads: *Vad bekymrar dig vårt tillstånd, du som aldrig sorg har
        smakat?/ Du som sitter på flodens brädd, vad vet du om törstens
        överväldigande makt?*

121   'Most people sleep themselves stupid' and 'Dear Sir, you
        simply begin' are quotations from Arnold Bennett's *How to
        Live on 24 Hours a Day* (1908, 1910).

121   *Giftas*, 1884 (*Getting Married*, English translation by Mary
        Sandbach, 1972) is a set of short stories by August Strindberg
        on the subject of modern-day marriage, and his somewhat
        reactionary take on the 'woman question'. An even more
        vituperative second volume appeared in 1912.

121   Ellen Key (1849-1926), educationalist and socio-cultural
        polemicist, wrote a sequence of essays about Elizabeth
        Barrett Browning and Robert Browning in her book
        Människor (People), 1899.

123   This sounds like a typical free church hymn of the
        nineteenth century, but does not seem to have survived, no
        longer appearing in Swedish-language Baptist hymn books.

124   Ida Aalberg (1857-1915) was the leading actress of her age in
        Finland and also performed abroad. The play Vega attends
        is Henrik Ibsen's *Et dukkehjem* (*A Doll's House, 1879*). The lines
        quoted are from the final act and the edition used here
        for the English-language versions is *A Doll's House and Other
        Plays*, transl. Deborah Dawkin and Erik Skuggevik, Penguin
        Classics, 2016.

126   The Finnish Women's Association (in Swedish: *Finsk
        kvinnoförening*; in Finnish: *Suomen Naisyhdistys*) was founded
        in 1884 and was the first women's rights organisation in
        Finland.

126   Sewing circles had an important role to play in securing
        women's suffrage in Finland. Maria Lähteenmäki and Ellen
        Rees, among others, have pointed out that Finnish women
        learned the basics of organisational work in temperance and

workers' associations, and members of small women's groups across the country eagerly practised the conventions and procedures of meetings. Women also became accustomed to association work in sewing circles and drama and speech clubs, these activities providing a cover for political activism.

129   Georg Carl von Döbeln (1758-1820) was a Swedish lieutenant general, notably lauded – not least by Finland's national poet Runeberg (see above) – as the hero of the Battle of Jutas in Ostrobothnia, Finland in 1808, at which he commanded the Swedish forces against the Russians. He had been shot in the head in an earlier battle and despite surgery the wound never properly healed, so he wore a concealing, black silk bandanna for the rest of his life.

129   The concepts of 'cosmic' and 'cosmos' and the spiritual unity of all existence are central to *Chitambo* and to the thinking of an author who was once dubbed 'the apostle of the life force' (Svanberg). For further discussion of Olsson and the concept of cosmos, see the Translator's Afterword.

130   Ateneum, in central Helsinki, is a renowned gallery which was inaugurated in 1887 and houses part of the national art collection.

138   This is in all probability a Biblical reference: 'For whosoever will save his life shall lose it', Matthew 16:25.

144   The Apache was a brutal and passionate dance that began in Paris nightclubs and spread to other European capitals in the early decades of the twentieth century. Modelled allegedly on gang fights, or fights between lovers or between pimps and whores, it was also known as the 'dance of the underworld'. Flat caps and neckerchiefs were sported by the male dancers.

163   *der seine Sache auf nichts gestellt*: who had put himself into the hands of nothingness. Possibly from 'Ich hab mein Sach auf Nichts gestellt', which is the first line of the Goethe poem 'Vanitas! Vanitatum Vanitas!' This is in turn Goethe's parody of the Christian hymn 'Ich hab mein Sach Gott heimgestellt'

by Johannus Pappus (1549–1610).

168   Söder, short for Södermalm, is a district in Stockholm, on elevated ground and thus visible from the water.

176   There seems to be some confusion in Livingstone sources as to whether Chitambo was in fact the name of a village or of its chief. Hagar Olsson, however, consistently treats it in this novel as the former.

177   'the open sore of the world, the Africa of the black man': attitudes to colonialism, racism and even eugenics and 'racial hygiene' that would be unacceptable today were relatively widespread in the Nordic region, as in other parts of Europe, in the 1920s and 30s. Interestingly, Livingstone's final words were said to have been 'The open sore of the world' (see www.westminster-abbey.org/abbey-commemorations/commemorations/david-livingstone). The addition of 'the Africa of the black man' must be Olsson's own comment, or have come from a Swedish translation of his words.

177   Vega Maria's 'dark continents enough in my own land' implies not a darkness of skin but 'hardship, darkness and night, enslavement and civil war'.
Links between primitivism and modernism are discussed in the Translator's Afterword.

Translator's afterword

Prolific and multilingual Hagar Olsson belonged to the Swedish-speaking minority in Finland, which has produced more than its fair share of literary figures through the years. Her *Chitambo*, written in 1933, is a multi-layered revelation, the work of a writer coming to the top of her game, and splicing her fiction writing with all that she had learnt as a critic and cheerleader of European modernism. Its themes are universal, international, national and personal, and many critics see it as her most important work of prose fiction. It is compelling storytelling, and full of scathing humour, particularly in the episodes in which the mature protagonist looks back on her own youth, episodes which Ellen Rees characterises as 'at times exuberantly comic, and always full of irony at the expense of the narrator's younger self' (2005, p. 133). Although, as the notes to this translation will testify, this is a novel bursting at the seams with references and quotations from very diverse sources, Olsson wears her learning, if not exactly lightly, then rather attractively, and the novel is eminently accessible.

Above all, it is an entertaining novel, and although the reader will readily absorb a lot about Finnish history, society and temperament as well as about girlhood rebellion and self-discovery, we are carried along by the story of Vega Maria, invigorated not only by the fresh breezes of a vividly evoked port city but also by the winds of change and revolution blowing across Europe.

The structure of *Chitambo* can be described as modernist in, among other respects, its departure from a traditional nineteenth-century chronological narrative. Although readers of today are very familiar with shifting perspectives and timelines, they still need to retrospectively construct the precise nature of the events that have caused Vega Maria such emotional anguish. Tancred's move to Stockholm, for example, so painstakingly orchestrated by Vega, and his subsequent betrayal in returning to Finland, to his mother and to war, is conveyed in nothing but a few disjointed glimpses.

Chitambo in fact seems a novel designed to dazzle and disconcert, and in doing so, it adopts an array of guises. George Schoolfield, whose 1973 article remains, for me, one of the most thorough and thoughtful English-language contributions to Olsson studies, notes that the title *Chitambo* brings to mind the name 'Chimborazzo', which had occurred in the work of several Nordic modernist poets over a decade earlier, and ponders why this Olsson novel had not, by the time he wrote his article, been rated as highly by the critics as some of her other works. He attributes it in part to the novel's refusal to be categorised:

> But what can be done with *Chitambo*, whose very title has the ring of modernism, yet which leads us into the world of nineteenth century explorers and beyond; where the time of narration embraces contiguous but distinct epochs in Finnish history; where the heroine's attitude towards a variety of matters [...] is by no means clear[...]? (Schoolfield 1973, p. 224).

Yet even before *Chitambo*, Olsson was not easy to pigeonhole. Her works in the preceding years were all very different from it, and from each other. In 1927, for example, inspired by playwrights such as Strindberg, O'Neill and Pirandello, she wrote her first play, *Hjärtats pantomim* (Pantomime of the Heart), a stylised drama in four tableaux about human emotions. In the novel *På Kanaanexpressen* (On the Canaan Express, 1929), by contrast, she used state-of-the-art stylistic devices of collage and photomontage to conjure up a nightmarish vision of people living as cogs in a machine, until chaos and hopelessness give way to a quest for light, ultimately making it a hymn to human bravery and clear-sightedness. She also wrote other plays in this period: *SOS* (1928) on themes of chemical warfare and pacifism; and *Det blå undret* (The Blue Miracle, 1932) about a sibling clash between Communism and Fascism. It is interesting that among the Finland-Swedish modernists, she was the only one to engage with the theatre.

Hagar Olsson is still little translated into English and little known in the anglosphere, but in working on this translation and Afterword I have gratefully drawn on the published research of several generations of Olsson scholars. Earlier studies took a traditional biographical approach, but more recent research has opened up interesting angles such gender ambiguity and queer theory. This is not a piece of academic writing but an introductory survey, intended to set Hagar Olsson and *Chitambo* in their wider context. It is also a chance to make a few personal observations and to reflect on the challenges and the pleasures of translating this compelling work, which in many respects still feels fresh and innovative. For those keen to know more, some suggestions for further reading follow the Afterword.

CHAMPION OF FINLAND-SWEDISH MODERNISM

In his introduction to Hagar Olsson in the database *Litteraturbanken* (The Swedish Literature Bank), Jonas Ellerström writes that Hagar Olsson 'did not content herself with standing right in the middle of her era. She was utterly determined to be part of influencing it, culturally, socially and politically. With her energy, organisational skills and international outlook, Olsson is one of the most important figures in early Swedish and Scandinavian modernism.' (My translation.)

Her early interest in the emerging modernist trend received a boost from the emotion and energy of her close friendship with the poet Edith Södergran, cut short by Södergran's untimely death. The relationship made a deep impact on Olsson's life, even though it only lasted from 1919 until 1923.

When the two of them first made each other's acquaintance via correspondence, initially as writer and reviewer, Södergran wrote: 'We'll be ruthless with one another and as sharp as diamonds' (Södergran 2015, p. 34).

Olsson was permanently employed as a reviewer by the left-wing paper *Dagens Press* from 1918. She was also much involved with the outward-looking and culturally radical little magazines *Ultra* (1922) and *Quosego* (1928–1929), publishing her work alongside other modernists such as Elmer Diktonius, Gunnar Björling, Rabbe Enckell and Henry Parland. One of the *Ultra* group's manifestos was expressed by Diktonius as 'the internationalism of the new art, and the universal unity of art-forms' (Wrede, 1976, p. 77).

Olsson felt herself to be in the vanguard of something huge and vital, writing in *Ultra* that art is no longer 'a flower in one's buttonhole but a necessity of life' (Holmström 2000, p. 105, my translation). In her collection of essays *Ny generation* (New Generation), published in 1925, she presented writers including Apollinaire, Blok, Joyce and Pirandello, and developed her views on modernism, always at pains to place the Finland-Swedish variety in its wider European context. Her internationalist approach included travel to gather cultural impressions abroad: to Switzerland and Paris in the early 1920s, and to Vienna in 1932.

She became a skilled and trusted reviewer, and actively championed many new writers. Ellen Rees (2005, p. 125) asks how a young female student could so quickly appropriate the avant-garde and maintain her dominance of it for decades, and attributes this in part to her sheer professionalism. Like fellow modernist Djuna Barnes, Olsson financed her literary career by writing for the newspapers, and like Virginia Woolf, she insisted on the importance of criticism as a profession.

Norvik Press has recently published a translation of another work by a female modernist writer of the period, Karin Boye. Her 1934 novel *Kris* is now available in an English edition, *Crisis*, translated by Amanda Doxtater. The two novels, the Finland-Swedish *Chitambo* and the mainland Swedish *Crisis*, differ in their renewal of traditional narrative approaches, but they are both novels of female development, springing from the same literary and cultural impulses, and can readily be viewed as a pair. These two writers were very much aware of each other's work. Olsson wrote about Boye in a review in 1927 and Boye subsequently gave *Chitambo* a favourable review in the magazine *Tidevarvet* (issue 45, 1934). Olsson reviewed *Kris* in *Svensk Press* (1.12.34), calling it a 'significant artistic victory' but finding it lacking in compelling insight or empathy, according to Margit Abenius's introduction to the *Samlade Skrifter* edition of *Kris* in 1948.

CHITAMBO AND MODERNISM

By the time Olsson came to publish *Chitambo* in 1933, her modernist credentials were probably second to none in the Nordic region. Little wonder, then, that *Chitambo* is full of references to the works of other authors.

It is a fascinating exercise to look at where *Chitambo* sits among the other Nordic, European and world titles – in prose, drama and film – published at around the same time, many of which have become part of the modernist canon. This brief overview combines elements of lists provided in the *Cambridge Companion to Modernism* (Levenson) and Ellen Rees's *On the Margins*, together with some other sources:

1930   W.H Auden: *Poems.*
        William Faulkner: *As I Lay Dying.*
        Tom Kristensen: *Hærværk* (*Havoc*).
        Hagar Olsson: *Det blåser upp till storm*
        (A Storm is Brewing).

1931   Karin Boye: *Astarte.*
        Sigurd Hoel: *En dag i oktober* (*One Day in October*).
        Fritz Lang: *M* (film).
        Eugene O'Neill: *Mourning Becomes Elettra.*
        Cora Sandel: *Alberte og friheten* (*Alberte and Freedom*).
        Virginia Woolf: *The Waves.*

1932   Bertolt Brecht: *Die Mutter* (*The Mother*).
        Elmer Diktonius: *Janne Kubik.*
        Louis-Ferdinand Céline: *Voyage au bout de la nuit*
        (*Journey to the End of Night*).
        Aldous Huxley: *Brave New World.*
        Hagar Olsson: *Det blå undret* (The Blue Miracle).

1933   Karin Boye: *Merit vaknar* (Merit Awakens).
        T.S. Eliot: *The Use of Poetry and the Use of Criticism.*
        Pär Lagerkvist: *Bödeln* (*The Hangman*).
        André Malraux: *La condition humaine* (*Man's Fate*).
        Hagar Olsson: *Chitambo.*
        Aksel Sandemose: *En flyktning krysser sitt spor*
        (*A Fugitive Crosses His Tracks*).
        Gertrude Stein: *The Autobiography of Alice B. Toklas.*

1934   Karin Boye: *Kris* (*Crisis*).
        Gunnar Larsen: *Weekend i evigheten*
        (Weekend in Eternity).
        Rolf Stenersen: *Stakkars Napoleon* (Poor Napoleon).

Formal experiment in terms of structure and language is the hallmark of the majority of these works. We can speak of a break with, indeed a revolt against, nineteenth-century narrative conventions. Michael Levenson identifies certain common devices and preoccupations in works of the time: 'the recurrent act of fragmenting unities (unities of character or plot or pictorial space or lyric form), the use of mythic paradigms, the refusal of norms of beauty, the willingness to make radical linguistic experiment, all inspired (in Eliot's phrase) to startle and disturb the public' (2011, p.3). Olsson scholars have been able to find almost all of these devices in operation in *Chitambo.*

Ellen Rees has made a close study of the novel's narrative structure. The novel is formally divided into two planes: first the present-tense frame narration, indicated by italics, and secondly the retrospective episodes of childhood and youth, narrated in vaguely chronological order, and termed 'development narration' by Rees (2005, p. 133). This juxtaposition reflects the non-linear nature of human consciousness, and the two planes allow two contrasting voices to be heard; the frame narration is more 'exalted' and emotionally intense, whereas the chronological section is mocking, full of self-irony and humour.

Rees also notes that in the frame narration, Vega has to undergo three symbolic trials at the hands of Tancred: (1) she sees him in the street and faints; (2) she sees him at the opera and is again felled to the ground and left unconscious; (3) she sees him arm-in-arm with another woman and has a hallucination of his disembodied head. This third encounter causes her to try to take her own life, a failed attempt which eventually leads to a kind of rebirth. But for Rees, *ambiguity* is the watchword of the novel, with its conflicts between different role models, different genders, different callings and visions of the future. She asks: 'how is it possible to be both woman and modernist writer, and how is it possible to be both critic and novelist? It is precisely the insistence upon vacillation and ambiguity between the two narrative planes – bitextuality, metaphoric bisexuality, not choosing – which makes *Chitambo* such an important modernist text' (1999, p. 205).

BILDUNGSROMAN OR DRESSING-UP BOX?

The sub-title of the novel is 'Vega Maria's Story', with the likely intention of pointing to her personal development as the central thrust of this genre-shifting novel. Is this some kind of *Bildungsroman*? Olsson scholars have increasingly chosen to use a less conventionally male term such as *Entwicklungsroman* – or to use the Swedish term, *utvecklingsroman*. Ellen Rees terms it a 'female novel of development'.

But complications threaten to block the path; Vega Maria has a dual personality foisted upon her from the outset, because of her parents' wrangling over her name (bold, adventurous Vega or cloistered, conformist Maria?) and their widely differing ideas of how to bring her up cast a shadow of discord and tension over her younger years. She lived her days, she says, in precarious balance, prey to sudden shifts of emotion, like a sailor in squally weather. Eventually, she thinks she has decided who she is: 'I am at the core of my being a Vega,' she says, and 'my father had hit the spot when he named me for the unknown and dangerous reaches beyond the boundaries of what lies closest to hand' (p. 30 in this volume). But subsequent events prove she still has a great deal to learn about who she is, trying to accommodate a multiplicity of identities. As the book progresses, we see her as an uneasy mix of naive hubris and ambition, and shy, inexperienced innocence.

Alongside the queasy ups and downs of young Vega's everyday life with her warring parents – Mr Dreary the junk dealer with big ideas but little common sense or stamina, and Mrs Dreary the miserable domestic drudge finding solace in the church's embrace – we are also offered a roll call of other role models. First, from her cradle onwards, come male warriors, adventurers and explorers, with Livingstone at their head. 'Every personality in the making is without a doubt a world conqueror in miniature' (p. 131 in this volume), she says. Later she discovers Ibsen's Nora and pledges herself as the knight of downtrodden womanhood; then she admires (until it is revealed as a sham) the strong and independent stance of her mother's unconventional unmarried friend Mildred Jonsson. Roles and costumes are donned and discarded one after another. As Eva Kuhlefeldt puts it in her English summary: '*Chitambo* can be read as an identity experiment during which different genders are being tried on in a literary dressing room' (2018, p. 295).

Kuhlefeldt stresses the performative nature of Vega Maria's behaviour. At her uncle's country estate, for example, she is not so much *being* a tomboy as *performing* the role of a young male. In her later emotional encounter with the actress playing Nora, and its aftermath, she is merely acting out the role of the women's champion, trying a feminist costume for size. 'Mimicry' (in English) was in fact one of the alternative titles suggested by Olsson for *Chitambo* as she was writing it. In some senses, this element of the novel is reminiscent of what Virginia Woolf does in her slightly earlier *Orlando* (1928) although *Chitambo* is, of course, not a fantasy with action spanning the centuries.

Is Vega a Napoleon or a Nora, an Atuahalpa or a General von Döbeln? Or does she, at some level, represent strife-torn twentieth-century Finland itself, trying out roles in the region, forced into them, and finally, painfully, forging some kind of self-helping identity of its own? In the end she opts to shoulder the mantle of a Finnish Livingstone. Her jubilation at finding herself still alive after her brush with death impels her at last to emulate her childhood hero and beat new paths through her own psychological jungle to devote herself to people in need, in her own land.

PRIMITIVISM AND MODERNISM

All the talk of Livingstone and his death at Chitambo, especially the closing chapter of the novel with its references to slaves and dark continents, gives this novel a distinct colonial undercurrent, locating it very much in its historical era. The same is true of Olsson's choice of vocabulary in this subject area. But research is increasingly confirming that a fascination with primitivism is also a hallmark of a modernist novel, and perhaps particularly of a female modernist novel.

Marianne Dekoven in her paper 'Modernism and Gender' looks at Joseph Conrad's novella *Heart of Darkness* (1899), in which Africa becomes what she terms 'the undecidable locus of empowerment of the maternal feminine as racially and geographically darker and lower down' (2011, p. 218). She writes of the 'triumphant masculinism' that became a defining feature of male modernist writers and their 'irresolvable ambivalence towards powerful femininity'. But she points out, too, that the period in which modernism emerged and entrenched itself, 1880-1920, was also the heyday of first-wave feminism and the suffrage movement. This is precisely the tension that Hagar Olsson, also fascinated by primitivism, dramatises and develops with such relish in *Chitambo.* Ellen Rees (2005, p. 136) argues that Olsson uses representations of primitivism rhetorically in her novel, to strengthen her own association with the avant-garde. She describes how Olsson employs various aspects of primitivism, such as borrowing from archaic traditions and the presentation of dream states and surrealistic images (for example in the 'trials' of Vega). She is struck by Vega's fascination, surely a deliberate choice on Olsson's part, with Aztec conqueror Fernando Cortez's locally born slave, concubine and interpreter Marina, also known as La Malinche. Marina has become, Rees explains, an ambivalent icon in Mexican culture: a traitor and whore, but also a representative of female access to power, and of the intelligence and skill of the indigenous people.

Rees also looks at the somewhat perplexing figure of Uncle Eberhard, who with his restlessness and campfires and outsider mentality symbolises a Finnish version of the 'noble savage'. He (or rather his spirit, appearing in a vision) is the one Olsson entrusts with bringing Vega back from the brink of death, and by the end of the novel, Vega is identifying with the primitive 'folk' of Finland, seeing herself in almost mystical terms as their saviour.

COSMOS AND UTOPIA

To Hagar Olsson, the concept of 'cosmos' expresses the spiritual unity of all existence. It was the Swedish journalist and critic Gunnar Brandell, quoted by Birgitta Svanberg (2012) who dubbed her 'the apostle of the new life force'. As Svanberg puts it: 'Her entire literary project is about faith in the life force, the power of the spirit to transform the world [...] the cosmos's great strength'.

According to eminent Finland-Swedish critic, writer and translator Thomas Warburton, in his foreword to the 1959 edition of *Chitambo,* this cosmic outlook finds its deepest expression in Olsson's confessional work *Jag lever* (I'm Alive, 1948). For him, the cherished underlying idea running through

Chitambo is 'that the world, existence, is part of a spiritual whole, influencing its smallest parts' (p. 6, my translation).

The enticing expanse of the cosmos also stands in stark contrast to the predictable, man-made monotony of daily life. The student Vega, her homework done for the following day, contemplates the room: 'On the shelf stood the alarm clock, ticking indefatigably – tick tick, tick tock – crumbling cosmic time into tame, tidy, foreseeable little units.' (p. 123 in this volume) And when spring comes to the city, and the sun shines, many a boy will mischievously misdirect its rays with his magnifying glass, his 'wonderful cosmic toy' (p. 150).

The Swedish Literature Bank is not yet a comprehensive database, but it is interesting that a search for instances of the word 'kosmos' among female writers shows Edith Södergran and Karin Boye as the most frequent users of the term. Hagar Olsson is also there, but to a lesser degree; by no means all of her works are yet uploaded to this digital resource. But in *Chitambo* alone, the words 'kosmisk' or 'kosmos' occur six times.

Another crucial concept for Hagar Olsson is that of utopianism, which Johan Wrede links to Olsson's attraction to collectivism. In the novel, the word actually only occurs twice, both times with reference to a (doomed) plan to create an all-male utopia. The mysterious so-called doctor's proposed utopian community, a dubious enterprise which turns the heads of both Fridolf and Mr Dreary, never materialises.

I would argue that we are later shown an existing, fully-functioning, all-female alternative in the shape of 'All those small sewing circles in Limingo, Suojärvi, Kangasala, Finby and Pargas, in the most remote rural areas and the largest towns in all corners of our land', where women were working away, 'organising their little projects to support poor mothers and children, provide work for destitute women, maintain children's homes, workhouses, weaving schools and libraries.' Vega admits her young self would have despised them, had she been aware of them, because she had:

> no understanding of what was really going on and did not
> see the wider context or realise the extent of the revolution

that was taking place, sometimes silently and covertly, sometimes with shouts and banners and hallelujahs, and least of all did I realise that labour, the secret freedom of labour, was at the core of this revolution as of all others'. (p. 126)

For Olsson, utopia is not something unreal, idyllic and out of reach, but the possibility of renewal and a new future. Vega's utopia at the end is represented as attainable, albeit messily and after much effort and struggle. Like Livingstone she will have to hack a path through the jungle – opening up the route to the interior of her own mind – before she can tackle the ills of her native country. The voyages and landfalls of the great seafarers were Vega's childhood idylls and utopias. The white sails which make their appearance in the opening chapter are evoked again in the 'Forward, comrade' with which the novel ends. As Vega realises with joy that she has survived her suicide attempt, her lifelong vision is of a utopia that is both within herself and across the wide water:

my Atlantis rising from the sea, beyond the horizon I perpetually scanned, we all perpetually scanned, Mr Dreary and Fridolf and Ta and I and the peculiar prophets, the proud and godless supermen from the idyllic era of my youth (p. 175)

To quote Judith Meurer-Bongardt in the English summary of her thesis on the subject of Olsson's utopias, *Wo Atlantis am Horizont leuchtet*:

Her major utopian idea is that of a new humanism with the creative and productive human being at its centre. [...] A person's ideas are never allowed to harm others. This means that utopia is a state of mind upon the basis of which a better world can be created. What this world will look like remains open (2011, p. 509-10).

TRANSLATING *CHITAMBO*

Any conscientious translator surely feels a distinct sense of responsibility when bringing a classic into English for publication for the first time, but that somehow did not lessen my enjoyment in translating the well-crafted prose of this moving and engrossing book. Although there are many claustrophobic indoor scenes, the adjective that most often seemed to be in my mind was 'breezy'. The waterside of Helsinki, open fields of Tavastia and skerries of Åland somehow lent their character to the whole enterprise.

That is not to say there were no challenges. For a start, the Finland-Swedish and mainland Swedish languages were not in 1933, and are not today, entirely the same, and my experience lies with the latter. I was grateful to have access to two online dictionaries made available by the Institute for the Languages of Finland: *Ordbok över Finlands svenska folkmål* (kaino.kotus.fi/fo/) and *Finlandssvensk ordbok* (kaino.kotus.fi/fsob/)

Name-giving was another challenge. Schoolfield talks about her 'name-magic', and tells us, 'names, and their usefulness in the creation of a literary work, have fascinated, or haunted, Hagar Olsson from the beginning of her literary career' (1973, p. 226). Name-giving in translation is something which experience has taught me to take on a case-by-case basis. If I make a hard-and-fast rule for a book I am working on, I invariably find I want to break it. In general, I try to leave as many names unchanged in a translation as I can, even if they have some part to play in characterisation, because unanticipated distortions can arise. Olsson was a fan of Mr Micawber, as she wrote in her *Möte med kära gestalter* (Encounters with Much-Loved Figures, 1963) and apparently allowed something of him to rub off on Vega's father, but I did not want to risk turning twentieth-century Finland into some jarring, sub-Dickensian realm. It seemed impossible, however, to skate over such a major protagonist as Herr Dyster in this regard, and after much experimenting with various alternatives, I alighted on the name 'Mr Dreary'. His personality and demeanour are so central to the narrative, and there are even sentences constructed around a play on his name, such as Vega's remark, 'At home, he truly was dreary' (p. 15).

But I was true to my own policy of inconstancy, or perhaps we should call it flexibility: the character became Mr Dreary, but the street where he lived remained Gräsviksgatan. When it comes to street names, I normally prefer to leave them untranslated, and have argued with editors over the desirability of doing so. I sometimes give the English-speaking reader a pointer and yet retain the original name, hence in my rendering of *Chitambo* we have examples like Kungsträdgården Park, Elisabet Square, Tölö Bay and Klovskär Island. I did feel tempted to translate Gräsviksgatan, for as Schoolfield says, 'Hagar Olsson is almost as careful with street names as James Joyce in *Ulysses*' (1973, p. 249). It was with a slight pang of regret that I robbed the street name in English of its bland, inoffensive, conformist associations, but somehow, a name like Grassy Bay Street would have introduced an entirely different flavour, and one which clashed with the topographical names still in Swedish.

Then there is the matter of what to to call the capital city. In the original novel, Olsson uses the Swedish form Helsingfors, whereas English usually uses the Finnish form Helsinki, and that is what I have also done.

Chitambo is inevitably something of a period piece in its attitudes and vocabulary, occasionally using, in the original Swedish, terms that can now seem outdated and even offensive, and this can pose a problem for the translator. I am grateful to Jeff Bowersox of the German department at UCL, a specialist in this area of research, for helping me to get my thoughts in order on the pros and cons of various potential translations for the original word 'neger' (negro) in Olsson's text. The elegant black man (as I called him) seated next to Vega in the episode set at the opera house (p. 96) offers a striking counterbalance, one could say, to the images of indigenous peoples that Vega has seen on her nursery walls, courtesy of her father's educational methods. But this urbane opera-goer's gleaming white teeth still reveal him as a stereo-type of his time.

Turning to the source text more generally, the edition I used to make this translation was: *Chitambo*, Schildts, 1959 (Finlandsvenskt Bibliotek 3), cross-referenced with the first edition of 1933, available here: litteraturbanken.se/författare/OlssonHagar/titlar/Chitambo/sida/3/etext.

This was, luckily, not one of those cases where some editions can prove to be unreliable or abridged. *Chitambo* seems to have been consistent through its various editions, and of course it is a boon, for a translator and for her editors (and I am extremely lucky in that both of mine can read and understand the source text very well), to have access through the Swedish Literature Bank to a searchable, digitised first edition.

Modernist writers were very conscious of typography, and visual arrangements were important to them, so this aspect was not something that I and Norvik's designer Essi Viitanen could be casual about. There are five chapters in the novel which appear in the original edition in italics, namely those set in the elder Vega's raw present, rather than the flashbacks to her past. Long passages in italics can be a little hard on the reader's eyes and we originally considered putting these chapters into a slightly different typeface, hoping this would maintain the contrast envisaged by the author. But as I came to do the background reading for this Afterword, I found so many references in the research literature to 'the chapters in italics' that I decided we could not pursue our original plan. I therefore asked Essi to try to find a typeface that was 'italic-ish' without being *too* italic. She came up with several suggestions and we decided on the one named Archer, which we have used here. The remaining chapters are in Gentium Basic.

So these were some of the challenges, but there was also much to delight the translator of *Chitambo*. For me, the wonderful strand of irony in the chapters in which adult Vega looks back on her more naive younger self was something to relish and enjoy recreating. Think, for example, of how the author describes the 'doctor' and his shabby apostles, one of whom Vega comes upon, 'his eyes burning like hot coals set deep in his bearded face, white with unaccustomed and over-intense brainwork, as a stream of menacing prophetic words issued from his lips', while she 'stepped bravely forward, firmly resolved to defy the spirits of the abyss itself for the doctor's sake' (p. 108).

Or here is Vega again, chafing against the soul-destroying chore of dusting:

> I detested all these things so profoundly that I would gladly have administered a kick or dashed them to the ground, had not fear held me back and forced me to do my rounds with a subservient expression, dusting and polishing in an idiotic and senseless fashion (p.30).

The claustrophobia of the domestic world is brilliantly evoked, and with wicked humour. Beyond its stultifying walls, *Chitambo* ranges far and wide, from battlefields and revolutionary Russia to South America and the jungles of Africa and back again, but the novel's real emotional home is Finland, its capital city, archipelago and countryside, and there are some wonderful passages of description. To me it seems no coincidence that Olsson uses the the adjective *gnistrande* (sparkling) so liberally in the novel, because that was how the text so often felt. See how the language dances to match Vega's rising spirits as Uncle Eberhard drives her in the creaky old cart through the countryside to her uncle's estate:

> Then suddenly we were in murmuring spruce forest with magical green hiding places, deep shade and cool air, and a pungent fragrance of conifers, marsh flowers and damp moss. My wonderful land opened its arms to me and let me experience its scents and enchantments, let me feel the play of its light and shadow as stabs of delight in my own blood (p. 69).

And my favourite sentence of all describes the arrival of spring in Helsinki:

> Spring came upon us early, in April, inundating us with its heat and intensity. My city awoke in that headlong way she does in spring, the white queen of the still-frozen waters, her crown glistening with sun and cobalt (p. 150).

FURTHER READING

Abenius, Margit, 'Anmärkningar' in *Kris. Samlade skrifter av Karin Boye*, Albert Bonniers förlag 1948, pp. 259-72.

Boye, Karin, *Crisis*. Translated from Swedish and with an introduction and afterword by Amanda Doxtater. Norvik Press, 2020.

Dekoven, Marianne, 'Modernism and Gender', *Cambridge Companion to Modernism*, 2nd ed., Cambridge University Press, 2011, pp. 201-231.

Ellerström, Jonas, 'Hagar Olsson: Introduktion'. On the website litteraturbanken.se/författare/OlssonHagar

Holmström, Roger, *Hagar Olsson och den öppna horisonten. Liv och diktning 1920-45*. Schildts, 1993.

Holmström, Roger, 'Modernisternas prosa', in *Finlands svenska litteraturhistoria*. Vol II. Svenska litteratursällskapet i Finland, 2000, pp. 104-22.

Irons, John, 'Lucidor "O Syndig Man", a wake-up call from before 1674.' bit.ly/3cvFX75.

Kristensen, Tom, *Havoc*. Translated by Carl Malmberg. Nordisk Books, 2016.

Kuhlefelt, Eva, *Dekadens och queer i Hagar Olssons tidiga prosa* (University of Helsinki, 2018). Available at: https://helda.helsinki.fi/bitstream/handle/10138/253488/DEKADENS.pdf

Lähteenmäki, Maria, 'Women workers and the suffrage issue', on the website *Centenary of women's full political rights in Finland:* www.helsinki.fi/sukupuolentutkimus/aanioikeus/en/articles/workers.htm

Levenson, Michael, ed., 'Introduction' in *Cambridge Companion to Modernism*, 2nd ed., Cambridge University Press, 2011, pp. 1-8.

Meurer-Bongardt, Judith, *Wo Atlantis am Horizont leuchtet, oder eine Reise zum Mittelpunkt des Menschen: utopisches Denken in den Schriften Hagar Olssons*, Åbo Akademi University Press, 2011.

Rees, Ellen, 'Hagar Olsson's "Chitambo" and the Ambiguities of Female Modernism.' *Scandinavian Studies*, Summer 1999, Vol. 71(2), pp.191-206.

Rees, Ellen, *On the Margins: Nordic Women Modernists of the 1930s.* Norvik Press, 2005.

Schoolfield, George C., 'Hagar Olsson's "Chitambo": anniversary thoughts on names and structure'. *Scandinavian Studies*, Summer 1973, Vol. 45 (3), pp. 223-262.

Södergran, Edith, *The Poet Who Created Herself: Selected Letters.* Edited and translated by Silvester Mazzarella. Norvik Press, 2015.

Svanberg, Birgitta, 'With responsibility for all humanity'. *The History of Nordic Women's Literature*: http://bit.ly/2TFtNQm.

Warburton, Thomas, 'Inledning', in *Chitambo.* Holger Schildts förlag, 1959, pp. 5-8.

Wrede, Johan, ed, *Modernism in Finland-Swedish Literature. Scandinavica* supplement 1976, pp. 1-4.

PREVIOUS OLSSON TRANSLATIONS

In 1995 Sonia Wichmann, then a graduate student of Scandinavian literature at the University of Washington in Seattle, won the 16th annual translation prize, awarded by the American-Scandinavian Foundation, for an English translation of *Chitambo*, but this has remained unpublished.

Extracts from *Chitambo* translated by David McDuff appeared in *Books from Finland*, 4/2008. The translations are available here: http://bit.ly/32QkMIo

It is interesting that McDuff, too, opted to translate the surname Dyster as 'Dreary', something I was not aware of when I made my own choice. There have been very few English translations of Olsson's work generally, with only two other works tackled so far. If these pages do not provide a full list, I will be glad to receive further information.

George Schoolfield translated *Träsnidaren och döden* as *The Woodcarver and Death* (University of Wisconsin Press) in 1965. The full text is now available here: http://bit.ly/2TmBdcg

'The Motorcycle', a story from Hagar Olsson's late story collection *Ridturen* (The Ride, 1968), translated by Susan Larson, was published in Ingrid Claréus (ed), *Scandinavian Women Writers: An Anthology from the 1880s to the 1980s*, Greenwood Press, 1989, pp. 139-46.

MY THANKS

I am extremely grateful to my editors Janet Garton and Claire Thomson for their generous multiple readings and invaluable comments. And thank you, Janet, for first introducing me to this exuberant novel. It has been on Norvik Press's classics wish-list for quite a few decades, and it is a pleasure to see it finally published in English.

Thanks also to:
Åbo Akademi, Finland, home to the Hagar Olsson archives, for permission to translate and publish this book.
The Finnish Literature Exchange (FILI) for the grant that made this translation possible.
The indefatigable Norvik office team for layout, design, marketing and publicity.
Agneta Rahikainen of Svenska litteratursällskapet i Finland, for valuable help with research literature.
John Irons for responding with alacrity to my wish for a translation of the Lasse Lucidor poem.
Dr Jeff Bowersox, Department of German, UCL, for advice on cultural history and European colonialism.
All those who helped in my efforts to identify quotations in the novel, including Helen Svensson, Maria Antas, Eva Kuhlefeldt, and Judith Meurer-Bongardt.
My husband John for reading and commenting on a near-final draft, and acting as my linguistic sounding-board throughout.

Sarah Death, February 2020

HENRY PARLAND
To Pieces

(translated by Dinah Cannell)

To Pieces is Henry Parland's (1908-1930) only novel, published posthumously after his death from scarlet fever. Ostensibly the story of an unhappy love affair, the book is an evocative reflection upon the Jazz Age as experienced in the Baltic. Parland was profoundly influenced by Proust's *À la recherche du temps perdu*, and reveals his narrative through fragments of memory, drawing on his fascination with photography, cinema, jazz, fashion and advertisements. Parland was the product of a cosmopolitan age: his German-speaking Russian parents left St Petersburg to escape political turmoil, only to become caught up in Finland's own civil war – Parland first learned Swedish at the age of fourteen. To remove Parland from a bohemian and financially ruinous life in Helsinki, his parents sent him to Kaunas in Lithuania, where he absorbed the theories of the Russian Formalists. *To Pieces* became the focus of renewed interest following the publication of a definitive critical edition in 2005, and has since been published to great acclaim in German, French and Russian translations.

ISBN 9781870041874
UK £9.95
(Paperback, 122 pages)

KARIN BOYE
Crisis

(translated by Amanda Doxtater)

Malin Forst is a precocious, devout twenty-year-old woman attending a Stockholm teachers' college in the 1930s. Confounded by a sudden crisis of faith, Malin plunges into a depression and a paralysis of will. Oscillating between poetic prose, social realism, fragments of correspondence, and imagined dialogues between the forces of nature, *Crisis* telescopes Malin's distress out into metaphysical planes and back, as her mind stages struggles between black and white, Dionysian and Apollonian, and with an everyday existence that has become unbearably arduous. And then an intense infatuation with a classmate reorients everything.

Karin Boye (1900-1941) was a poet, cultural critic, journalist, feminist and literary intellectual often credited with bringing high modernism to Sweden. *Crisis* epitomises Boye's capacity to write in a way that is queer, cerebral, imaginative, moving, sometimes formally estranging, sometimes sweepingly beautiful, and above all, wild.

ISBN 9781909408357
UK £11.95
(Paperback, 192 pages)

ELLEN REES
On the Margins:
Nordic Women Modernists of the 1930s

This study examines the work of six women prose writers of the 1930s, placing them for the first time within the broader context of European and American literary modernism. These writers - Stina Aronson, Karen Blixen, Karo Espeseth, Hagar Olsson, Cora Sandel and Edith Øberg - have been doubly marginalized. Their work has long been viewed as anomalous within the Scandinavian literary canon, but, apart from Karen Blixen, it also remains marginalized from examinations of women writers produced outside Scandinavia. This is a 'connective study' which examines the literary strategies, preoccupations, and responses to changes in society shared across national boundaries by these writers. They all sought inspiration from foreign literature and culture, and made themselves literal or figurative exiles from their homelands. Themes in their work include representations of consciousness, hybridity, and experimentation with literary forms. Each writer's work exhibits a strong sense of ambiguity, which takes many forms and challenges received notions about identity.

ISBN 9781870041591
UK £14.95
(Paperback, 208 pages)

EDITH SÖDERGRAN
The Poet Who Created Herself:
Selected Letters of Edith Södergran

(translated by Silvester Mazzarella)

This anthology of the poet's letters, with commentary by her friend
and fellow writer Hagar Olsson, illuminates the passionate and
contradictory nature of Södergran's poetry. Her vital, compelling
and very personal poems have been translated into many languages,
and several times into English. Written for the most part when she
was dying of tuberculosis in a remote Finnish frontier village only
a short train journey away from revolutionary Petrograd, they are
a major contribution to European modernism. These letters are
almost all that remains to us of her work, apart from the poetry.
They are unusually spontaneous and show Södergran in many moods,
passionate and caring, intransigent, desperate for human contact,
and racked by religious doubts that threaten to stifle the very poetry
for which she lived. The collection is accompanied by an introduction
and notes which both contextualize the letters and greatly enhance
our understanding of Södergran's life and poetry.

ISBN 9781909408210
UK £12.95
(Paperback, 244 pages)

Ingram Content Group UK Ltd.
Milton Keynes UK
UKHW010655210323
418913UK00014B/711

9 781909 408555